Grace from the Grave

Songs of Grace Series
Book I

CINDY H. FLOWERS

REIGN OF GRACE PUBLISHING
** USA **

Grace from the Grave
Cindy H. Flowers

Published by:
REIGN OF GRACE PUBLISHING
** USA **

13 Digit ISBN: 979-8-9887373-0-8
Library of Congress Control Number: 2023913889
Copyright © 2023 Cindy H. Flowers – All Rights Reserved

Cover Design: German Creative

Printed in the United States of America

Grace from the Grave

CINDY H. FLOWERS

Foreword

I've had the enormous honor of calling Cindy Flowers a friend for several years. We first met when she showed up at one of my early Becoming a Novelist sessions I host at our local library. During the first several months of Cindy's faithful attendance to my class, I could count how many times she spoke openly about her writing on one hand; in fact, I could count those times on no hands. To say the least, she was reserved; therefore, I began a quest. I was determined to convince Cindy to tell me about her story, but she was a worthy opponent. Finally, in frustration, she pulled back the curtain, ever so slightly, and admitted that she had a story inside her head that seemed to want out, but there was no chance she would ever show it to anyone, and that Stephen King would write a heart-warming children's book before anyone would ever get to actually read Cindy's story, even if she mustered the courage to write it all down.

As they say — whoever they are — admitting you have a problem is the first step to recovery, and I considered Cindy's timid admission that she couldn't get the story in her head to leave her alone a fabulous sign that she was stricken with an affliction for which there is no cure: the dreaded character voices in her head.

As time went on and I continued conducting the writing class,

Cindy began taking notes and asking amazing questions that I wasn't smart enough to answer. One of the best things about being a novelist is getting to make stuff up, and that stuff doesn't have to be based on anything meaningful, but of course I would never commit such an unforgivable atrocity as encouraging a fledgling writer to actually listen to those mysterious voices and write down what they say. Okay, maybe I would make such a vile suggestion. After a few months of asking her about her story every time I saw her, I believe she began to enjoy sharing tidbits about how much fun it was to let the story come out and play. That was my cue to initiate phase two of my diabolical plan.

"If you'll send me just a few pages of your story, I promise I'll never tell a soul." Such are the egregious lies of us novelists, but it worked. She actually sent a sample, and I panicked.

What if she can't write at all? What if it's terrible? How can I possibly tell this delightful lady that her story is garbage?

Boy oh boy, was I ever relieved. Not only was her story not garbage, but it was magnificent. She'd committed many of the same boo-boos we all made when we wrote our first novel. The difference between what Cindy had written and what comes out of most first-time novelists' fingertips was that her story was solid, beautiful, and bore a depth that is rare, even from seasoned novelists with a dozen titles under their belt. This discovery made me panic again.

I was terrified I had plunged myself into a pit of my own unworthiness. I write action-adventure novels in which I blow things up and shoot bad guys. Anybody can write that stuff, but what Cindy was creating was art, and although I may have the résumé to teach basic writing and publishing classes, I'll never be qualified to teach an art class of any kind. So, I made a judgment call and stopped trying to teach Cindy, and instead, began simply encouraging her.

Fast forward through the Covid pandemic and a few hundred hours of Cindy listening to her characters and learning a little more every time she finished a new sentence. Soon — okay, maybe not soon, but eventually — her story became a manuscript, and I was one of the fortunate few who got to hold it in my hands and experience the magnificent piece of art she had created. Over the coming months, my wife and I helped find the perfect editor and held Cindy's hand a few times when she wanted to strangle that editor. (Every writer knows that feeling all too well.) Now that both the author and editor have survived the process, the beautiful story Cindy created from deep within her soul is now in your hands, and I'm honored beyond words to open the door and welcome you across the threshold of the world into which Cindy will take you with this marvelous and unforgettable story. I know you will enjoy the experience as much as I've enjoyed watching a wonderful friend grow from a shy, timid potential writer, into a novelist of remarkable talent, passion, and beauty. Let Cindy take you by the hand and lead you through the world of her magnificent story, and just like me, you will soon fall in love with every word she writes. Please enjoy *Grace from the Grave*.

— Cap Daniels

I waited patiently for the LORD; And He inclined unto me, and heard my cry. He brought me up also out of an horrible pit, out of the miry clay, And set my feet upon a rock, and established my goings. And He hath put a new song in my mouth, even praise unto our God: Many shall see it, and fear, and shall trust in the LORD.

Psalms 40:1-3 KJV

My God out sings every other god.
Not because He's the God I've chosen,
But because He's the God that chose me.

I

The Invitation

The shadow drifted along the sidewalk of Clifton Street, mimicking every move of the figure it followed. Pausing at the corner, the figure turned left and moved toward the target: the house at 1517 Piedmont Drive. Its perfectly manicured lawn allowed it to blend seamlessly with the pasture-like lawns of the other expensive homes around it. For days, he'd wanted to take a shovel to that yard. He wanted to dig holes, trample flower beds, hack gaps into the perfectly even hedges. He wanted to destroy the beauty, just like she'd destroyed his life.

Maybe he'd have his chance, but it would have to wait. Destruction was not his priority ... at the moment. For now, he was confirming what he already knew. And on schedule, the front door opened, and the two teens walked out, bickering playfully, leaving their mother home alone.

He continued his walk as if he belonged on the street, merely out for a morning stroll. As usual, people were too comfortable in their own world, oblivious to the dangers lurking about. Literally in their own front yard.

He laughed to himself as he rounded the corner at the end of the block and saw the collection of cigarette butts that had accumulated at the base of a light pole. All left by him, of course, discarded one by one as he stood in the shadows, day after day, night after night.

* * *

As soon as Grace broke out into the chorus of "Danny Boy," Daniel threw the covers aside. He bolted to the edge of the bed and planted his feet on the floor, his tousled blond hair hanging over his sleepy blue eyes.

"I'm up, Mom, I'm up. Just ... don't sing. Please," he groaned.

Grinning, she pulled the door closed. Mission accomplished. She headed downstairs, knowing Daniel's sister would already be out of bed. Always the early bird, Lucy was likely well into her morning ritual of priming, primping, and perfecting.

Grace popped four slices of bread into the toaster, then walked over to the stainless-steel refrigerator and grabbed the orange juice. She poured two glasses and set them on the bar, making a mental note to buy more when she stopped by the store later. As Daniel and Lucy got ready for school, the familiar, telltale sounds drifting from upstairs told her exactly what each of her two children was doing. The running water directly above her told her Daniel was in the shower. At seventeen, he was more aware of his appearance than he'd ever been. He was no longer the little boy who had to be bribed into a bath after a sweaty baseball game. Grace was certain girls had something to do with her little boy growing up.

On the opposite side of the kitchen, a soft creaking above the breakfast nook told her Lucy was pacing in front of her closet. The fifteen-year-old had enough clothes to outfit an entire cheer squad, but she never had anything to wear. Grace sighed, shaking her head. Oh, how she loved those kids. They were growing up way too fast. Daniel would graduate in a few months. Where had the time gone?

Daniel appeared in the kitchen, his hair still wet. "Morning, Mom," he said as he grabbed his glass of orange juice and chugged it.

"Hey kiddo." Grace took the toast out of the toaster and placed two slices on a plate. "You want some eggs?"

"Nope, this is fine." He picked up the grape jam—his favorite. "Do we have any peanut butter?" Grace passed the jar to him and watched her handsome son sit down at the bar and make a PB and J on toast. Maybe her little boy was still in there somewhere, after all. Lucy came into the kitchen on a wave of Victoria's Secret Bombshell, causing Daniel to wave his arms and fake cough. "Man, did you really have to bathe in that stuff? I mean, I can taste it now!"

Lucy walked the long way around the bar to a bowl of fruit, ensuring she passed right behind her brother. She grabbed an apple from the bowl and made a show of inspecting it for bruises. She paused behind him, spinning around and waving her arms.

"You are NOT getting in my truck smelling like that," Daniel said. "It'll take me a week to get that smell out."

Lucy bit into her apple and rolled her eyes. Grace just shook her head and set about washing the few dishes in the sink. Those two were always at it, each seeming to get better and better at getting the best of the other.

Lucy slung her book bag over her shoulder and headed for the door. "Let's go, Danny Boy. We have to pick up Sara on the way."

"Great. More skunk spray in my truck. Grab a muzzle, would you? That girl talks way too much." Daniel pretended to be disgusted as he picked up his bag and followed Lucy through the door.

"Have a great day, you guys," Grace called as they left. She closed the door behind them and leaned back against it, sending up a silent prayer asking God to keep her children safe. Returning to the kitchen to finish cleaning up, she made a mental list of everything she needed from the market and reminded herself to drop Danny's suits off at the dry cleaners.

After showering and dressing in a simple flower print dress, she was brushing her hair when her phone chirped. It was a text from a number she didn't recognize.

Surprise, I'm back. Dolby Park. Noon. Don't be late. Bring it with you.

A chill crept down her spine as an old fear snaked up her throat from the pit of her stomach. A fear she'd buried years ago. Dropping the phone on the bed as if it had shocked her, she ran into her closet. If she hurried, she could be long gone before anyone missed her. She yanked her suitcase from the rack above Danny's suits and stopped. Her hand reached out for a white linen sleeve and sanity took over. She could never leave Danny. With her eyes closed, she forced herself to take a deep breath, hold it for a few seconds, then let it out. As her heart rate slowed, she pushed the suitcase back in place and stepped slowly back into her bedroom. She sat on the bed, leaning forward with her face in her hands. It was impossible, she thought, after all this time. Feeling her fingers tremble against her skin, she let her hands drop to her lap, alarmed at how quickly her safe, secure world had nearly crumbled.

When the initial panic had subsided, she realized it was probably a wrong number, someone reminding someone else of a previously planned meeting. Or maybe it was Lizzy. Her best friend, the best prankster she knew. She must be back from California already, she thought. She'd play along. Chuckling to herself, she typed:

Invite accepted. I'll bring a picnic lunch; you bring cold drinks. :)

Lunch with Lizzy would be nice. They hadn't had girl time in weeks. Lizzy's job tore her away from home for sometimes months at a time, and Grace missed her company dearly. After dropping Danny's suits at the cleaners, she'd go by her favorite deli and pick up sandwiches and chips. Sliding her feet into a pair of flats, she dropped the phone into her purse and turned to the door.

2

Buried

An unfamiliar voice reached out to her through the fog. It was singing. Something about ten thousand souls. Grace struggled to open her eyes. Her lids were like lead weights sinking in murky water. Thick, black water that pulled her farther down the harder she tried to swim. Not swim; swimming would be pleasant. It was like crawling or climbing—no—clawing her way out of a deep, dark hole. Like a grave. Panic rose, but she broke through the surface and opened her eyes. Surprised not to be standing in a graveyard, she took in the white room. An elderly woman looked at her from the corner. The silver strands of her hair tied in a low bun caught the sunlight shining in through the window. The small, seemingly frail woman clutched a long stick or cane in her hands. The woman smiled, then took a step toward Grace before everything faded to black.

When she woke again, the old woman's words still echoed in her mind. This time, her eyes opened with less effort. A horrible pain sliced through her head when she turned toward the beeping sounds coming from somewhere on her left. "Aagh!" She grunted, lifting a hand to her forehead as tears sprung to her eyes. What happened? she thought as her fingers explored the bulge of the bandage that was wrapped around her head. Something tugged at her hand, and she noticed the plastic IV tubing was caught on the bedrail.

"I thought I heard you. Here, let me get that." A nurse had stepped into the room and was smiling down at her. She had a pleasant face with big blue eyes, and dark hair pulled back into a thick ponytail swung softly over her left shoulder. The nurse made some adjustments and released the tubing, giving her enough slack to move her arm freely. "My name is Leah. How are you feeling?"

"Thank you. My head hurts." Her raspy words barely escaped her dry throat.

"I'm going to go tell the doctor you're awake, and I'll bring you something for your pain." Then the pretty nurse hurried out of the room before Grace had a chance to ask what had happened to her and why she was in a hospital bed with a bandage on her head.

A few minutes later, there was a soft knock on her door and Leah stepped back in, followed by a dark-haired man she introduced as Dr. Whittaker. He wore a white lab coat over gray scrubs and a black stethoscope around his neck. The badge clipped to his coat collar read Michael Whittaker, MD. Underneath his name was Chief of Neurology. He smiled and took her hand in a firm but gentle grip.

"Good morning. We've been waiting for you to wake up. Leah tells me you have a bit of a headache." When she nodded slightly and winced, he continued. "That's to be expected. Before we give you any medication, I need to perform a short neuro test to check your reflexes. I'll start by shining a light into your eyes to check the reaction of your pupils. And I need to ask you a couple of basic questions." She nodded as he took a light out of his pocket and shined it into each of her eyes. He instructed her to follow his finger as he moved it up, down, and diagonally. Then he took her hands and asked her to squeeze. After a few more simple commands she easily followed, he began with his questions: "Can you tell me your name?" He watched her expression shift and leaned toward her, cocking his head.

Her bottom lip quivered as she softly responded, "I was hoping you could tell me." Holding her breath, she watched as a look of concern washed over his face.

He studied her face and cast a swift glance at the nurse, who made a note on the clipboard she held. To Grace he said, "Don't worry, it's common to have some confusion after a head injury. Let's begin again with a few different questions. Do you know where you are?"

"I'm in a hospital," she replied, and in her peripheral vision, she saw the nurse glance at the doctor.

"That's right. But can you tell me where this hospital is located? In what town, or which state?" He waited for her response, but when tears appeared in her eyes, the corners of his mouth fell.

"I don't know," she said, clutching the bedsheet tightly in her hands. "What happened to me?"

Dr. Whittaker reached out and took her hand again. "Your name is Grace Bradford. The police think maybe you were attacked. I don't know all the details, but you were found lying near your car, and you had hit your head. You've been in a coma for four days." She gasped and put her hand over her mouth to cover the small cry she had failed to hold back. He squeezed her hand tighter. "I know this is a scary time, and I'm sure you have a lot of questions. We'll work through them all one at a time and try to get you answers." He released her hand. "On a positive note, we didn't find any broken bones or other serious injuries—just a lot of scrapes and bruises. An especially nasty one above your left knee."

Dr. Whittaker gestured to the nurse. "Leah's going to give you something for your pain. Nothing too strong, just enough to make it more tolerable so you can rest." He gave her shoulder a reassuring pat before he stepped out of the room.

She shook her head in denial when Leah asked her if she was nauseated, and she agreed to try some soup. Her body trembled as the nurse walked away, but she was unsure if it was due to the coolness of the room or the fear of the unknown lying before her.

Holding back threatening tears, she took several calming breaths and looked toward the bathroom. Why bother the nurse? Grace pushed the bedcovers back and gingerly slid her legs over the side of the bed, using the bedrail to pull herself into a sitting position. It took a few seconds for the room to stop spinning, then she slowly stood, pausing to be sure her legs would hold her. Everything seemed to be in working order. She grabbed her IV pole with one hand and her catheter bag with the other and took the few shaky steps to the bathroom. She gave the pole a painful tug as it caught on every unseen bump on the floor. Reaching the bathroom, she wedged herself and the pole into it and closed the door. Afraid to step in front of the mirror, she took a moment to smooth her hair with her free hand. As she worked up her courage, she told herself to expect to see bruising and maybe some stitches besides the bandage on her head. She could do this. Grace stepped forward, closed her eyes, and turned toward the mirror. With a deep breath, she slowly opened her eyes and looked into the face of a stranger. The woman peering back at her was a wreck. Her blond hair hung in tangles, and one side of her face was swollen. The bandage on her head added to the horror of her reflection. She grabbed a nearby washcloth and moistened it under the faucet. Wiping her face, she winced as she rubbed across the tender areas. She struggled to remember the woman staring back at her. Her image blurred as her blue eyes filled with tears, and she choked back a sob. She placed a palm against the mirror, as if making contact with her reflection would spark a connection. Who are you? she wondered.

A loud beep startled her, and she grabbed at the sink to steady herself. The IV pump was screaming for attention. Struggling with the tubing and the stubborn wheels, she made it back through the door just as her nurse entered the room.

"What are you doing out of bed?" Leah demanded with her arms crossed.

"I had to um—" She didn't finish, unsure what to say.

Leah stared her down for half a minute before she relaxed and smiled. "I understand, but you should've waited for me. Your first time out of bed in several days can be tricky." She paused when Grace didn't look at her. She softened her voice. "You won't be a stranger to yourself for long. Let's get you cleaned up, so the next time you take a look, it won't be such a shock."

Leah took the soiled gown and the wet towels and washcloths to the bathroom and deposited them into a yellow bag. "That's the best we can do for now until you're allowed a real shower."

"Thanks, Leah. I really appreciate your help. I feel so much better now."

"No problem at all. Now, how about some lunch?"

* * *

Grace pushed the lunch tray away, leaving the Styrofoam bowl of lukewarm broth mostly untouched. Closing her eyes, she leaned back against the bed and sighed, ignoring the single tear that escaped down her cheek. She'd begun a mental list of questions she planned to ask Dr. Whittaker when he returned. Most important on her list was, *Who am I?* She needed more than a name. Opening her eyes, she looked around the small hospital room, thankful that most of the wires and tubes had been removed. She only wore a heart monitor now and still had an IV access in her left hand. Leah had disconnected the tubing and capped it off with a plastic hub when she'd brought her soup. She glanced at the phone on the bedside table and her lower lip trembled as the gravity of her situation weighed on her. She didn't even know anyone to call. The doctor had told her that she in fact had family and they'd be back that evening to see her. Her husband, he said, had been by her side for most of the past few days. Husband. How could she not remember she had a husband? The word alone unleashed anxiety that tangled with the worry already churning inside her as she imagined how their next visit would play out. Dr. Whittaker wanted to see her again before she had any visitors, presumably to prepare her. As if anyone could be adequately prepared for such an unbelievable situation. She pulled the blanket up over her shoulders and closed her eyes, letting her thoughts drift to the small old woman she'd dreamed about while she was in a coma. Or was it a dream? she wondered. It had seemed real at the time, but then again, who was she to decide what was real or not at this point? The peaceful words from the woman's song lingered as she drifted off to sleep.

A gentle touch on her shoulder stirred Grace, and she opened her eyes and saw the nurse smiling over her. "That was beautiful," Leah said.

"I'm sorry?"

"The song you were singing when I came in. It was so beautiful I didn't want to interrupt you."

"Oh, I must've dozed off. I didn't realize I was singing," she said, embarrassed. She imagined she could still hear the faint echo of the old woman's song, but not singing it herself.

"Well, it was beautiful. Anyway, the doctor will be in shortly. My shift is almost over, and I wanted to see if you need anything before I left."

Shaking her head, Grace replied, "No, I can't think of anything. So, I'll have a different nurse now? You've been so kind today." She was just getting comfortable with Leah.

"Yes. Teresa will be your nurse for the rest of the night. She's very sweet and will take good care of you. But I'll be back on duty in the morning at seven." She smoothed the blanket as she talked and went about straightening items on the bedside table before looking back at her. Leah offered Grace a reassuring smile.

Grace returned her smile and lifted her hand in a small wave as Leah turned and left the room. She rested her head against the pillow and closed her eyes, trying to quell the anxiety creeping up to overcome her. Her name was Grace, but it didn't seem familiar to her. She had a family. Children! But how could she not remember her own children? She reached up and gingerly touched the bandage on her head. And what happened to her? How did she end up lying injured in a parking lot?

The soft squeak of the door opening interrupted her thoughts, and a smiling Dr. Whittaker approached her bed. He sat on the edge of a chair and rested his elbows on his knees, hands clasped in front of him. "How are you feeling, Grace?"

Grace thought for a moment before she responded. "I'm not sure I know how to answer that. I'm scared, I think. Other than my name, I don't know who I am or where I am Not knowing what happened to me or why ..." She paused and took a shaky breath. "And a family. You told me I have two children. Forget how this is making me feel. What about them? How in the world do you tell children their own mother doesn't remember them?"

Dr. Whittaker straightened in his chair, his expression thoughtful. "Your answer is interesting. Since you didn't mention a headache or any new symptoms, may I assume that you aren't in any pain?"

She nodded. "Not enough to complain about."

"That's good to hear. Since your pain is under control, I'm confident we don't need to run any tests other than the scans we've already scheduled." He leaned forward again and put his fingertips together. "Grace, listen to me. You may not remember your family right now. You don't even know their names. But listen to yourself. You're more concerned about them and how they're doing, and you're the one lying there in that hospital bed. That's a good thing. It tells me that mentally, you're stronger than I gave you credit for. And that's important for me to be certain you're ready to face your family."

Her eyes widened, and her pulse quickened. "Now? What do I do? What do I say? Are you positive he's my husband? How do you know for sure?"

"We're sure. He provided all the necessary proof. There's no script for this. Play it by ear, okay? That maternal instinct is still there. And somewhere inside"—he tapped his own temple with a finger—"all your memories are there. We just have to be patient. Your husband and children are eager to see you. If you feel up to it, I'll go and get them. But I think we should take it slowly. Maybe it's best if your husband, Danny comes in alone at first."

Grace nodded. "Okay. Um, I think that's a good idea." While the doctor left to get her husband, she took a deep breath and closed her eyes, trying to summon enough strength to get through the next few minutes.

"Grace." A deep voice spoke softly from the doorway. She looked up to see a tall, sandy-haired man stepping into the room. She noted (how could she not?) that he had a handsome face and solid build. His face was drawn with worry. The bags under his eyes were evidence he hadn't slept well in days. He cautiously stepped closer to the bed. "Hey. I'm so glad you're awake. We've been so worried. I'm sorry I wasn't here when you woke up." His voice cracked, and she noticed the tears in his eyes threatening to spill.

It took a moment for Grace to respond. Nothing about him was familiar. Oh, how she wished she could remember! She'd hoped seeing him would trigger something. Anything. "Hi. Did-did Dr. Whittaker tell you—" She hesitated.

Danny saved her the discomfort. "He did. He explained to us that you have amnesia. He said that in most head injuries the events before and after a traumatic event are mostly clear, but the brain tends to block out the event itself and the few minutes right before. In your case, he said you can't remember anything at all. Is that true?" He fidgeted with his keys as he waited for her answer. There was no way she couldn't remember him. They'd built an entire life together. She'd know him, he thought. She had to.

"Yes. I'm so sorry. I feel so useless." She began to sob.

He moved toward her and took her in his arms. He felt her flinch, but he didn't let go. He couldn't let go. He'd almost lost her once. Danny gently rubbed her back and waited until her shaking subsided.

It was hard to process all the emotions running through her mind.

She didn't know this man. Didn't he understand how awkward this was? Not wanting to offend him, she let him hold her, but she didn't return the gesture. Grace sensed it wasn't the first time he'd comforted her this way. She squeezed her eyes closed, trying desperately to remember even one of those times.

His voice broke through her sobs. "You have nothing to apologize for. This isn't your fault. We'll get through this. Together." His affirmations calmed her momentarily. She pulled away from him and wiped her face with the back of her hand.

"I'm so sorry, I—"

"No more apologies. I'm here for you, and like I said before, we'll get through this. The kids and I have been praying. Our friends and everyone at church have been praying as well." Danny fished his wallet out of his back pocket and thumbed through it. "Here, I have something for you." He pulled out a photo and studied it. A smile relaxed his face, and he held the picture out to Grace. "This was taken last year. I keep this in my wallet and another one in my office."

Grace accepted the photograph and held it up to see four faces smiling back at her. She ran her finger lightly over her own image, smiling in front of a waterfall. Danny was standing to her right with a boy and a girl in between them. They were all dressed in shorts and hiking boots.

"You can keep it with you," he said when she held it out to him. Nodding, she laid it on the blanket covering her lap.

"The kids are anxious to see you. I know all of this is overwhelming, and if you don't feel up to it, they'll understand."

She shook her head. "No, let them come in. I'm just nervous and don't know what to say. But this must be so hard on them. I hope it's not too uncomfortable." Despite her discomfort moments before, Grace sensed Danny was genuine and felt a little more at ease with him. Not familiar, but he was easy to talk to.

"Don't worry. I'll go get them and explain that they can only stay a couple of minutes. They'll be relieved to see you with their own eyes, and that'll satisfy them enough that maybe they can get some sleep."

Grace stopped him as he turned toward the door. "Um, I know this is going to sound horrible, but can you tell me their names?"

Danny closed his eyes and groaned. "Now I'm the one who should apologize." He returned to her bedside and sat back down. "We have a boy and a girl. Daniel is seventeen and a senior in high school. Loves sports and girls. Lucy is fifteen, a sophomore. She's a cheerleader and has a passion for art. And shopping. That girl really loves to shop. And they both love you. They are your world." He choked on the last word. The realization of how close they'd come, how close he'd come, to losing her hit him like a train. He squeezed her hand to ward off his tears and to pass that emotion to her without saying any more words. He rose and swallowed the lump in his throat so he could reintroduce his wife to their children.

As he left, she closed her eyes and said a quick prayer. She assumed she prayed. Danny said they'd been praying for her. She thought it strange that she remembered God and prayer but couldn't remember if she routinely prayed. To calm herself, she softly hummed a few words of the song that still haunted her thoughts.

Grace sat up a little straighter in the bed as the door crept open. Her breath caught at the sight of the pretty face that peeked around the door. Her daughter.

"Mom?" she softly said and moved cautiously into the room. Then she ran over to the bed with tears streaming down her face. "Oh, Mom!" She sobbed as she leaned over the bedrail and pushed her face into her mother's shoulder. Grace's instinct was to hold her, so that's exactly what she did. She put her arms around her daughter and gently rubbed her back. She looked past her to the handsome young man that seemed to be waiting his turn. He ran a hand through his unruly blond hair and gave her a timid smile. He was slim and towered over his younger sister by at least a foot.

"Hi Daniel," she said. His eyes widened at the sound of his name.

Lucy's head snapped up, and she looked hopefully at her mother. "You remember his name?"

She didn't want to hurt them. Again, Danny came to her rescue. "No honey. I prepped her a little before I called you in." Lucy's shoulders dropped and disappointment flooded her face, but she recovered. Grace could tell she was trying hard to be brave. She looked at her mother and nodded toward her bandage.

"Does it hurt?" she asked.

"Only a little," Grace answered. "The doctor said the bandage can come off in a day or two."

Daniel spoke up. "When are you coming home?" His eyes widened and his face looked stricken when he glanced at his father. "She *is* coming home, right?"

Danny shifted his weight. He hadn't discussed bringing his wife home. He didn't know if she would even be comfortable staying with them, who to her were essentially strangers. His family didn't deserve this. What had they done to provoke such severe punishment from God? He swallowed. "We still have a lot to talk about. Right now, we need to head home and let your mother get some rest. The doctor said we don't need to overwhelm her right now."

Daniel and Lucy looked disappointed, but they didn't argue. Lucy leaned over and kissed her mother on the forehead, telling her she would see her soon. Daniel gifted her a shy smile as he followed his sister out of the room. Danny followed them to the door, reminding them to be careful. He told them he'd meet them at home and would bring dinner with him. When he turned back to Grace, he smiled. He wanted to reassure her but needed his own encouragement. Who would tell him his wife wouldn't always see him as a stranger?

She returned his smile but words escaped her. His words confirmed he knew what she'd been thinking. "Grace, we do have some things to work out. I can't imagine how you feel right now, and I know you're scared. This will be difficult for all of us, but somehow we *will* get through it."

Afraid of the answer but needing to know, she asked, "Why has no one else been to see me? Don't I have any other family? Parents? Or brothers and sisters?"

A trace of sadness crossed his face. "Your parents died in an accident before we met, and you're an only child. You told me they were only children as well, so I've never met any of your family. Not even distant cousins, if there are any. Our pastor has been to see you every day, but Dr. Whittaker limited your visitors while you were in a coma. It'll be up to him to lift that restriction. And now that you're awake, I expect the police will want to speak with you."

Her eyes went wide. "The police?" She wrung her hands.

"There are a lot of unanswered questions regarding the attack. The police haven't gotten very far in their investigation."

"Can you tell me anything about what happened?"

Danny reclaimed his chair. His jaw tightened as he contemplated his words. "We don't know much. Two women showed up for their walk and found you alone and unconscious. They told the police that the area of the park where they found you was empty when they arrived. They called 911 and waited for the paramedics."

Grace swallowed. "I went there alone?"

"It looks that way." He dropped his eyes to his hands.

"Is that something I normally do?"

Danny took a deep breath, cheeks puffing as he let it out. "It's not unusual for you to go for a walk during the day, but the only shoes you had with you were the flats you were wearing."

"That doesn't make sense. Why was I there?"

Danny lifted his hands, palms up. "You're the only one who can answer that."

"Except I can't remember. So whoever did this to me what—just gets away with it?"

"The police have your phone, but it was smashed. Their IT department is working on trying to get any information they can out of it. We're hoping you had a call or text that might shed some light. For now, the phone is their only lead. There's really nothing to prove it was anything more than a random attack."

Grace pressed the heel of her hand to her head, where it had begun to throb. "It seems so sinister."

"I'm sure they'll come up with something. I'd sure like to get my hands on whoever did this to you." The flash of anger that crossed his face faded as quickly as it had appeared. "You need to get some rest. I'll be back tomorrow, and we can talk more. I'm sure you have a lot more questions." After a slight hesitation, he offered, "Unless you want me to stay."

Um no, ah, I'll be okay," she stammered. "Really. You need to be with the kids."

He watched her hands twist the bedsheet, and his own insides twisted with it. "Okay, if you're sure." He leaned forward, then stopped, his body hovering awkwardly above her. Even the right to kiss his own wife had been ripped away. Life with Grace was always clear, and now it felt muddy. He straightened. "I'll see you tomorrow then. Have a good night and call me if you need anything." He found a pen and notepad in the nightstand drawer and scribbled a few lines. "Here are the numbers to the house and my cell. I'll need to check in at the office, so I'm adding that number too, just in case. Call anytime at all." When she nodded and said she would, he pictured Grace, the sassy waitress he'd handed his number to so many years before. He hadn't expected a call then, either. He dropped his head and quietly left the room.

Danny leaned against the wall of the elevator as the doors slid closed. He was torn between celebrating and mourning. She's alive, but she's not his wife. On the outside, she was the Grace he knew and loved, but on the inside, she was a stranger to him. "God, help us." He'd muttered the same words a thousand times since he learned of the attack, and he felt as helpless now as he had four days before.

3

The Nut

Pressure on her shoulder roused her from sleep. When she opened her eyes, she jumped at the sight of the strange man at her side and recoiled from his touch. The dim glow of the bathroom night light wasn't enough for her to make out any details of his face in the dark room. Of course, he was a stranger. Everyone was. But somehow she knew this wasn't a friendly visit. His gravelly voice was angry, and she could practically feel the menace when he said, "Tell me where it is. You should have listened." She noticed the faint squeak of leather as his grip on her shoulder tightened.

"Where is what? I don't know what you're talking about." Her voice shook with fear.

"Don't play games. As soon as you get home, you'd better get it to me. Or else I'll put you right back in here with worse than a little bump on your head."

A knock on her door startled her, and she woke gasping for breath and her hand clutching at her chest. "Good morning!" called Leah's cheerful voice as she came through the door carrying a breakfast tray. With one look at Grace's face, she put down the tray and hurried to her side. "Grace, what's wrong?"

Grace took a couple of deep breaths, trying to slow her racing heart. She glanced around the room, but the man was gone. "Did you see that man? Where did he go?"

Leah's forehead wrinkled in confusion. "What man, Grace? There's no one here."

Grace shook her head. "There was. He was wearing a dark leather jacket and was standing right there, threatening me." She indicated the spot where Leah now stood.

"I've been outside at the nurse's station for the past half hour. No one has come in." Grace's confusion faded, and she recognized the brightness of her room. The sun was shining through her window. It must have been a dream, she thought. It was dark when he was here. But it seemed so real. She could even smell the cigarettes on his breath.

"I guess it was just a dream," she replied. But she still couldn't shake the fear that gripped her.

"You've been through a lot these last few days," Leah said. "It's not surprising you'd have bad dreams. Dr. Whittaker's making his rounds, he should be by shortly." She noticed Grace rubbing her left shoulder. "Is your shoulder bothering you? Can I get you something for it?"

Grace hadn't realized what she was doing, and when she thought about it, she had to admit it was a little sore. She must have strained it somehow during her accident. Maybe the pain had triggered that horrid dream. "No, it's fine. Thank you, Leah."

Leah pulled a chair a little closer to her bed. "I have a few minutes. Do you want to talk about anything?"

Grace smiled her appreciation. Leah was so sweet and obviously had found her calling in nursing. "I wouldn't even know where to begin. I met my children last night. It sounds strange to say it that way, but that's essentially what happened. Meeting my children for the first time." She felt her eyes fill with tears and she looked down at her hands in her lap. When Leah placed her hand on Grace's arm, she clutched it and said, "I don't want to disappoint them, but I'm scared. I don't know who I am. I don't know who they are. I mean, they seem nice enough. And my husband"—she let out a short breath and looked up toward the ceiling—"that sounds so bizarre. Danny was very sweet and encouraging, but I don't even know *if* I'll get my memory back, let alone when. And if I don't ..." Grace dropped her head into her hands and let the tears flow through her fingers.

Leah moved to sit on the edge of the bed and wrapped her arms around Grace. She squeezed her and said, "Well, I do know one thing about you." Grace looked up hopefully as Leah stepped back. "You have a beautiful voice. I'd be willing to bet you sing in a church choir."

"Choir?" That didn't sound like anything she'd do. She didn't think so anyway. But then, how would she know?

"Yes, choir. After all, you were singing 'The Lily of the Valley' when I walked in yesterday."

Grace remembered the old woman she'd seen in her room. She remembered that she'd been singing but couldn't recall the song. She considered asking Leah about the woman but didn't want to sound totally bonkers if it was just another dream.

"Leah?" A pale face peeked around the open door. "Um, could you go to the staff bathroom? Pregnant Kelli is losing her breakfast." Leah moved from Grace's side and turned to leave, explaining on her way out. "We have two Kellis on this shift. Pregnant Kelli and Bossy Kelli. And Weak Wendy can't stomach the retching," she added with a whisper and a point toward the door.

As soon as she disappeared, another visitor entered, still talking to someone in the hallway. "Yes, ma'am, I get it ... I understand ... I *won't* ... I promise. Geez," he finished as he closed the door. "What's wrong with those people?" He approached her bed and pulled up the nearest chair. Staring at her, he waved a hand in front of her face. "Danny said you were awake, how are you feeling?" he asked.

Grace was stunned into silence. Who was this man? He wore a blue windbreaker with *Alaska* embroidered on the left pocket area. He was average height, and clean shaven with a bald head. Clear blue eyes returned her gaze, as if able to peer past the surface, deeper to the outer skirts of her thoughts. It was unsettling.

"Um, okay, I guess." She swatted his hand away. "I'm sorry, what are you doing?" Grace replied, waiting for him to introduce himself. She didn't peg him for a doctor.

"I'm checking to see if you can see. And I'm glad you're better." Rolling his eyes, he said, "You should be rested up. You slept long enough." He leaned forward and rubbed a hand over his face, then looked around the room absently, avoiding her eyes.

Grace was dumbfounded. If this man hadn't mentioned Danny's name, she'd swear he'd wandered out of the psych ward. "I'm not blind," Grace said slowly, hoping he'd give her at least a clue to his identity.

He looked back at her, seemingly clueless. "Oh yeah, that was the patient on the *fourth* floor. I really need to write this stuff down," he said as he patted his pockets.

Was this guy serious? Grace thought. "Who *are* you?" she asked.

The man stopped his search for a pen and had the audacity to look hurt. "You don't know me? We're like best friends. You invite me over for dinner all the time, we text, we talk on the phone. I mean, we're so close I'd buy the house next to you if I could get that other family to move out."

Speechless, Grace could only stare at him. Finally, she managed, "You're insane."

She jumped when he bolted from his chair, pointed at her, and said, "I knew you were faking! I knew it!" Catching himself, he flopped back down and lowered his voice. "Listen, milk this for as long as you want. Your secret is safe with me."

Grace had had enough. This man really was a patient, and he must have overheard someone say Danny's name. She reached for the nurse call button, but before she could push it, he burst out laughing. "I'm kidding, I'm kidding! It's me, Joe!" To her blank look, he said, "Your pastor?" as if it was obvious.

"My pastor. You're kidding." To his credit, he looked a little sheepish.

"Yes, I'm serious. I'm sorry, usually you love my teasing."

"Danny should've warned me about you." Her initial shock had begun to wear off. "He said you've been here every day. I appreciate that. I'm sorry I don't remember you."

"You're apologizing to me?" he said incredulously. "Same old Grace, whether you remember yourself or not. Yes, I've stopped by every day." And with another roll of his eyes, he said, "It's kind of my job."

Grace snickered with him, somehow knowing he was kidding. She liked him but wasn't quite ready to let him know it.

Dr. Whittaker's knock interrupted their visit. "Hey, Joe, how are you today? Up to more shenanigans, I bet," he said, and they laughed.

Joe said, "No more than usual. Listen, I'm gonna get outta here. There's nothing wrong with her. But do you mind if I pray first?" They all bowed their heads as Joe said a short, simple, yet moving prayer for Grace's healing.

When the preacher had left, the doctor turned to Grace and said, "How are you feeling this morning? How did your visit with the family go? Not too upsetting or stressful, I hope."

Grace sighed and repeated the concerns she'd discussed with Leah. She told him she'd had a nightmare but left out any details. He reassured her it was common to have nightmares after a head injury and that unfortunately it was possible they may persist for a while. "But then again, you may not have any lingering symptoms once you've completely recovered."

Danny entered the room just then, and after greeting him, the doctor continued, "I was about to tell Grace her scans show the swelling in her brain has decreased. Usually when the swelling goes down, the memory returns. All the other tests are normal." Looking back to Grace, he said, "Other than removing those sutures in a few days, the only concern I have is your memory. Time will tell us how that's going to go. It could take anywhere from a few days to several weeks."

No one missed the disappointment that played out on Grace's face.

"Grace, how do you feel about going home? I think you're doing well enough that it's perfectly safe, and physically you would be much more comfortable. Emotionally, though, I want to leave that up to you. Insurance companies these days seem to control our patients' length of stay, but under the circumstances, I don't feel they would have a problem with a couple more days. But I'll let you two talk about it and I'll see you tomorrow." He shook Danny's hand and left the room.

When Danny turned to Grace, her hesitation was written on her face. "Grace, we don't have to discuss this right now. You can sleep on it, okay? We don't have to rush." Grace didn't hide her relief, grateful Danny was sympathetic to her feelings.

She nodded her agreement, ready to change the subject. "Pastor Joe came by."

Danny hung his head. "Yeah, I ran into him downstairs. He didn't tell me what he did, but judging by the way he couldn't keep a straight face, I'm sure he did something."

Grace laughed softly, still somewhat shy around her husband, then recounted the unusual visit.

"That's our Pastor Joe. He's quite the prankster. He's a bit unconventional, but he has a heart for God. All the kids love him, and he loves them. Sometimes I think he relates better with the youth than the adults. He loves to have fun, loves to lift others up. Basically, he's a nut."

Smiling, Grace replied, "That's exactly how I pegged him."

4

Home

Home. Grace honestly didn't know how she felt about going home. But if she had to leave the hospital, she most certainly didn't have anywhere else to go. Or did she? She reached over and picked up the pen and pad from the table and started a list of questions she'd ask Danny when he came back.

1. Close friends?
2. Do I sing in the choir?
3. How old am I?

She laid the pen on the pad in her lap. There was so much to consider she couldn't even think of which questions she wanted to ask first. Going home with Danny and the kids would be like moving in with strangers. On the other hand, so would staying with anyone else. To them, it wasn't even a question. Lost in her thoughts, she didn't hear the woman enter her room and approach the bed.

Grace jumped when she saw the old woman from her dream standing by her bed. The woman nodded and smiled, then reached out and patted her shoulder. Grace said, "I know you. I dreamed about you. You were singing."

The woman smiled and replied, "Songs aren't dreams, child. They're praises. And there's a reason for every song worth singing. I'll go now, things to do, you know. I'm glad you're okay." Without another word, she turned and walked quietly out of the room, leaving Grace with even more questions.

She shook her head and thought back to her first memory of the woman singing by her bed. As she recalled the comforting words, she succumbed to fatigue and let the song soothe her to sleep.

"'The Lily of the Valley' must have some significance to you," Leah told Grace later when she brought her dinner tray.

"Why do you say that?"

"Well, because when I checked on you a little while ago, you were singing it again. And, I must say, it was beautiful. Did you ask your husband if you're in the choir? Because if you didn't, you should."

Grace shook her head. "I didn't think of it, but it's on my list of questions. But I do have one for you. I may have been dreaming again, but before I fell asleep, I'm sure there was a woman in here. I thought I'd dreamed about her before, but then she showed up here in my room. She didn't say much, but the little she did say didn't really make sense. It was almost like a riddle. She didn't even tell me who she was."

The nurse smiled and nodded as Grace described her visitor to Leah. "That would be Miss Eva." She chuckled. "She's one of our volunteers here and likes to go around checking on our patients. The cane, or staff, you thought she had was probably a broom. Miss Eva says the housekeeping staff isn't worth the dirty water they dip their mops in. Nothing is ever clean enough for her. She's super sweet and very wise. And harmless. Likely, one day when you least expect it, her words will make sense. Now, I'll be back when you've finished your dinner, and we'll get that bandage off."

With the bandage gone, Grace could shower as long as she didn't get her stitches wet. Unfortunately, that meant she couldn't wash her hair. That was a disappointment, but the hot shower more than made up for it and felt wonderful on her aching body. Leah returned to her room later with dry shampoo and helped her clean her matted hair as best she could.

"Just a couple more days and those stitches will be out. Then you'll be able to give your hair a real washing," Leah told her as she gently tugged on a tangle. When she was done, Grace was exhausted. She still hadn't regained all her strength.

She napped fitfully off and on until the early afternoon, when Danny showed up with a small bouquet of flowers. He'd left work early so he could be there when Dr. Whittaker stopped by during his rounds. The doctor reported that everything continued to look normal and told Grace she was progressing well.

"Except for my memory," Grace said, and accepted his reassurances with a grim smile. "I've been thinking some," she began when he paused. "I think I'm going to go home with my family." She glanced at Danny. "Maybe we can discuss alternative arrangements in case it doesn't work out or if it's too uncomfortable."

Danny let out an audible breath and grinned from ear to ear. "Absolutely. We'll do whatever we need to do to help you feel safe." He looked at Dr. Whittaker and waited for his response.

Dr. Whittaker nodded. "I think that's a good plan. If you'd like, I can place a consult for social services to stop by and see you before you leave. I'm sure they have some resources that will help you adjust. Also, I'm going to give you the number of one of my colleagues. She's a psychiatrist, one of the best in the area. Aside from following up with me, I recommend you get established with her for counseling. You'll benefit from some guidance over the next few weeks, and she may have some techniques to work on getting that memory back." He pulled a business card out of his pocket and handed it to her. She read the name. Monica Hyatt. Grace agreed to make an appointment as soon as possible.

* * *

Grace watched the scenery unfold through the passenger window as Danny drove. Nothing was familiar to her. She couldn't believe she was letting a stranger take her to a house she didn't remember. Full of things she didn't remember and people she didn't remember. It was all too much. Her unease grew by the minute. Her heart raced. She couldn't catch her breath.

"Pull over," she panted. "Please." When the car stopped, she flung the door open and sunk her feet into the gravel. Her back found the car, and she slid down, head between her knees.

Danny rushed around and knelt without crowding her, then laid a hand on her shoulder. He'd be a wreck if he were in her shoes.

Grace slid from under his hand, stood, and paced alongside the car.

"Grace, it's okay to be scared. We can take this slow. Would you be more comfortable if we found a hotel nearby? You can come for dinner and hang out with the kids but sleep on your own." He ducked to catch her eye.

Something in his gaze calmed her. He wasn't pressuring her or expecting anything. The tightness in her chest loosened, and she took in a full breath of air for the first time since she'd walked out of the safety of the hospital.

"I want to do this. I didn't expect to feel so overwhelmed."

He smiled.

She didn't want to go back to the hospital and there was no way she wanted to be alone. Grace hadn't told anyone she'd had another dream about the strange man in her room. This time he'd been standing at the foot of her bed, staring at her. She'd woken up gasping for air. Feeling as though she'd had no other choice, Grace forced herself back into the car. She could always leave if it got too bad. That thought made the situation a little less terrifying.

Danny offered her a sympathetic smile and opened her window a crack. "The fresh air might help," he said. As they headed out of town, her view changed from busy streets and storefronts to green lawns and fences.

"Do I work?" Grace asked as Danny turned his SUV into a neighborhood with two-story homes and well-kept lawns. In the driveways sat minivans, SUVs, and sedans. The occasional Jeep or flashy sports car made Grace wonder briefly if those homes housed teenagers or young couples, maybe even middle-aged divorcées going through the proverbial midlife crisis.

Danny glanced at her and smiled. "You tutor high school and college students."

Grace furrowed her brow, thinking about his response.

"You're a teacher," he said, "but you stopped working full-time when Daniel was born. You make your own schedule now, and only charge what your students can afford." He paused as he slowed and rounded a curve in the road, then added, "We have a good life together. You'll remember soon." He reached over and squeezed her hand, then pulled his own hand back.

Two left turns later, Danny pulled into a curved driveway that led up to the two-car garage of a large two-story brick house. Charming was her first thought. The garage face was earth-toned stone, with arches made of a darker stone over each door. Looking to the left at the front of the house, she saw the same stonework with brown shutters hugging the upstairs windows. Someone had taken great care choosing the shrubbery, plants, and flowers that perfectly accented the larger plants and trees along the border of the yard. She could see large stones here and there in the flower garden.

"What do you think?" Danny asked. "Anything familiar?"

Glancing at him, she said, "No, I don't recognize anything. It's beautiful. We obviously have great taste." She smiled, not wanting to disappoint him. Opening her door, she stepped out of the car just as Lucy came running out, closely followed by Daniel.

Lucy ran right up to her mother and hugged her. "It's so good to have you home, Mom." Daniel also stepped forward and gave her a shy, one-armed hug as well. Grace could tell he was a little more hesitant than his younger sister. Maybe it was a boy thing.

Danny came around the car and suggested they go inside and get their mother settled.

They led her through the front door into a foyer that opened up to a large staircase leading to the second floor. Looking up the stairs, Grace could see a collection of black-and-white framed photos arranged on the wall to match the incline of the stairs. From where she stood, she couldn't tell who or what was in the photos, but assumed they were of her, Danny, and the kids. Moving forward and to the left, they stepped into an inviting living room. It was tastefully decorated with neutral colors of beige and white, with accents of teal and red.

Danny watched her with hope as she looked around. "What do you think? You decorated the house yourself, down to the last detail. While it was being built, you pored over magazines and websites, searching for just the right furniture and decorations." He picked up a carved elephant from the sideboard and showed it to her, then pointed to a painting on the wall. "You wanted everything to be perfect and wouldn't settle for anything less."

Grace wished she could recall something. Anything. This couldn't be her home, she thought. She'd never been here. Had she? She hadn't given up hope, of course. It was only a matter of time before her memory returned. She hoped.

"Let's go through the rest of the house. Maybe something will click."

Grace agreed, and she followed Danny through the lower level with Lucy in tow. Daniel had disappeared when they'd begun the tour. The kitchen and laundry room and their obvious uses were first, then the den. It was strange for Danny to be giving Grace a tour of her own house, pointing out closets and spaces she'd used a million times.

"This is your favorite reading spot." He pointed to a chair by the window with a matching ottoman. There was a soft throw draped over one arm. Built-in bookshelves spanned the wall behind the chair.

Grace stepped toward the shelves and let her fingers glide over the spines of books on the nearest shelf. Lysa TerKeurst, Priscilla Shirer, Cap Daniels, and Harlan Coben were only a few of the authors in the impressive collection. Her expression didn't change as she skimmed the titles.

Grace turned to Danny. "Have I read all these books?"

Danny's shoulders dropped and he nodded. "You have." He pointed to one section of the shelving. "That's where you keep your to-be-read books. Notice how they're turned backward? You always said you had a hard time choosing what to read next, so you'd turn them like that and choose one at random."

The crease between Grace's brows deepened. "Hm. Seems like a good idea."

They completed the ground floor tour and made their way upstairs. Lucy led the way into her room and when Grace asked about a trophy and some blue ribbons on a shelf, she said with a smile, "I won those in an art show."

"That's incredible. I'd love to see your work."

Lucy's smile widened. "I mostly do charcoal drawings, but about a year ago I started painting with acrylics. I've only done a few. A couple of them are on display in the art department at school." She gestured to the awards. "The one I got those for was bought at a silent auction fundraiser. I'm not sure where it ended up. I'm working on a new piece. I'll show you when it's done."

"I can't wait."

They found Daniel simultaneously stuffing clothes into a drawer and closing the closet door with one foot. His bed was made but rumpled. Grace grinned at his effort. That's why he'd disappeared.

Danny didn't comment on Grace's hesitation when they entered the master bedroom. "Your closet is over there, and the bathroom is through that door. I want you to be comfortable here, so I'll be sleeping downstairs in the guest room for now."

Grace pressed her lips together and let out the breath she'd been holding. "Thank you," she said, swallowing a lump. She'd been worried about the sleeping arrangements. She was grateful she hadn't had to bring it up.

"I'm feeling a little tired. Do you mind if I lie down for a while?" Dr. Whittaker had told her to expect episodes of fatigue in addition to headaches and other symptoms she couldn't recall. Danny nodded and told her to rest as long as she needed. Lucy squeezed her hand and kissed her cheek as she left the room. She watched them walk away and closed the door. Her fingers hovered over the lock, but she didn't turn it. Dr. Whittaker and the preacher trusted Danny. She should try too.

Two hours later, Grace opened her eyes, disoriented for a moment before realizing where she was. Startled by a slight movement on the bed beside her, she turned, surprised to see Lucy lying next to her.

"Hi. I didn't mean to wake you." A combination of sadness, hope, and fear played across her young face.

This was a girl who needed her mother and was afraid of losing her. Grace reached out and gently brushed a lock of hair away from Lucy's face. "You didn't wake me, I'm happy to see you." Seeing the tears well in the girl's eyes, she continued, "I know how hard this must be for you. Soon I'll have my memory back and everything will be back to normal."

Lucy closed her eyes tightly and said, "But what if you don't? Didn't the doctor say that could happen?" Her voice cracked, and Grace felt her heart break along with it.

"He did say that, but it's rare. We don't know how long it will take, or what might trigger it. But I'm here and things will be okay. You'll see. Come here." She lifted her arm, and when Lucy moved into her embrace, she held her tight. Lucy sobbed as she admitted to her mother how afraid she'd been when she thought they'd lost her. Grace shushed her, stroked her hair, and sang.

Lucy listened in awe, but kept her face hidden from her mother. She didn't want her to stop but wondered where this came from. Her mother didn't sing. Not out loud anyway, especially where anyone could hear her. If she hadn't witnessed it for herself, she would never have believed this was her mother's voice.

* * *

"Yes, Dad, *singing*. And it was good. Really good." Lucy sat on a barstool at the kitchen island while her father prepared dinner. She'd come downstairs to talk to him while her mother was in the shower.

Danny stopped slicing a tomato and laid the knife down. "So you're telling me that your mother, the woman who *never* sings because she doesn't like her voice, sang to you. Out loud." He stared as Lucy nodded, bewilderment still on her face. "Well, what did she sing?"

Lucy looked toward the ceiling and tapped her fingers on the counter, trying to remember the name of the song. "You know the song Sherry and Dianna sang last year at Homecoming? About the river?"

"Down to the River to Pray?"

She slapped her palm on the counter. "Yes! That's the one."

Before he could respond, Grace walked into the kitchen. "Hi," she said, somewhat shyly. She paused when she saw Danny and Lucy staring at her. "Is something wrong?" she asked. "I found some clothes in the closet. I hope that was okay." She suddenly felt like she had two heads.

"Um, of course, that's okay. They're your clothes. Come on in and have a seat. I'll have some burgers ready in a few minutes."

She sat down, noticing that Lucy was still staring at her. Self-consciously, she raised a hand to smooth her hair.

"So," Lucy began, "that song was really pretty. And you remembered the words."

Grace gave a short laugh. "Yeah, I guess I did. The odd thing is I don't remember singing it before, but the words were just there in my head. I don't understand it."

Lucy looked at her dad and, seeing the slight shake of his head, didn't say anything further. "Lucy, why don't you go get your brother for dinner." She didn't waste any time hopping off the stool. She couldn't wait to tell him.

Dinner was pleasant. Danny and the kids answered several questions Grace had about herself, and they filled her in on their lives and told her about the after-school activities that kept them busy. They'd agreed earlier not to mention anything about her singing, Danny and Daniel wanting to witness it for themselves.

After dinner, they moved to the living room and Lucy pulled photo albums from a bookshelf. Grace relaxed and laughed as her family pointed at pictures, describing the places where they'd vacationed and recounting some of the more hilarious excursions which had prompted some of the candid photos. She listened intently as they pointed out different people that appeared again and again in the photos. "I've got to meet this Lizzy," she said, after one particularly amusing story of Lizzy and a curious skunk while camping in the mountains. Lucy giggled when she pointed to a picture where Grace stood frowning at the camera. She was covered in white powder and Lizzy stood nearby with a hand over her mouth. She looked up at Lucy, curious.

"Well, that would be the work of our very own pastor." Then she proceeded to tell how Pastor Joe had dumped a giant cup of flour over Grace's head in retaliation for a prank she had pulled on him.

"Pastor Joe? Hmm, that explains a lot," Grace said, remembering the odd visit from the man she'd thought was a psych patient. "He seemed nice enough, although a bit ... strange."

Daniel snickered. "Strange? Yes. Nice? Now that's a bit questionable. But whatever you say."

Secretly, they'd hoped the photos and stories would trigger a memory, but so far, they were disappointed. Danny kept an eye on the kids, and his chest tightened when he saw his own anguish reflected on their faces.

Grace soaked in every detail about herself and her family. Later after saying good night, she laid down on the bed and stared at the ceiling, feeling both enlightened and saddened by the evening. She and her family obviously had a full, happy life together, but it was disheartening to not be able to remember any of it. So many moments of their lives captured and frozen in time, never to be forgotten. How ironic it was that she couldn't recall even one of those moments. Closing her eyes, she prayed for her life to return to normal. As long as her memories remained a mystery, not only would she struggle to move forward, but her family would as well. To her, even though she would never say so, it felt as if someone had chosen a family and home for her at random and placed her there without asking for her input, then expected her to live that life without complaint. She wondered if this was how young people of other cultures felt when their marriages were arranged. Did they just accept what was handed to them without question? And how does she even know there are cultures that practice that custom? How was it that she could know things, but not remember *how* she knew them? With a sigh, Grace laid her arm across her eyes, fighting the pressure in the back of her skull she'd come to recognize as a warning sign of a migraine.

* * *

Studying Danny's profile as he drove, Grace wondered what he was thinking. They were on their way to see the psychiatrist Dr. Whittaker had recommended. Danny was optimistic Dr. Hyatt would help coax her memories out of hiding, but Grace didn't want to get her hopes up. It had been nearly three weeks since her accident and she hadn't remembered a thing. She and Danny had eased into a simple daily routine, but at times, she still felt like a guest in her own home. Grace did the laundry and cleaned, even though Danny had told her he would handle it. She needed to be doing something other than sitting around all day waiting for a memory to surface only to have it no-show. Still, she felt like she was doing someone else's chores in someone else's home. She yearned for normal. But what was normal? Maybe this was her new norm. Destined to be a character in a movie sequel where everyone but her had seen the original film. Just wandering around the set without a script, waiting for someone to give her a hint on her next line.

"Hey, we're here." Danny's voice jerked her back to reality. Shaking her head clear, she opened her door and stepped out of the car. She looked up at the white stucco building in front of her and wondered if inside she would find a clue to the mystery her past had become. Danny came around the car and lightly touched the small of her back. "Ready?" She nodded and let him lead her up the walkway.

As she watched their reflections approach the double glass doors, movement behind Danny caught her eye. Someone standing in front of the coffee shop across the street. Someone familiar ... not familiar. That was the man from her dream.

Danny noticed her stiffen as she stopped in her tracks. When he touched her elbow, she whispered, "That man across the street."

As Danny turned to look behind them, he moved into her line of sight. "What man? There's no one there."

Grace spun around in disbelief. She had seen him right there. She stared at the spot where he'd stood under the awning.

"Who do you think you saw, Grace?"

Anger and frustration flashed across her face. "I don't *think* I saw anyone. I *know* I saw a man. And I saw him before, at the hospital." When Danny opened his mouth to respond, she shook her head and turned back to go into the building. "I don't expect you to believe me."

Danny followed her inside, puzzled. It wasn't like Grace to anger so quickly, especially over something so minor. As they stepped into the elevator and he pressed the button for the third floor, he tried to remember if the doctor had said anything about sudden mood changes. He'd been so relieved to have her home he hadn't thought about her mental stability.

By the time the elevator stopped, Grace's rattled nerves had settled to a mild tremble. She knew Danny meant well, and it wasn't his fault the man had disappeared. But she was sure she'd seen him. He'd been standing there, watching them. The same fear and tightness in her chest she'd woken up with in the hospital overtook her when she saw him. But she didn't want to worry Danny, and she didn't want to be told she was imagining things, so she dropped it even though she was certain of what she'd seen.

When they stepped into suite 303, the contrast of the office to the building's exterior surprised Grace. She had expected a harsh, sterile setting. Not the warm, inviting room she now stood in. The receptionist looked up and smiled. "Hi, you must be Grace. My name is Amanda." Grace smiled and let Danny handle signing her in and offering insurance and demographic information. As she looked around the room, the warm tones of the furnishings and the soft lighting eased her anxiety from moments before. All the paintings on the wall were nature scenes; one from the perspective of someone sitting on a porch and looking out across a field scattered with horses. On a hill in the distance stood a lone white cross. Of everything in the painting, and despite how small it was, that was what seemed to be the focus. Something pulled her into the scene, something familiar about the view. Whether it was the cross or the scenery itself, she wanted to be there. She saw herself walking up the hill, then kneeling at that cross. Even though it was too far away to see on the canvas, Grace knew there was a bed of wildflowers at its base. She shook her head. The artist was good. So good she could place herself in that field, could almost hear children laughing as they played on the grassy slopes. There was nothing on the frame indicating who the artist was, not even a signature on the painting itself. Interesting. She thought she'd like to have something like it of her own.

Danny studied Grace as she stared at the painting. He touched her arm. "It's good, isn't it?"

"Yes, I love it. It seems—almost familiar."

Danny stood straighter. "You recognize it?"

She shook her head. "No. I can't explain it, but it feels like I could step into it and know where I was."

"Mrs. Bradford, Dr. Hyatt is ready for you."

Grace nodded and followed the receptionist. As she led her down a short hallway, Amanda said, "After your appointment, you'll go out through another door. Your husband will be waiting for you there."

"Thank you." The knot in her stomach tightened as she stepped through the office door.

"Hello, Grace. Come on in." The woman held out her hand and gestured toward a comfortable chair. Instead of sitting behind her desk, the doctor sat in an identical chair facing Grace's. Unruly curls hung loose and reached to just below her shoulders, each lock seeming to do its own thing. Not all the curls twisted the same way, some even threatened to not curl at all. The look was very becoming to the doctor. It must be natural, she thought, and commented on it.

Dr. Hyatt smiled and reached up to touch her hair. "Yes, it's natural. I used to call it a curse, but I gave up trying to tame it a long time ago and learned to let it do what it wants. Now, let's talk about you."

The doctor eased Grace into smooth conversation with a few questions about her children.

Grace's face brightened at the mention of her kids. "Daniel and Lucy are amazing. They've been doing everything they can to help me remember. Especially Lucy." Her smile faltered.

"What is it?"

"I've failed them."

"Why do you say that?"

"I can't remember anything." Tears threatened to spill, and she reached for a tissue from a box on the desk. "They don't say it, but I can see the disappointment on their faces." Grace dabbed at the corners of her eyes. "They show me pictures and tell me stories and nothing rings a bell. Nothing. They've all been great, but I'm living with strangers. And sometimes I start feeling smothered. Like Danny's my babysitter or something."

Dr. Hyatt's voice was gentle. "Do you want to leave, Grace? Are you uncomfortable there?"

Grace shook her head. "No, I wouldn't say uncomfortable. Not really. Just—off. But even if I wanted to leave, there's nowhere else I could go. Everyone's a stranger. Even the city. If anyone trusted me to drive, I wouldn't know how to get to the nearest store. That is, if I could even find my way out of the neighborhood."

"That's something you can start with. Familiarizing yourself with your neighborhood. Have you tried going for a walk?"

"No." Grace widened her eyes. "Please don't tell Danny, but I'm afraid to go out alone. What if I'm attacked again?" Her hands twisted the tissue she held.

"Why don't you want Danny to know you're afraid?"

Grace dropped her head and pressed her lips together. Fresh tears rolled down her cheeks.

"Grace, after what you've been through, it's natural to feel uneasy." When Grace didn't respond, she continued. "Do you have a reason to believe it wasn't a random attack? Has something else happened?"

"There was a man." Her breath hitched. "In my room at the hospital."

Dr. Hyatt leaned forward. "Did he hurt you? Did you tell anyone?"

Shaking her head, she said, "No. He didn't hurt me. At least I don't think so. I'm not even sure he was real. I think I was dreaming. But then I saw him across the street on our way in here today. When I looked back at him, he was gone. Danny said no one was there." Grace rocked back and forth in her chair. "I feel like I'm losing my mind." She flattened a palm on either side of her face and groaned.

The doctor touched Grace's wrist and gently tugged her hand from her face. "Look at me." She waited until Grace turned toward her and didn't react to the pained expression pleading for help. "I believe you."

A soft cry escaped her throat. "You do?"

"I do. I can't say who it was or if it was the same individual who attacked you, but I believe you when you say someone was there. But let me say this. With the type of injury you had coupled with your memory loss, it's not unusual for your mind to play tricks on you."

Grace's shoulders slumped. "Great. Now I'm hallucinating."

"That's not what I meant. I believe you saw someone outside. But could there have been something similar about him that reminded you of the man in your hospital room? The color of his shirt? Or maybe a beard or the length of his hair? Anything like that?"

Grace's brow furrowed. "It looked like he was wearing a leather jacket." She closed her eyes. "Maybe that's all it was. Maybe I'm trying too hard to remember?"

The doctor smiled. "Maybe, maybe not. And I'm not saying that you should dismiss what you saw and chalk it up to mind tricks. I'm saying it's one possibility. I don't want you living in fear, but you still need to pay attention to your surroundings."

"I understand."

They spent the rest of the session discussing the need to increase her sense of independence and techniques to use when she felt claustrophobic. They talked at length about her headaches, and the doctor laid out a plan to monitor them.

"Remember," Dr. Hyatt said at one point. "Danny and the kids are dealing with a loss too."

Before she knew it, she was walking out of the office with Danny. As they stepped back into the sunshine, Grace scanned the street for the man she'd seen earlier, unable to shake the feeling that someone was watching her. She kept her worries to herself and was relieved when they were in the car and turning onto the street. Neither noticed the gray car that pulled out of the lot behind them.

On the drive home, Grace told Danny about her session with Dr. Hyatt, and how she was optimistic Grace would get her memory back. They'd discussed her injury and the symptoms she was having. The doctor had assured her that even though there was no way to predict what would eventually happen, they could work on dealing with her symptoms in the meantime. She wanted to meet with her every couple of weeks to monitor her headaches and to be sure Grace didn't slip into depression. She was to start a diary of her headaches to catalog severity, frequency, how long they lasted, and what made them better or worse. And she was to report any new symptoms immediately. Grace felt like it was homework, but it would at least feel like she was *doing* something.

Danny agreed the diary was a good idea and said he would also write down any symptoms he noticed that she might not be aware of herself. "Hey," he said. "Do you feel up to a visitor this evening?"

"A visitor? Who?" she asked.

He told her a friend wanted to stop by that evening to see her. "Lizzy's your best friend and has been for years. She has some errands to run first but wanted to stop by if you're up to it." Grace recalled the pretty face from their evening of perusing the family albums and found herself eager for someone new to talk to.

"Well, I think you all have sheltered me long enough. I'd like to meet her." Then she let out a short laugh, part amusement and part sadness. "It seems odd that I'm going to be meeting my best friend for the first time."

Danny reached over and squeezed her hand. "Maybe she'll jog that memory of yours awake." He gave her a smile. "Oh, I almost forgot. I have something for you. Open the glove compartment."

She did as he asked and pulled out a cell phone. "I had to get you a new one. The police weren't able to get any of your contacts or photos off your old phone. I've put in my numbers, and those for the kids, doctors, and of course Lizzy's. You two would talk or text nearly every day."

"Were they able to get anything else from my phone? For the investigation, I mean?"

Danny shook his head. "No, the phone was a total bust. I was able to get phone records from the cell company. There weren't any unusual calls, but it looks like there were a couple of texts the morning you were hurt. One incoming and one outgoing." He studied her face.

Grace frowned. "Meaning what?"

"Meaning someone texted you and you replied. I searched back a few months, and as far as I can tell, it wasn't a number you'd communicated with before. I tried calling the number, but it was no longer in service. I handed the records over to the police so they can look into it further." He placed a hand over hers. "We'll figure it out."

She gave him a weak smile and lowered her eyes to her new phone. She touched the screen and a beach scene appeared with the time and date across it. A few more touches and swipes and she found the contacts. "Thank you," she said. She didn't think she'd need it but had to admit she felt safer knowing it would be available if she did.

5

Write Your Story

Lizzy kicked the back wheel of her shopping cart for what felt like the millionth time. How did she always end up with the one with jacked up wheels, she thought with a final kick. As she walked, she pulled out her clicker and popped the trunk.

"Looks like you might need a hand," said a deep voice behind her.

Already irritated, Lizzy wasn't in the mood to be hit on today.

"I can manage," she snapped without turning around. "It's just groceries."

"I meant your flat," he persisted.

"What?" He had her attention, and she dropped two plastic bags into the open trunk and peered around the car at her completely flat back tire. "Great."

"You must have run over a nail or something. Let me help you get the spare on." The man was tall with hard features, and was dressed as if he'd just been working out.

But he looked harmless enough. It was broad daylight, and she still had to take these groceries home and change before her interview this afternoon with the Director of Nursing at the hospital; all before she was finally able to see Grace. That was one visit she refused to miss. "Thanks, I'd really appreciate it. You're sure you don't mind?"

He flashed her a smile. "Not at all. Here, let's get these bags back out." Thirty minutes later, she was on her way home with groceries and a dinner date for that evening.

* * *

Back in her den at home, Grace stood in front of the bookcase that framed the fireplace and perused the shelves. She reached for one of the books that had been placed spine in. She took the novel and sat in a chair by the window. The book lay in her lap, but she hadn't yet opened it. She shook her head, thinking she could've chosen any of the other books. It wouldn't matter if she'd already read it. It would be new to her, regardless.

"Grace?" She turned to the voice at her door and smiled at the pretty redhead peeking in. The woman wore jeans and a flowing pink blouse, and her hair hung loose around her shoulders.

"Hi. You must be Lizzy," Grace said and was rewarded with a bright smile. However, Grace didn't miss the wetness in the other woman's eyes.

"That's right. I'm so happy to see you." She walked over and sat on the footstool in front of Grace's chair. She reached out to take her hands. "Woman, don't you ever do this to me again. I don't know what I'd do if I lost you." Then without warning, she pulled Grace into a tight hug. "I'm sorry I haven't been by sooner, but I was in the middle of a six-week assignment in San Diego." As soon as she spoke the words, Lizzy realized her mistake. Holding a palm up and shaking her head, she said, "Sorry. I'm a traveling nurse, and I take six- to twelve-week assignments all over the country. That's why I haven't been here before now."

Grace was surprised at the boldness of her visitor but replied, "Well I assure you that if I had any clue what I did to end up in this mess, I most definitely wouldn't repeat it."

Lizzy chuckled, then pulled back to look at her friend. "It's so good to see you. I've missed you. This last assignment was a tough one."

Curiously comfortable with her, Grace asked, "Will you tell me about how we met? How we became friends?"

"Sure." Lizzy leaned forward and rested her elbows on her knees. "Let me see. Back when you were still teaching high school, before Daniel was born, I was the school nurse. We ended up at the same table in the lunchroom one day, and I was complaining about the meat loaf. You offered to share your lasagna, which was *amazing* by the way, then we started talking and hit it off. I'd found out rather quickly that being cooped up in school was not for me. I love being able to move around, taking care of actual patients. The sick ones, you know?" Holding a palm up, she clarified, "Not that students don't need nurses from time to time, but reviewing shot records and handing out Tylenol wasn't my thing. I wanted a challenge. So, about the time you left to be a stay-at-home mom, I started travel nursing." When she'd finished her story, she looked at her friend with concern. "Now tell me, and be honest, how are you feeling? And don't put on a brave front like you always do. Tell me the truth." She looked at her pointedly.

"Do I really do that?" Grace continued without waiting for an answer. Obviously she did, or Lizzy wouldn't have said it. "Physically, I feel okay. The doctors say that I'm recovering well, and other than my memory loss, I'm practically back to a hundred percent."

Lizzy stared at her and pressed her lips together before she responded. "I didn't ask what the doctors said. I asked you how you're feeling. How are *you* doing?"

Grace let out a nervous laugh. "Are you always this forward and blunt?"

Her friend sat a little straighter and crossed her arms. "Yes. I am. And one of these days you're going to remember that. Now, fess up. Talk to me."

Grace felt a bond with Lizzy she couldn't explain. Though she remembered nothing about their relationship, she sensed Lizzy was one

who would challenge her, keep her on her toes. Maybe she was grasping at anything that resembled an anchor, anything to stabilize the
turmoil in her mind. She wanted to feel a connection. "Honestly, I
don't know. One minute I think I'm fine, and the next ..." She shook
her head and looked out the window into the backyard. "Danny and
the kids have been great and are definitely more patient than I deserve.
This is so unfair to them." She glanced back at Lizzy. "But what can I
do? There are times when I think I'm losing my mind."

Lizzy held up a hand to interrupt. "Uh, correction, my friend. You
literally *did* lose your mind."

Grace chuckled and dipped her chin in acknowledgment.
"Touché."

Lizzy picked up the book still lying in Grace's lap. "You know, you
love reading." She ran her hand over the cover and opened it. "All you
have to do is open the cover of a book to step into another life, and
that journey becomes yours. The characters become your best friends.
You can travel the world, explore the unknown. You slip into the
minds of the characters, feel what they feel. Fear what they fear. You'll
love, laugh, cry, and hurt right along with them. Every time you turn a
page, you open a door to a new experience. A new adventure. Every
page has a secret to reveal. Sometimes it's so good and so real you don't
want to leave that life and step back into this one. You want that story,
that moment, to continue." She gently handed the book back to her
friend and met her eyes.

"It sounds like you love to read too."

Lizzy gave her a sad half smile. "You could say that. It's one of the
things we have in common. Grace, when you woke up with no memory, you essentially stepped into another life. Just like opening a new
book. Except this one you won't be reading. It's yours to write. Now
you can either start filling in those blank pages and make it a best seller,
or you can sit here waiting around for that noodle of yours to get un-
tangled enough for your memory to find its way back. What's it gonna
be?"

Grace felt as if she'd been kicked in the gut. She sat there and processed the dam of emotions Lizzy's words had released. "You're right. I've been feeling sorry for myself, living day-to-day, waiting for a memory. Hoping to wake up in the morning and be back to normal. Whatever that is." She paused for a moment. "I don't want to live like that. Afraid and unsure. I want to do everything I can to make sure those blank pages are filled. Danny and the kids deserve that."

"*You* deserve that," Lizzy said.

"I'll work on it." Grace studied the cover of the book she gripped. "Can we take a walk? I'd like to get some fresh air."

"Of course we can. Let's go."

As they reached the end of the driveway, Grace lifted her face to the sun. "Oh, this feels wonderful. Thanks for this."

"Tell me this isn't the first time you've been out."

"No, Danny and the kids walk with me sometimes. But I don't like to bother them."

Lizzy looked at her and frowned. "They don't want you going out alone?"

Grace didn't meet her eyes. "It's not that. I just haven't tried it on my own." She changed the subject before Lizzy could question her. "Can I ask you something?"

"Sure. Anything."

"Are Danny and I happy?"

"What do you mean?"

"Well, you're my best friend, right?"

"That's right."

"So you'd know if Danny and I were having trouble, if we were going through something?"

"I'd like to believe that I'd know, you and I talk about everything. But as far as I know, everything was great. If there was ever a perfect couple, it would be you two. I mean, Danny has had his moments, times where he'd get frustrated. And he's been known to have a bit of a temper."

Her stomach tightened. "Temper?"

"Yeah, just quick to anger, you know? But I've never seen him out of control. Like the time Daniel left his basketball gear in the garage and forgot to move it. The next morning when Danny backed over it, you said he really lit into Daniel about being irresponsible. By that afternoon, he'd gotten over it and he and Daniel were in the driveway shooting hoops."

"So not violent or anything?"

Lizzy felt a nervous quiver in her stomach. She chose her words carefully. "No, never. At least you've never said anything. Has something happened?"

Grace shook her head. "No, nothing like that. I just don't know him and I don't know what to expect. Can you tell me about him? What he's really like?"

Lizzy relaxed her shoulders. "Danny's very much a family man. You're both involved with all the kids' activities. When you aren't at a school-related event, you're usually hiking or camping. Danny is very protective of you and the kids."

"What about you? I've seen a lot of pictures of you with us on camping trips and stuff, but only you. No husband or kids. Why is that?"

Lizzy was quiet as she continued to walk, watching her feet on the sidewalk. When she lifted her face, she appeared sad and wistful. "I was engaged once, but it didn't work out. The traveling I do with work isn't conducive to relationships. And I can't have children."

"Why not?"

"Endometriosis. And something about the weird shape of my uterus." She lifted a shoulder. "It's okay. Daniel and Lucy have been my honorary babies since they were born. Every summer, I take them on a mini vacation. It's kind of our own little tradition."

"I'm so sorry. And here I am whining about myself."

"Listen, I know this is shocking and new to you, but to me, it isn't. I learned this a long time ago and I've accepted it." Lizzy paused and held Grace's eyes with her own. "Talk to me, Grace. Has something happened? Why are you asking these questions about you and Danny?"

"It's just that everyone seems to be walking on eggshells around me. How am I supposed to find out who I am if everyone continues to treat me like I'm going to break? Am I really that fragile?"

Lizzy scoffed. "No. You're the strongest woman I know, always levelheaded. You're involved and supportive of everything, but you prefer to stay behind the scenes."

Grace tilted her head and thought about Lizzy's words.

"Have you talked to Danny about this?" When Grace shook her head, Lizzy laid her hand over Grace's and caught her eye. "You might want to think about that. Give him a chance."

"I'll think about it. What about me? Was there anything unusual going on with me lately?"

"Unusual in what way?"

"Well, the police say I was at the park alone but not dressed for walking. When Danny told me about that, I got the feeling he was suspicious of something."

"Suspicious of what?"

Grace lifted her shoulders. "Why I'd be alone at the park if I wasn't there for exercise. My phone was demolished but the phone records showed one text that I replied to. Danny said he searched back several months and that was the only time that number showed up. And I had picked up lunch for two on the way. The bag was still in the car."

Lizzy wrinkled her brow and frowned. "Hm, that's odd. It would be very unlike you to meet someone out of the way like that if it wasn't someone you knew."

Grace nodded and turned to meet Lizzy's eyes. "Okay. I need you to help me with something. And I need to you to promise you won't say anything to Danny."

Lizzy tucked her chin and lifted her brows. Sucking in her bottom lip, she gestured for Grace to continue. "When I said I feel like I'm losing my mind, I meant it. Sometimes I think someone is watching me." She looked down at her feet and didn't notice the dark cloud that crossed Lizzy's face. When she looked back up, Lizzy was staring at her.

"Tell me what you mean by that."

Grace told Lizzy about the man she thought she dreamed about in the hospital, then continued with how she thought she'd seen him outside the psychiatrist's office. "That's why I don't walk alone. I'm afraid. But please don't tell Danny. I don't want him worrying any more than he already does. But I swear I've seen him a couple of times here at home, standing at the end of the street staring at the house." She paused and ran her hand through her hair. "Please tell me you believe me, Lizzy. Danny thinks I'm stressed and imagining things. I haven't told him about seeing the guy outside here."

Lizzy took a deep breath and let it out slowly. "Okay," she said, drawing out each letter as if trying to buy time to decide how to answer. "I believe you. But why not tell Danny? He needs to know."

Grace closed her eyes and sighed. "He'll just brush it off and say it's a neighbor or something. Or that my mind is playing tricks." She lifted her hands. "Maybe it is. Regardless, I don't want him to worry over something that might not even be real. I'd like to figure it out first." She covered her face and groaned. "All this makes my head pound."

Lizzy wouldn't patronize her. Grace was already insecure and tense. "We'll figure this out, okay? Maybe you could try to snap a picture of him the next time you see him. Then we can go from there."

"I could try that."

Lizzy looked at her watch and said, "Listen. There's somewhere I need to be. Let's keep this between us for now, okay? Let me think on it, and I'll stop back by in a couple of days, and we can talk about it some more." Putting an arm around her, she drew her in close and led her friend back to the safety of her home. "Everything's going to be okay."

6

The Voice

"I'd like to go to church tomorrow." Grace looked up from her plate of pasta to gauge her husband's reaction. Danny looked surprised but pleased.

Nodding, he said, "Of course, that's a great idea. We can go to worship service and go out for lunch after."

"Dad, can we go to Jolene's? It's Mom's favorite." Lucy looked at her mother with a smile. "If Jolene's fried chicken doesn't trigger your memory, it'll definitely trigger those taste buds."

"Okay, Jolene's it is. But only if you two clear the table and do the dishes after dinner." His terms elicited the expected groans from Lucy and Daniel, but they knew better than to argue. Satisfied, Lucy stabbed a piece of shrimp with her fork and Daniel sipped his water.

"I've been meaning to ask you," Grace began. "Do I sing in the church choir?" Daniel sputtered and the water he'd sipped spewed straight toward Lucy.

"Daniel!" Lucy scolded her brother as she wiped her arm with a napkin.

Grace jumped at Lucy's shriek.

He choked out a weak "sorry" as he dabbed at his mouth and chin. They both looked at their father.

Even though Danny wanted to laugh, he somehow knew his wife was serious. He hid his amusement by clearing his throat with a fist in front of his mouth. "Um, no, you don't sing in the choir. Why do you ask?"

Grace pushed her pasta around with her fork. "Ever since I woke up in the hospital, these songs have been in my head, so I just thought maybe there was a reason. That's all. Maybe I can join."

Daniel's head snapped up and Lucy's pasta suddenly became very interesting. Both sets of eyes were wide as they waited for their father's response. "Well, um, why don't we take it one step at a time? You don't want to overwhelm yourself."

Grace thought for a moment and then smiled. "Maybe you're right. We'll see how tomorrow goes. Will you at least point out the choir director so I'll know who to go to when I'm ready?"

Glancing at the kids, and unsure of what else to say, he said, "Sure." Looking back at them, he shrugged his shoulders as if to say "what was I supposed to say?"

* * *

Grace didn't know what she'd expected, but she was pleasantly surprised when she stepped into the small church. She accepted and returned numerous hugs and handshakes, smiled at all the "welcome backs and good-to-see-yous," and thanked all the well-wishers for their prayers. The pastor had been keeping the congregation updated on her progress since the accident, so nearly everyone knew about her amnesia. Thankfully, they all refrained from asking prying and awkward questions. Still, she felt the stares they didn't think she noticed, but she understood their curiosity. It wasn't every day one encountered an amnesiac. Someone who'd known you for years and suddenly didn't recognize your face. Danny led her to a middle pew on the right side of the sanctuary. She settled herself on the green cushion and examined her surroundings. Light shone through the stained-glass windows, casting warm rays of color across the room. Each window was bordered by open white shutters that reminded her of angel wings. She'd hoped coming here would trigger something in her memory, but she hid her disappointment, knowing she couldn't rush it. A few more members paused to speak to her, and then the room grew quiet as a group of people entered the choir loft from a door to the right.

When they'd taken their seats, the pastor stepped to the podium and welcomed everyone with a big smile and cheerful greeting. The crowd's response matched his enthusiasm. He bowed his head and led the congregation in a short prayer, where he thanked God for the beautiful morning, new beginnings, and answered prayers. As he walked away from the pulpit, he glanced at Grace and she returned his smile with brief a nod of her head, silently thanking him for not drawing attention to her specifically.

A heavyset woman with a helmet of brown curls replaced Pastor Joe at the podium. "Good morning, everyone! It's good to see you all here today. If you would all stand and turn to page 238 in your hymnal, let's all sing 'Nothing but the Blood.'"

Grace picked up a hymnal from the back of the pew in front of her and flipped to the correct page as she stood between Danny and Lucy. She sang along softly, noticing that Lucy kept looking at her expectantly throughout the song. Assuming she was waiting for some evidence of recognition, she leaned over and whispered, "I guess I don't remember this one." Lucy just smiled in return and turned back to her own hymnal as they finished the song.

Grace listened with rapt attention to the sermon that followed, noting it was coincidentally appropriate for her current situation. She suspected the pastor had intentionally written his sermon with her in mind, as he made multiple references to scripture that reminded believers to "remember to continue to worship the Lord even in times of trouble." His words hit close to home for Grace, specifically when he read from the book of Thessalonians:

Rejoice always, pray continually, give thanks in all circumstances; for this is God's will for you in Christ Jesus.

The words comforted Grace, and a peace overcame her. It was the first time since waking up after her accident that she felt, and truly believed, there was a reason for what had happened to her. She closed her eyes and sent up a silent prayer of thanks, and when the lady with the helmet hair returned to the pulpit, she stood with the rest of the congregation to sing the invitation song. As they sang "Great are you Lord," Grace closed her eyes and let the words of life, love, and hope envelope her.

A warmth started in her chest and spread through her, reaching all the way to her extremities. As the sounds around her faded to the background of her mind, she felt like she was standing alone on a hill in warm sunshine.

She tilted her head back, and the warmth fell on her face. As it flowed around her, she sensed an energy filled with love, hope, understanding, goodness, and power. She lifted her arms to accept it, and suddenly it was as if she was standing with the arms of God wrapped around her, granting her the comfort she'd been so desperately craving. Grace smiled as these invisible arms embraced her with a divine tenderness she couldn't have explained if she'd tried. She stood there filled with joy and peace, letting the words cascade over her.

Grace opened her eyes as the song ended and was surprised to find her hands raised and tears streaming down her face. As she lowered her arms, she turned to see most of the congregation, including her own family, staring at her. She couldn't read Danny's face, but she didn't miss the tears in his eyes. Lucy's face was also wet, and Grace could've sworn she saw pride shining behind her tears. Daniel stood on the other side of Lucy. His jaw hung open. Then Lucy jabbed her elbow into his rib and hissed, "I told you!"

* * *

Silence weighed heavily in the car. Pastor Joe had promptly begun his closing prayer, and Danny had ushered his family out the door and to their car practically before the amen had left the preacher's mouth.

Daniel tried to voice what he knew everyone was thinking. "Well, that was—"

"An amazing service. Yes, it was, son."

"But Dad," he tried again, but Danny cut him off yet again, and threw him a cautioning glance in the rearview mirror.

"So, do we all still agree on Jolene's?"

Daniel and Lucy took the hint and mumbled their agreement while Grace remained quiet in the front seat. When Danny touched her arm, she smiled and nodded, but then turned back to gaze out her window.

An hour later, Grace pushed her plate away. "That was delicious," she said. "You were right, Lucy."

"I told you you'd like it." What Lucy didn't say was that she'd been hoping her mother would remember something about the place. Anything. She looked away and Danny caught her eye with a smile, his silent signal telling her he understood.

Danny tried to keep the mood light during lunch, but the cloud hovering over them kept everyone tense and hesitant to talk. He'd been contemplating how to handle the matter and struggled between a head on approach or continuing his current course of trying to protect Grace at all costs. He knew her mental status was delicate right now, and he was unsure how much she could actually bear, despite her claims of not wanting to be sheltered any longer. Eventually, if she didn't get her memory back, they'd have to come to terms with it and move on. Hadn't the doctor said to keep things as normal as possible? His decision made, he picked up the check and stood to leave. Now he had to decide how best to broach the subject. With a sigh, he gestured for his crew to go ahead of him, and he followed them to the car.

Back at home, Danny sat in his office chair thinking about what they'd experienced at church and how he should talk to Grace about it. The sight he'd witnessed was nothing short of astounding, and as hard as he tried, he couldn't make sense of it. He sent up a prayer asking God to guide him and also to lend his family strength throughout the days to come. Then he called a family meeting.

They all settled in the den, Lucy and Daniel on the sofa and Grace in the chair by the window. Danny chose a chair near Grace and perched himself on the edge. "I think we need to talk about what happened at church today."

Grace held up her hand to stop him. "Wait. May I say something first, please?" Daniel held his hands out palms up, motioning for her to go ahead. "Let me apologize to all of you. I'm not sure what happened, and I honestly didn't even realize I was singing out loud. I know that my being there today was awkward enough, having to be seen with 'The Amnesia Lady.'" She made invisible quotes in the air to emphasize the name she'd given herself. "And then I made it worse by making a spectacle of myself and embarrassing you. I am so sorry." Tears filled her eyes as she looked at each of them. Where she expected to see disgust and disappointment, she saw only confusion.

Danny, Lucy, and Daniel all looked at one another. Lucy opened her mouth to speak but nothing came out. Danny, always to rescue, spoke for them. "You think you embarrassed us?" He shook his head. "What makes you think that?"

"Well, I saw how everyone was looking at me." She picked up a pillow from beside her and hugged it to her chest, then turned to look out the window.

"Look at me," Danny said. When she turned back to him, he continued. "What I was trying to say was that we don't understand what happened in church, where all that came from. But I assure you what you saw on our faces wasn't embarrassment. It was awe. We were completely and utterly amazed. Everyone was."

"Amazed?" Now it was Grace's turn to be confused. "I don't understand. What was there to be amazed about?"

"Your voice, Grace. It was beautiful."

"It's not like you've never heard me sing before."

Daniel stole a glance at Lucy and said, "Um, yeah, we've heard you sing." She elbowed him for the second time that day, and they tried to hide their grins.

Danny cleared his throat. "That's kind of what we need to talk about." Grace shook her head, still not understanding. "Ah, well, you usually don't sing in church. Actually, you don't sing at all. Ever." He paused, waiting for her response.

Grace wrinkled her forehead as her brows came together and she stared at each of them in turn. "I still don't understand what you're trying to say. What do you mean, I don't sing?"

Her husband laced his fingers and tapped his thumbs together. "Well, first of all, you've always avoided drawing attention to yourself. You've always been"—he tapped his fingers on his knee searching for the right word—"reserved. Very reserved. You never even sang much here at home with us, much less in front of anyone else."

"Why not?" She still couldn't grasp what Danny was trying to say. Why didn't he come right out and say whatever it was?

"Because you sound like a goat on crack."

"Daniel!" Danny's voice was sharp and caused Grace to jump.

"Well, not *today*," Daniel rushed to correct himself. "Today you sounded great, Mom. It was incredible. Just like Dad said. I'm just saying before ... well, before you sounded ... bad. That's how you'd get me out of bed every morning. It was the only alarm that worked."

She was stunned. Of all the things Danny could have said, this was not what she expected. "I'm trying to understand. So, what you're saying is that before the accident I didn't like to sing. Couldn't sing, in fact. And now ..." She lifted her hands and dropped them back into her lap.

"Now you need to audition for *The Voice*," Lucy said. "That's how good you sang today."

"The Voice?"

"It's a reality show on TV. Basically, a talent show where people compete for money and a record deal."

"But none of this makes any sense." Grace put a hand to her forehead and then kneaded the back of her neck. The headache that had been threatening since lunch was now hammering at her skull from the inside.

Danny noticed her discomfort. "Okay guys, meeting's over," he announced. When the kids had left the room, he turned back to his wife. "Grace, why don't you go lie down for a bit? This is a lot to take in and none of us understands it. We can talk more later."

She didn't have the strength to argue. She stood, and the room began to spin. She staggered and reached out when she feared she was going to fall. Danny caught her and eased her back down into the chair. Leaning forward, with her elbows on her knees, she placed her head in her hands.

Unable to hold it in any longer, she sobbed. Danny sat on the ottoman in front of her and placed his hands on either side of her face. He rested his forehead against the top of her head, whispering soothing, reassuring words. They sat there together for several minutes until her sobs had subsided, then he gently helped her up and walked with her up the stairs. She lay down on the bed, and he pulled a blanket from the foot of it to cover her. Smoothing her hair, he said, "I love you, Grace. I promise we'll figure this out. Now get some rest." He kissed her lightly on the forehead and left the room. Grace closed her eyes and soon drifted off to sleep.

7

A Memory

She fought to break the grip of the hand on her arm as she tried to run. Another hand pulled her back by her purse strap. Her attacker wanted something, was furious that she hadn't brought it. He shoved her against the car, slamming her left shoulder against the doorjamb, causing her to yell out in pain. When she tried to kick him, her knee rammed into the door and she lost the momentum she needed. Her attacker grew angrier and jerked her backward against his body. She couldn't make out the words that he hissed into her ear, but she had no doubt that whatever threat they promised would become a reality if she didn't escape. He pulled her away from the car. She didn't know what was going to happen, but she knew that if she didn't do something, it would end badly. Very badly. She stopped fighting and allowed her legs to go limp. He dragged her across the pavement, scraping her legs raw. She dug her heels into the ground, but her efforts were futile. Then they stopped. His grip on her upper body tightened with a vicious squeeze before he brutally thrust her toward the ground.

Grace woke with a sharp intake of breath. Her heart beat like a bass drum at halftime in her chest. The splitting headache she'd had was only slightly better. Groaning, she forced herself to sit up and rolled her neck from side to side, trying to loosen her tight muscles. When she saw the glass of water on the nightstand, she knew Danny must have come in to check on her. She shook two pills from the bottle beside the glass and washed them down with the water.

In the bathroom, she peered into the mirror as she brushed her teeth, trying to make sense of the images of her dream. As the chaos dissolved into clarity, the hand holding her toothbrush slowed. She stared at her reflection, eyes wide. She spit out the toothpaste, rinsed her mouth, grabbed the towel from the rack, and tore out of the bathroom, down the stairs in search of her husband.

She found him in the kitchen. "Danny! I think I remembered something." Twisting the towel that was still clutched in her hand, she told him about her dream. "I know it's not much. But it's something, right?" she asked hopefully.

"I'm sure it has to be," he replied. He took a pen and a small notebook from a drawer behind him. "Tell me again exactly what you remembered and take it slow. Let's figure out as many details as we can and write them down." She relayed everything she could remember about the dream, stopping to repeat specifics when Danny interrupted with a question. The attorney in him knew what questions to ask and within minutes, they had a list of every detail she could recall. Finally, she could see a glimmer of hope beyond the cloud that had become her life.

Danny took a deep breath and let it out, his cheeks puffing. "Okay. So from what you've told me, the car you were pushed up against in your dream was yours. Come on, I want to show you something." She followed him into the garage. He turned the light on and walked to the driver's side of her car.

She hadn't driven herself anywhere yet and hadn't noticed it when getting in and out of Danny's SUV, because he parked on the passenger side of her car. But there, in the middle of her door, was a slight indentation right where her knee would connect. She reached out to touch the area, recalling the pain and bruising she had when she woke up in that horrid hospital bed.

"It really was a memory," she whispered. "It was real." She turned to Danny as her excitement swirled, and she smiled. "I remembered something!" She threw herself into his arms and wrapped her own around his neck.

Danny hardly had time to return her embrace before she pulled away. "Oh, I'm so sorry," she began. "I didn't mean to—I was just so excited."

"Don't be sorry. This is great!" His hands were still on her waist, and he reluctantly pulled them away. If she only knew how he'd longed to hold her again. But he wouldn't push her. His family lived on Grace time now. But this was a step in the right direction, albeit a small one. Small steps led to bigger steps, steps toward a full recovery and getting his wife back.

8

Take a Walk

"Lizzy's going to stop by later. We're going for a walk around the neighborhood. I'd like to get out of the house for a bit."

Danny looked up from his computer with a frown. "Why didn't you say something? I could go with you or take you anywhere you want to go. You aren't a prisoner here, Grace. You can go out anytime you want."

"I know. But I thought it would be nice to have some company, and I didn't want to take you away from your work." Danny had been working from home as much as he could but planned to return to the office as soon as she felt comfortable being left on her own. Grace didn't mention her fear of leaving the house alone. She hadn't ventured any further than the back deck unless Danny or one of the kids was with her. There had been no sign of the man on the street in the past few days, and Grace wondered again if he was a figment her imagination had conjured.

Danny studied her face. "I appreciate that, but it's no trouble. Is there—" The doorbell interrupted what he was about to say and Grace seized the opportunity to avoid any discussion about her fears.

"That must be Lizzy." She darted from Danny's office.

She opened the door and greeted Lizzy's smile with one of her own. Lizzy held up a Starbucks cup. "Caramel Macchiato, no whip—your favorite."

Grace accepted the warm cup. "I'll take your word for it. Come on in. I'll tell Danny we're heading out. You don't mind if we walk while we drink, do you?"

"No, not at all." She heard Grace's muffled voice, then Danny's deeper one.

"Hey, Liz!" Danny called from down the hall.

"Hi, Danny!" Lizzy called back.

The women silently agreed on a slow pace and sipped their coffees as they walked. Lizzy was the first to speak. "How's it going? Have you seen any more of the mystery man?"

Grace shook her head. "Maybe it was my imagination after all."

"That's a relief. I was beginning to think I was going to have to set up a stakeout and watch your house. Seriously, though. Are you feeling safer?"

"I am. I wanted to go out today to get a feel for the neighborhood without Danny. I figure if I don't get the jitters, I might try it on my own tomorrow."

"I think that's a good idea. Staying cooped up in that house isn't doing your mental health any good. You've gotta get out and let your brain breathe."

Grace laughed. "Let my brain breathe?"

"Yep, it's a medical fact. Take it slow at first. Stay within a couple of blocks from your house for the first few days and work your way up."

"I'll try that." They walked three blocks, then turned left so they could circle and approach the house from the opposite direction. Grace appreciated her friend and was about to say so when Lizzy stopped with a huff.

"Why do people do that?" Lizzy pointed to the ground at the base of a light pole. Someone had discarded a convenience store coffee cup and several cigarette butts were scattered in the grass. Lizzy poured out the last swallow of her coffee and began scooping the butts with her empty cup. When she'd finished, she picked up the discard cup and placed it into her own.

"Sorry, but people have no respect. You ready to head home?"

Grace nodded and shifted her gaze from the pole to her house down the street. "Lizzy, this is where I saw that man standing."

Lizzy followed Grace's line of sight. "Here? At this corner? You're sure?"

Grace nodded. "I'm sure."

Lizzy held up the cup in her hand. "These look old. They could've been there for a while. If I hadn't seen the cup and stopped to get it, I probably wouldn't have noticed them."

Grace looked, and Lizzy gave her a halfhearted smile. "You know, you're right. I'm reaching. I haven't seen that guy around in a while. That could be anybody's trash."

Telling herself she was being silly, she fell in step with Lizzy as they made their way back to the Bradford home.

9

A Gift from God

Grace stepped out of her closet dressed in a simple gray T-shirt and navy leggings. For the first time, she'd finally slept through the night without running from invisible monsters or digging through mountains of blank paper, searching for her memories in her dreams. The headache that had become a nearly constant companion seemed to be sleeping in and hadn't yet started pounding on the door of her head, demanding attention. The kids were at school and Danny was at work, so she had the house to herself. She'd finally ventured on short drives to the market and doctors' appointments on her own. Her appointments were done for the week and the few chores that had become her routine were complete. Over the weeks she'd begun to get restless, and at times felt like the walls were closing in. When she wasn't looking through photo albums, she was cleaning, and when she wasn't cleaning, she was reading. She'd spent countless hours sitting on the swing on the back deck reading from the collection of novels on the bookshelves, hoping to get a glimpse of who she used to be. And singing. She sang often, needing to satisfy the overwhelming urge to get the songs out of her head.

Whispers of her predicament had begun to spread until rumors of her story had ended up on social media. Danny had tried to shield her from most of the rumors, but curiosity had gotten the best of her and she'd created an account for herself and found some of the posts. According to some, she'd been drinking and driving when she'd wrecked and hit her head. In another version, she'd fallen down the stairs and some suspected she'd been pushed. Still others claimed she was faking the amnesia, hoping to gain attention and notoriety, although their suspected reasons were unclear. A few posts defended her and offered support, praising her new ability while skeptics continued to scoff. Danny's secretary had intercepted several phone calls from churches and other organizations inviting her to sing and tell her story. As if she was some kind of circus side show. A freak. She'd made it clear to Danny that she had no desire to perform for anyone. As for social media, they'd ignored the accusations and rumors until the attackers finally gave up and moved on to the next unfortunate target.

She still didn't understand what was happening to her and no one had been able to explain it. Not even Dr. Hyatt, who'd told her to accept what she couldn't change and live her life. The doctor remained hopeful her memory would return, but Grace had begun to accept the fact that it might not. She'd decided to take Lizzy's advice and refused to sit quietly waiting for something that might or might not decide to join the party. Which was exactly why she'd decided to get out of the house. Her body had healed, but she decided she needed to be stronger. And on days like today, when she had so much nervous energy she felt like she could run out of her own skin, a long walk was the only thing that could keep her sane.

Grace was about four blocks from her house when she saw Mrs. Cooper walking down her driveway. The short, round woman wore an outfit exactly like every other one Grace had seen her in on her walks. The velveteen pantsuit she wore today was green. Christmas green. And it didn't go at all with the pink canvas tennis shoes she wore on her feet. "Hi, Mrs. Cooper," she called out.

"Hello, Grace. How are you? It's a gorgeous day for a walk." The eccentric woman was always so pleasant, and Grace enjoyed their little talks. "If you have a minute, I'd like to talk to you about something."

"Sure, I have nothing but time."

"Well, before I say anything, I want you to know that you can refuse, and we won't be offended in the least."

"We?" Grace's curiosity was piqued. "Yes. The WAG group at church."

"The WAG group? I'm not sure ..." She had no idea what the woman was talking about.

"Oh, pshaw. Listen at me." She waved a hand in front of her face as if she were erasing a chalkboard. "Women and God. WAG. That's what we call the women's group. Some of us, especially the younger women, have been wanting to change the name for years, but as long as old Mavis Cummings is around, it'll stay WAG. The men in the church like to say they named our group because all we do is sit around and wag our tongues. But I beg to differ. We do a lot of work, we do." She emphasized her proclamation with a firm dip of her chin.

Grace nodded, amused. "I'm sure you do. So ... the question?"

"Oh! Yes. We'd like to know if you would be willing to speak at our monthly meeting next Tuesday." She waited hopefully.

Grace cringed inside, her amusement at the woman turning to dread. "Me? Speak? About what?" she asked. She didn't want to be rude by immediately refusing.

"Well, yourself, of course. We're all amazed at the change in you since your accident." She lowered her voice on the last word as if she were telling a secret. By now, surely everyone knew what had happened to her. "Now, I don't expect you to reveal details of your experience and your personal life, just maybe how you're dealing with it." She leaned in and again lowered her voice to secret level. "And if you wanted to sing a song or two, we wouldn't object to it."

She thought back to her conversation with Lizzy during her first visit to the house and remembered her promise to keep moving forward. She decided to fill in another blank page of her story, starting with a group in her own church. "I'd be happy to speak at your meeting, Mrs. Cooper."

The woman practically squealed with excitement. "Oh, thank you, dear! I'm going to go in right now and call the girls to let them know. We'll have cake and cookies, and I'll make my famous punch. Mavis swears I spike it, but I assure you I do not. She just wishes I did. Enjoy your walk!" She waved as she hustled back up the drive.

Grace smiled as she continued down the sidewalk and thought about what she'd say to a room full of strangers. At the next intersection, before crossing, she looked to her left and right. Someone darted onto the sidewalk behind her. She turned around, but no one was there. She turned back and was sure she saw a figure duck behind one of the cars parked on the street. The hair on the back of her neck stood and a ball of dread formed in the pit of her stomach. Her first instinct was to run, but unwilling to succumb to her fear, she stepped forward. She scolded herself for not bringing her phone. Maybe she could've snapped a picture. Taking slow steps, she clenched her keys in a fist with the tips protruding between her closed fingers to form a makeshift weapon. With a quick intake of breath for courage, she jumped around the rear of the car, ready to defend herself. There was no one there. Grace swiveled in a 360 turn, scanning the streets. It was empty but for a young woman jogging down the sidewalk across the street with a German Shepard trotting at her side at the end of a short leash. Relief, dismay, and apprehension twisted together in a medley of emotional struggle. She knew she'd seen someone. What was happening to her?

Choking back a sob, she curved a hand around the back of her neck where she felt the fingers of another headache beginning to close like a vise. Backing away from the car, Grace found a bench nearby and sat down, taking a few moments to steady her nerves.

After a full minute of focused breathing, she stood. Reversing her direction, she made a beeline for Piedmont Drive, turning frequently to check for a pursuer. She forced herself to focus on the relaxation techniques Dr. Hyatt had taught her, and by the time she'd retraced her footsteps to her front door, her nerves had calmed significantly. She was relieved to be home without another encounter. Her headache still lingered but had diminished from a pounding force to an irritating nag.

Placing her keys on the table by the stairs, she went straight to the kitchen for a bottle of water and some Tylenol. Grace held the cold bottle to the back of her neck for a moment before placing it on the counter. "Next stop, hot shower," she said to herself.

Her hair was still wet when she returned to the kitchen dressed in jeans and a long-sleeved T-shirt. Lunch was a small salad with grilled chicken breast left over from the previous night's dinner. Deciding to eat on the back deck, she picked up her bowl and reached for the bottle of water she'd left on the counter. It wasn't there. Grace turned in a circle, glancing at all the countertops. No water. She mentally retraced her steps, sure she'd left it *right there* after taking her Tylenol. Baffled, she stepped to the fridge to get a fresh bottle and froze when she saw the half-empty bottle sitting on the shelf inside. A bottle she knew hadn't been there earlier. She picked it up and closed the door, looking around the empty kitchen as if she'd find someone else there with her. Knowing Danny would say she was being irrational, she took it to the sink and poured the water down the drain, then threw the empty bottle into the trash. Grace had been so sure she'd left the bottle on the counter. Of course, there were a lot of things in her life lately she couldn't explain, and maybe she *had* put it in the fridge. Shaking her head, she pushed her thoughts aside and grabbed a fresh bottle from the fridge. An elusive bottle of water was the least of her worries. Taking her cell phone with her, she took her lunch out to the deck and texted Lizzy. After a few messages back and forth, they settled on a lunch date following her next appointment with Dr. Hyatt.

* * *

Sipping on a cup of coffee, she listened as Dr. Hyatt explained to her why she thought speaking to a room full of strangers was a great idea. "Talking about your experience with people outside of the circle you've placed yourself in will be good for your therapy. Talking with me is one thing. But talking to others, people who you . . ." Grace interrupted her.

She held up a hand when Grace opened her lips to object. "Even if you don't know them, Grace. You may learn some things about yourself that you wouldn't think to ask."

Grace wasn't so sure about that but kept her thoughts to herself.

"I wish I could understand all of this and why it's happening. It's just crazy, you know? How I didn't sing before, but now I can? And speaking of crazy, maybe I am. I mean, I keep seeing this man, but I don't know if he's real. Is it all in my head? Am I hallucinating?"

"You've seen the man again? The same one?"

Grace heard the concern in the doctor's voice. "Yes. Well, I'm not sure. I thought I saw someone following me the other day when I went out for a walk. But when I decided to confront him, there was no one there. Either he was really good at hiding or it was my mind playing tricks again."

"First of all, I'm happy to hear you're getting out of the house. Second, while I'm proud of you for being willing to defend yourself, you need to be careful about confronting strangers on the street. If the man who attacked you is following you, he could be dangerous."

"I understand. But just when I think I've convinced myself he's all in my head, I think I see him. I don't ever get a full look, only a glimpse out of the corner of my eye. During my first appointment, you told me there could be something familiar that would trigger my brain into thinking it was the same man. That could still be the case."

"You're right, it could be. But that doesn't mean you can let down your guard. Remember F-A-V-E. Stay focused, stay alert, stay vigilant, stay extra."

"Extra?"

"Yes. Extra focused, extra alert, extra vigilant."

"Right. I will."

Dr. Hyatt spoke softly. "I know you're frustrated, Grace. But much of the brain is a mystery to us. And even the best of us can't explain how a lot of it works. What's happening to you is possibly what we would call a phenomenon. Like someone who's never touched a piano, being able to sit down at one for the first time and play Mozart. Or maybe you could sing all along and your singing voice was hiding deep inside. Or maybe," she paused, "God has gifted you with this voice."

Grace lifted her head and looked at the doctor. "Do you really believe that?"

Dr. Hyatt sat back in her chair. "It doesn't matter what I believe, Grace. The point is, we don't know. But if God has given you a message, it's up to you to deliver it."

"What message?"

The doctor lifted her hands and turned them palms up. "I'm here to help you work through questions and to help you through this process, but I don't have all the answers. I'm giving you possibilities. But think about this. Move forward with the belief that you *will* get your memory back. And who knows? Maybe you'll find a message hidden in there for yourself as well."

Grace sat back in her chair and sipped her coffee. Great. More riddles, she thought. "This new life of mine has been one question after another. I hope the answers start coming soon." She smiled halfheartedly and rose to return her cup to the tray near the door.

10

Silver Lining

Grace laughed and wiped tears from her face as Lizzy recounted the famous "skunk story." "I'm sorry, but that's hilarious! How did you get rid of the smell?" She leaned back in her chair and took a deep breath, trying hard to control the fit of giggles threatening to start up again. It was a welcome distraction after her emotional session with Dr. Hyatt.

Lizzy took a sip of her coffee. "Let's just say I had to invest in a new tent." She laughed. "And a new sleeping bag. And a backpack." Lizzy laughed again. "I tossed almost everything I took with me that weekend. You had to loan me clothes to wear, and we rode all the way home with the windows down. It was freezing! Lots of vinegar, baking soda, peroxide ..., I tried just about everything." Her voice trailed off as she wiped her own face with her napkin. She leaned forward and placed a hand on Grace's arm. "I sure have missed this. Listen, I leave in two days to visit my parents. While I'm there, I plan to do a lot of thinking about the future and whether or not I want to continue travel nursing." At Grace's surprised expression, she said, "I've been thinking about taking that supervisory job at the hospital. I love the traveling, but it's getting old, you know?"

Grace returned Lizzy's gaze for a moment, then lifted her arms with her palms up and laughed again. "I have absolutely no idea."

Lizzy shook her head and laughed with her friend, thinking how wonderful it was to be able to spend time with her. She leaned forward, placing her elbows on the table. "Listen, Grace, there's actually another reason for me to stop traveling so much. I've met someone. We only met a few of weeks ago, but I'd kind of like to see where it goes." She watched Grace's face to gauge her reaction.

"Really. Well, tell me about him." Grace listened intently as Lizzy gushed about the new man in her life. Her only concern was that he sounded almost too good to be true. "So, when do we get to meet this mystery man?" she asked when Lizzy paused.

"I'm glad you asked. I know this is short notice, but would you and Danny like to come over for dinner tonight? Vince is grilling steaks and I've been wanting us all to get together. And don't worry, I haven't told him about your amnesia. He knows you had an accident, but that's all I've said. I know you're still a bit uncomfortable with the questions."

Grace wasn't expecting the sudden invitation but recovered. "I don't see why not but let me check with Danny. The kids are going to a youth gathering this evening and I'm not sure if we had anything planned for dinner. And thanks for not saying anything. It does bother me, but I'm hoping talking to those ladies at church tomorrow will help me with that."

"Great," Lizzy said. "I'll text Vince and let him know it'll be a party of four." Her thumbs flew over her phone screen. "So tell me about this tongue waggers' group you're joining."

Grace snickered. She was finding she could always count on her friend's brashness to make her laugh.

"WAG. And I'm not joining, only speaking. I don't even know what I'll say."

"Oh, don't worry about it. You'll do great." Lizzy picked up her phone when it vibrated on the table. "It's Vince." Her smile faded and her shoulders slumped as she read the message on her screen.

"What is it?"

"Change of plans. Vince has to leave town for a few days. Apparently, a coworker came down with the flu and couldn't make it to a conference where he was supposed to give a presentation. Vince has to cover for him." Lizzy looked disappointed but seemed to be sympathetic. "He sends his regrets and asked for a rain check. He was really looking forward to meeting you both."

"It's okay. We'll get together another time. Tell me more about this Vince," Grace said.

It worked. Lizzy's face brightened as she went on and on about her new beau. When they finished their coffee, the two women gathered their jackets and paid their bill. There was shopping to be done. Neither noticed the man watching them from the corner of the coffee shop. He sat holding a menu in front of him and had a cup of coffee and his phone on the table. When the women had passed by the window, he slid from his booth, tossed a bill onto the table, and exited through the door after them.

* * *

What she'd expected to be an afternoon of awkward introductions, hesitant hellos, and polite how are yous, turned out to be what felt to Grace like a happy reunion with old friends. The tangle of nerves knotted in her gut loosened. When it was time for her to speak, she inched to the front of the room, where someone had placed a stool and a podium. After taking a calming breath and exhaling slowly, she perched herself on the stool and spoke.

"Hi, everyone. Thank you for inviting me here today. I hope I don't disappoint you. Um, I admit I was nervous at first, but you all have made me feel welcome and at home here. So. By now, you all know that I had a head injury several weeks ago, and you also know that I have amnesia." Nods and quiet affirmations told her she had everyone's attention. "What many of you may *not* know is that since I woke up in the hospital, I've been singing. Now, I know, that by itself isn't anything remarkable. But if you knew me before the accident, you probably know that I didn't sing. At all." With a snicker she said, "At least that's what they tell me." A few chuckles prompted her to say, "It's okay, you can be honest with me. My son says I sounded like a goat on crack." That was all it took to release laughter around the room. "Maybe as I get to know you, I know that sounds crazy, you can fill me in on some details of myself since many of you know me, let's face it, better than I know myself. I'm told that the old Grace was not one to speak in front of a crowd, let alone sing. But I can't deny whatever this is. All I can do is go with it and see where it leads me.

"I wish I could describe how odd it is to be introduced to people who already know me." Mumbles of agreement and nodding heads urged her on. "My family included. Y'all, my children have known me all their lives, but I just met them a few weeks ago. How insane is that? Every conversation, every experience with them, is new. I can't remember their first steps, but they get to see me take first steps almost every day." She looked aside and put the back of her hand to her lips. "Forgive me if I get emotional. I sniffle and tear up at everything these days." Words of encouragement drifted to her from across the room, and someone handed her a tissue. "Apparently, the old Grace held everything inside and kept her emotions in check. Never let her feelings show." She waved a hand in the air. "But there are some advantages. When Danny tells one of the kids 'no,' and they say, 'but Mom told me weeks ago I could,' I can honestly say, 'I don't remember that conversation.'" Her own laughter set off a myriad of cackles, squeals, and table slaps. The remainder of the meeting flew by as Grace answered a multitude of questions, and at some point, began asking some of her own. A request for her to sing was inevitable, and she gladly complied. She stuck to the older hymns such as "Amazing Grace" and "Victory in Jesus," inviting them to sing along with her.

When Danny picked her up, she was exhausted, but had a huge smile on her face. He thought she looked beautiful. Listening to her animated chatter on the drive home, he could almost believe it was the old Grace sitting beside him. Except his Grace wouldn't have been so willing to speak in front of a crowd. Who was this woman? She'd voiced many times how she wished she was the type of person who could stand in front of an audience and speak without getting butterflies. His Grace was always the quiet one in a group and was never one to share her personal life. He remembered how he practically had to wrestle her number out of her when they met.

"It was amazing. Everyone was so nice. I was nervous at first, but when I started talking the words just flowed! And then they asked me to sing, and I agreed without thinking. But Danny—" She looked at him, eyes wide. "I knew the words! How is that even possible?"

"I'm as baffled as you are. But I'm happy to see that shine back in your eyes. I knew it was in there somewhere." Danny winked and turned his attention back to the road.

* * *

Cheers erupted as Daniel dribbled the ball down the court toward the goal. He faked to the right, sidestepped to the left, then bolted forward to make his shot. There wasn't a soul in the gym that didn't imagine they could hear the swoosh of the net as the basketball passed through it without touching the rim. Grace jumped to her feet along with hundreds of others, adding her own shouts and applause to the already deafening noise in the gym. The halftime buzzer sounded, and Danny offered to go to the concession stand for cold drinks.

Hearing her name, she turned toward another smiling parent. "Looks like these boys are going to take us all the way to the finals. That Daniel has really shot up this past year. He's a good player."

Beaming with pride, Grace returned his smile. "He's been working hard and practicing almost nonstop." She didn't comment on the growth spurt that she had no memory of. Glancing toward the door that opened into the concession stand, she caught a glimpse of Danny as he stepped through. To her horror, the man from her nightmare stood right beside the door. He wore the same leather jacket, but had added a blue baseball cap. He looked straight at her with an evil grin and followed Danny out of her sight. No, she thought as she jumped up and made her way to the aisle, leaving her and Danny's jackets on the bleachers. She darted through the crowd, trying not to push and shove. Bursting through the door, she scanned the mob of people in the lines waiting for drinks and food, but Danny wasn't there. She looked back and forth, not knowing what to do or who to go to for help. Panic gripped her chest. She could barely catch her breath. In the depths of her mind, she knew she was on the verge of an anxiety attack and tried to tell herself to focus on her breathing the way Dr. Hyatt had shown her. But she was more concerned about Danny right now. She had to find him before—before what? She had no idea what this guy wanted, but she couldn't let him harm her family.

There. Near an exit door, she spotted a security guard. Surely he could help her. "Grace!" She nearly jumped out of her skin when the hand closed around her arm. With a shriek, she drew her opposite hand back, ready to throw the punch of her life. It was Danny. He stepped back with his hands up. "Whoa, there. It's just me. You okay? You look terrified."

Flooded with relief, she put her arms around him and buried her face in his chest. Only when his strong arms hugged her tight did she feel safe and began to calm down. Danny led her to a corner away from the crowd and made her look at him. She knew he wanted an explanation, but she couldn't tell him she was losing her mind. Before he could ask, she said, "I'm sorry. I, uh, popcorn. I wanted some popcorn and thought I'd catch up and wait in line with you. Then when I got down here, the crowd was-was so big. And I guess I panicked. Dr. Hyatt warned me it might happen sometimes. I guess this is sometime." She tried to laugh it off, and he seemed to buy her story.

Danny took her hand in his, and they got in line. He didn't buy her story at all. Something was wrong. Something more than claustrophobia had terrified her. But what? He casually looked around the crowded room but saw nothing out of the ordinary, only people like himself waiting in line for cold hot dogs and stale popcorn.

As they waited in line for their drinks and the popcorn she didn't really want, she continued to sweep the throng of spectators in search of the stranger. He was gone. But what did he want? More importantly, why did he follow Danny? To her, that raised the stakes—it was a threat. She knew she should tell Danny, but she couldn't face him not believing her or telling her she was overreacting. Maybe she was crazy? Had she really seen him? If she had, she needed to find out what he wanted. Soon.

By the time Daniel's team achieved their victory, she had relaxed enough to enjoy the celebratory cheering. She and Danny joined everyone else on the gym floor to congratulate the team, and she didn't hesitate to get her own sweaty hug from her son.

"Great job, Daniel! I'm so proud of you!" She beamed up at him. His face practically glowed with excitement.

"Is it okay if I hang out with Coach and the guys to celebrate?" The question was directed at his father.

Danny said, "I'm fine with it as long as it's okay with your mom." He glanced at Grace and grinned at her surprise.

Grace looked up at Daniel. "Um, yeah, sure. That's fine with me too." This was new territory to her, though she was sure she'd done this a thousand times. "Just be careful, okay? And not too late?"

Daniel's smile widened, if that was possible. "Got it. Thanks!" Then off he ran to catch up with his teammates.

Grace fell into step beside Danny as they headed for the parking lot. "Thanks for that." He smiled and draped an arm across her shoulder.

Back in the quiet comfort of their home, Grace stood in front of the fireplace, studying the photos on the mantel. So much had happened over the last few weeks. Her feelings for this family had grown exponentially, and although at times she still felt out of sorts, she never thought of leaving them. Even if she had somewhere else to go. They had each claimed a space in her heart, and their love for her surrounded her like a shield, protecting her from any source that threatened to harm her.

"One day you'll remember, Grace." Danny placed a warm cup of tea in her hand.

Turning to face him, she offered a sad smile, then stared down into her cup. "I was thinking how hard this all must be for you and the kids. To have someone you care about in your life, in your home, who doesn't know who you are or anything about you. Your entire lives have changed because of me. And the kids. How heartbreaking to have a mother who doesn't remember their first steps or their first words. Not even when they were born, Danny." Grace swiped at the tears she was unable to stop.

Danny took the cup from her hands and gently placed it with his on the mantel. He took her face in his hands and said, "Grace, you're here with us. That's what's important. This could've turned out so much worse. I didn't have to tell our kids you were dead, and we didn't have to go to your funeral and bury you. You didn't leave us behind trying to figure out how to go on without you. I don't even want to think about what could've happened."

Her tears were now flowing through Danny's fingers on her cheeks. She hadn't considered what impact the alternative would've had on them.

"So you don't remember us. *We* remember *you*. And we've never stopped loving you. God has given us a lifetime to make new memories. Memories we won't take for granted. Ones that we'll cherish even more than the ones you lost." Leaning his forehead against hers, he whispered, "Trust me."

Grace looked up at him and nodded. "Okay," she whispered. Then he placed a soft kiss on her lips.

Later, Grace lay awake, thinking about Danny's words and praying. "God, what did I do? Why has this happened to me? I don't understand, and I can't fix it or make up for it if I can't remember what it is

I've done. But surely Danny and the kids didn't do anything. They don't deserve to suffer this pain. If there's a lesson I'm supposed to be learning, please, God, please reveal it to me so we can move on." Grace had thought she was out of tears, but they flowed freely, soaking the hair at her temples. She turned to her side and pushed her face into her pillow to muffle her sobs.

II

Book of Bads

Two weeks later, Grace stared at the painting in Dr. Hyatt's lobby as she waited for the doctor to call her back for her appointment. Again, the scene was familiar. When she closed her eyes, she could see the wildflowers at the base of the cross, could almost smell their sweet aroma mixed with the earthy odor of the grass in the field. The harder she tried, the further the memory slipped away. If it was even a memory. She had no idea, but her frustration grew. The episode at Daniel's game had triggered something in her mentally, and she'd become increasingly agitated. Grace felt as if she had been thrown into a raging sea in the middle of a storm. She battled the ups and downs of her emotions as a boat would fight the rise and fall of giant waves. She was exhausted but did everything she could to hide that fact from her family. Relieved when she heard her name called, she followed the doctor into her office and took her usual seat. She accepted the offered cup of tea and began to speak.

"Everything was going so well. Or so I thought. Then I thought I saw that man again at Daniel's basketball game, and something in me changed. I went after him, but he was gone. How do I know if he was ever there? Or if it was just an innocent spectator that my mind turned into something evil?" She briefly relayed the events of the awful evening. She had considered not mentioning the sighting, but what good would that do?

"Some days are so great and so perfect I feel like everything's going to be okay. Like nothing can get in the way of the future. Then there are times I feel like I'm sinking, being pulled down into thick black mud by something evil I can't see, but I know is there.

"On the outside, things are great. Everyone has been so patient with me, and they at least seem to try to not expect too much too soon. But here, inside me"—she placed a hand on her chest, felt the tears burning her eyes—"I expect more. I want more. In here, I'm reaching, clawing, trying desperately to get out of this hole, and I can't. I feel stuck. When does it end? And how do I look at this from a religious standpoint if I can't remember where I stood before the accident? All I know is what everyone tells me, but how do I know in my heart what is real?"

Grace had begun referring to the events leading up to her coma as an accident; calling it the "attack" somehow made her feel weak and vulnerable. She felt keeping a positive outlook seemed like the right thing to do, but she was finding it more and more difficult to maintain the bubbly persona she thought everyone expected. "I don't expect an easy answer, I really don't."

Dr. Hyatt waited as Grace released several weeks' worth of frustrations, then spoke softly, her voice gentle and soothing. "Venting our apprehensions and feelings is a form of therapy, Grace. It helps us tremendously, even when there is no solution. Before we go any further, I must recommend that you tell Danny about what you saw last night. Maybe even talk to the police. You said before that the investigation wasn't progressing as well as you hoped. Is that still the case?" Grace nodded. "Then this may give them additional clues to follow up on. With your description, maybe they could find him on camera footage, and at the very least, take him in for questioning."

A glimmer of hope stirred in Grace, but trepidation swallowed it whole. Would it prove her right? Or insane? "I didn't think of that."

"I believe it's time to start thinking about it." Dr. Hyatt wouldn't push her. She could only make recommendations. "Have you been journaling as I suggested?"

Grace glanced down at her hands and offered a sheepish half smile. "Some. At first, I did really well and wrote something every day. Then it became every other day, then occasionally, and then nothing. I found myself only writing the positive things that I knew would make everyone happy. All the other stuff, my misgivings, my worries ... all of that I kept to myself like I was afraid someone would read it and be disappointed in me."

The doctor leaned forward in her chair. "That's completely normal. Here's what I want you to do. Try again, but this time include all the negatives as well. You can try separating the ups and downs into different journals if that helps, but don't get discouraged if the 'Book of Bads' fills up faster than the 'Pad of Positives.' It's only release therapy, not an indication of how your life is going or a reflection of you personally. If it makes you feel better, you can journal on a computer or iPad, and then set it up so that it has to be accessed with a password." She laid a comforting hand on top of Grace's. "You are not a failure. For the time being, your memory has failed you, but you have no control over that. You haven't failed your family, but you *will* fail yourself if you continue to carry this burden."

Relief washed over Grace, but it didn't entirely eliminate her doubts. She glanced up into her doctor's eyes and saw the genuine compassion there. "I'll work on the journaling. Thank you for listening. I don't know what I'd do without you."

Smiling, the doctor said, "You'd do fine. But I'm here for you and I'm going to help you work through this." Grace smiled in response, unwilling to voice her growing concern that there was no one with the ability to help her at this point. She politely declined the doctor's offer of another cup of tea and rose from her chair to leave. Then, as if reading her thoughts, Dr. Hyatt placed a hand on her arm and said, "Grace, I understand your fears and your concerns. They're completely normal. I need you to trust me on this. Whatever you do, don't let yourself sink any further into that hole you described. Let me help. And when you feel yourself sinking, reach out. Ask for help. Okay?"

Grace nodded. "I will. Thank you." She lifted her purse and placed the strap on her shoulder, then turned and left the room.

As she approached her car, a surge of anger rushed over her, replacing her despair with a sudden determination to take back her life. It may only be temporary, she thought, but at least it's something. Before she could change her mind, she turned left out of the lot instead of the right that would take her home. She steered her car toward the place where her nightmare had begun. Dolby Park. Danny had shown her where it was weeks before at her request, but she hadn't had the nerve to pull in and stop. Today that would change. Hadn't Dr. Hyatt told her in one of her sessions to face her fears? Maybe, just maybe, something would jolt her damaged brain and kick it into gear. So far nothing else had worked, what could it hurt?

As she came upon the entrance to the park, Grace's pulse quickened and she concentrated on her breathing. You can do this, she told herself. She turned in and crept along the pavement, her courage fading as fast as it had hit her. Grace eased the car into the same parking spot in which it had been found a few weeks prior, then taking a deep breath, she opened the door and stepped out.

The wind was cool as it hit her face, blowing through the hair hanging loosely around her shoulders. Turning clockwise, Grace spun a full 360 degrees. Her surroundings neither looked nor felt familiar. Discouraged, but not yet ready to give up, she glanced toward a path that led around a small pond. A wooden bridge was built over the pond with a small, covered area in the middle. Stepping onto the path, she headed toward the bridge. Her destination was one of the benches nestled into each corner of the covered section. One side opened toward a playground, while the other would allow her an open view of the opposite side of the pond and the path that continued around it. That was the side she chose, settling herself on the bench with her sweater wrapped around her. The sun reflected off the surface of the pond, the ripples in the water caused by the wind twinkling like tiny diamonds. Grace watched as a couple ran side by side along the path, separating to allow another runner heading the opposite way to pass between them. As she watched the couple continue on the path, she saw the man lift his hand in a casual wave as they passed a bench where a man sat alone, one arm draped across the backrest. He bobbed his head, acknowledging the joggers.

Grace sucked in a breath and froze. The man across the pond stared back at her, and she knew instantly it was the man from her nightmare. He wore the same blue cap. It had to be him. Grace shot up from her seat, intent on getting to her car as fast as she could. As she took her first step, she saw him stand as well. He was coming for her. Grace quickened her pace, wondering if anyone was close enough to hear her if she screamed. What was she thinking coming out here alone? The park was nearly deserted, the joggers no longer in sight. Get to the car and you'll be fine, she told herself. Grace tried to focus on her destination but couldn't resist looking back to see where he was. He was headed her way! Running now, her shoes thumped loudly on the wooden bridge. Grace patted her pockets, only to realize she'd left her phone in the car. How stupid could she be?

As her foot finally reached the path at the end of the bridge, she heard a scream. Grace wanted to run faster, but her conscience wouldn't let her. She had to help if she could. Maybe she could find a stone or a fallen limb to scare him away from his victim. She spun toward them. There he was, but the woman she expected to see struggling in his lethal grip wasn't there. Instead, he lifted a little girl into his arms, her own wrapping around his neck. Behind her were two ducks in pursuit, causing her to run screaming to her father. Grace stood there, dumbfounded, watching as the man comforted his daughter. When the ducks lost interest and made their way back to the pond, he gently lowered her to the ground, and they continued on the path toward the playground.

Grace let out a shaky breath, wondering what was happening to her. Was she completely losing it? Seeing her attacker in every inno-cent man in a cap? She swiped at her wet face, unaware she'd been crying. She squeezed her eyes shut, trying to stop the flood before it got worse, but eventually gave up and let the tears flow. Tilting her head back, she looked up to the sky and whispered, "Please." One word. That was all she had left in her. Then spent, she trudged her way back to her car.

Grace pushed the button to start the engine but sat with her fore-head resting on the steering wheel, unwilling to shift the car into gear. She felt hopeless, like she was caught in a riptide with no energy to swim her way out. She tried to recall the anger she felt earlier when she'd left Dr. Hyatt's office, desperate to feel the intense determination to fight for her life. For her sanity. She hated the feeling of despair that overcame her now, the fear that had gripped her so fiercely moments ago.

The buzz of her phone vibrating on the console interrupted her thoughts, and she picked it up, swiping the screen with her thumb to answer the call from Danny.

"Hey, how'd your appointment go? Everything okay?" he asked.

"Um, yeah. Yeah, it was fine. I'm heading home now."

"Okay, great. I just wanted to check in with you. Hey, Daniel men-tioned wanting to see the new Avengers movie tonight. You up for it?"

Grace leaned her head back against the headrest and closed her eyes. Her head was pounding, another migraine likely triggered by her or-deal in the park. "I don't know, maybe. Today has kind of worn me out. Maybe if I lie down for bit ..." She let her words trail off.

"Are you sure you're okay, Grace? Did something happen at your appointment? A memory?"

She swallowed the lump in her throat, determined not to cry again. Why worry him with things she couldn't explain or understand? She'd have to find a way to work through whatever was going on in her head. "No, nothing happened. It's just one of those annoying headaches that comes out of nowhere. I'm sure it'll be fine." She tried to sound cheerful, but naturally, Danny wasn't fooled.

"Grace, you need to rest. Why don't you stay home and relax while I take the kids to see the movie? We'll bring dinner home after. How does that sound?"

A quiet evening sounded wonderful. Relieved, she said, "Are you sure you don't mind?"

"It's settled. No more discussion. We'll get out of your hair for a few hours while you rest. See you at home in a bit." The call disconnected, and she wondered again how he could stay so attentive when surely he had to be sick of the emotional roller coaster she had her family on. With a despondent sigh, she buckled her seatbelt and put the car into gear.

Danny ended the call and prayed he'd made the right decision to leave Grace alone. He'd sensed a shift in Grace's demeanor over the weeks since Daniel's basketball game. Where she'd seemed to be making progress, she was now restless and on edge. He still hadn't been able to figure out what caused her to panic, and she changed the subject each time he'd brought it up. Maybe the headaches had worsened, and she was trying to hide them. He wished she would stop hiding from him. He wanted her back—needed her back.

* * *

The storm stirred uneasiness in Grace. She walked around the house inspecting window locks and closing curtains, cringing at every crack of thunder and every flash of lightning. She desperately wished she'd chosen to go with Danny and the kids instead of opting to stay home. Sitting through a movie had seemed too much for her aching head to handle at the time, and she'd wanted nothing more than to lie down for a blissful nap. She was so sick of the blasted headaches and longed for a few consecutive days of relief. The sleep had helped, and she was thankful for that. It seemed like she had to remind herself more and more these days to be thankful, especially on her worst days. Grace was well aware that even her worst day was a blessing when compared to what could've happened.

She paused at each window as she wandered from room to room, peering out into the darkness through the sheets of rain. Lightning lit up the sky in bursts as quick as flashbulbs, with blasts of thunder on its heels. Another bolt flashed as she touched the lock on Daniel's bedroom window, illuminating the street in front of the house. Grace did a double take when she saw a figure standing under the streetlight at the corner. Gripping the curtain, she held her breath as she waited for the next flash. When it came, the sidewalk was empty. She watched through two more flashes, and still seeing nothing, she hurried through the rest of the upstairs bedrooms, checking the locks. Only when she was satisfied the house was secure did she venture downstairs to the den. Curling herself into her chair with a blanket over her lap, she sat in the dim glow from the fireplace to wait. Her eyelids, heavy with fatigue, closed against her will and she laid her head back against the chair while the storm continued to rage outside. Yet another crack of thunder rattled the windows. Her eyes flew open and toward the back of the house when she heard the jiggle of the doorknob. Afraid to get up, she stayed where she was and listened. It jiggled again, this time without the cover of thunder. She couldn't be sure, of course. The storm was so loud. And who would be crazy enough to be out in it? Pushing the throw aside, she rose from her chair and tiptoed toward the door, trying to work up the nerve to peek through the blinds. She took a deep breath, and in one swift motion, pulled the cord down. Just as she pulled it, the door to the garage flung open and a giggling Lucy burst in. Another clap of thunder sounded and lightning illuminated the back deck. Turning to the sound of Danny's voice, she missed the silhouette standing by the rail.

"We brought pizza," he announced. In his hand was a large pizza box, and the kids wore smiles.

Grace shoved her trembling hands into her sweatshirt pocket.

Danny laid his hands on her shoulder. "Everything okay? Are you feeling better?"

"Great. How was the movie?" She didn't want to scare them or for them to think she was crazy. Danny looked at her with concern for a moment as Daniel started raving about the Avengers, while Lucy said she would've preferred the sci-fi film in the next theater.

Grace managed to force a slice of pizza down her throat as they recounted the highlights of the movie. Inside, her stomach was churning. She was no longer sure she'd seen anything but shadows under the streetlight. The storm had rattled her nerves, that was all. She needed to get a grip.

12

New Memories

Danny chuckled at Daniel's playful snarl when his golf ball jumped over the divider between the greens and rolled to a stop against a fat gnome with a purple plaid hat.

"This isn't the PGA, son, it's Putt-Putt," Brother Joe said.

Grace laughed. She enjoyed watching her family have a good time. She needed these evenings out, and journaling was controlling her anxiety—as Dr. Hyatt said it would—and leveling out her emotional roller coaster. She might have even been having fun.

Joe positioned his club to take his shot as Daniel went to retrieve his ball. "Let me show you how it's done." Wiggling his feet and glancing dramatically between the ball and the hole, the pastor talked to himself under his breath. "There isn't a peep from the crowd as he prepares to take his shot. He measures the distance and slope with a mere glance ..." In exaggerated slow motion, he raised his club over his right shoulder and brought it down for the swing. His ball approached the hole under the lighthouse, teetered on the edge, and dropped in with a clink. "And the crowd goes wild!" The pastor ran from one "spectator" to the next, giving high fives.

"Way to go, Tiger. Get your ball outta there. It's my turn." Danny took his shot and also got it on the first try. The rest of the game turned into a competition between the guys, with Grace, Lucy, and Tammy, the pastor's wife, hanging back and having their own. By the end, the guys had cheated so much on their tally sheets no one knew who won, and they didn't really care. They were all hungry and made their way to the snack bar for burgers and fries.

Lucy and Daniel had run into some friends from school, and when they had finished eating, they'd gone into the arcade to hang out.

"So Grace, do you think you're up to it?" Brother Joe dipped a fry in his ketchup-mustard mixture and waited for her response.

Danny watched as she wiped at the condensation on her cup, lost in thought. When she looked up, he could see the indecision in her eyes.

"Don't let this old fool pressure you," Tammy said. "You do whatever you feel in your heart."

Grace closed her eyes, and with a quick nod of her head, she decided. "I'll do it."

The preacher slapped the table. "Yes! This is awesome! Now don't sweat over it or worry about it. I've been telling you that God has something big planned for you. And we'll be with you every step of the way." He swung his legs over the table bench and walked away without another word.

"He's such a kid. I knew he wouldn't be able to stay away from those games. In a few minutes, we'll hear him yelling at the Foosball table," Tammy said. She tilted her cup so the straw was pointing at Grace. "But he's right, you know. God has a plan for you." Grace smiled back at her, and the conversation moved to what she'd sing at church on Sunday morning.

When it was time to leave, Grace slung her small backpack over her shoulder, thinking it felt heavier than when she walked the golf course. They chatted as they strolled to the parking lot and paused to say their goodbyes. Why was this thing so heavy? she wondered. Frowning, she let her pack slip from her shoulder and set it on the hood of Danny's

Yukon. Unzipping the bag and pulling it open, she gasped and looked up at Danny, perplexed.

"What's wrong?" he asked.

She opened her mouth, but nothing came out. She reached into the bag and pulled out ... a napkin holder. She held it up for the others to see and they all burst out laughing. A blue pickup drove by with their pastor laughing out the window. Grace could see his wife shaking her head in the passenger seat. Turning back to her snickering family, she laughed. "Well, that's a first."

"Ha," Lucy said. "That's just the first you remember. It might be a good thing you don't remember everything he's done. The week before your accident, you were planning your revenge."

"Revenge?"

"Yeah. For one of his pranks," Lucy said as she opened her door.

When they were all buckled in, Grace asked what prank the pastor had pulled. Danny groaned.

Daniel volunteered to recap the tale. "Well, you'd loaded his sweet tea with salt at some dinner we had—"

"Wait. I'd never do that!"

Grace looked at her family in disbelief, but she was rewarded with a collective, "Yes, you would!"

"Anyway," Daniel continued, "a few weeks later, on a Saturday, our doorbell rang at like dark thirty in the morning. Dad opened it and there was this lady standing there holding a lamp, wanting to know how much we wanted for it. Dad got all bent out of shape and woke you up asking why you didn't tell him you were having a yard sale. Come to find out, Pastor Joe took a bunch of junk out of his garage and set up tables in our yard. Then he put yard sale signs down the street and had his grandson stand out there like he was one of us. He even put an ad in the paper the week before."

Grace shook her head, mouth open. "Are you serious? That's a bit over the top, don't you think?"

"Not for Pastor Joe," Danny said.

"What was I planning to do to him?"

Danny shrugged. "You wouldn't tell anyone. Whatever it was, you said you were using the hundred bucks you made off that yard sale."

* * *

Joe called Grace the following morning, and she readily accepted an invitation to lunch. They met at a small café downtown and chose a booth where they could talk without the noise of the main dining area. When they'd placed their orders, Joe spoke. "I wanted to take the time to talk to you away from family and church. I know I kid around a lot, but I'd like to know how you're doing. And I want to thank you for agreeing to sing this week. I understand how hard it was for you to agree to put yourself out there like that."

She'd been expecting a simple friendly lunch, not a serious discussion, but was pleased to hear they'd be having an adult conversation. "I'm doing okay, I think. And yes, it was hard for me. Singing is easy. It's the rest that gets me." She paused. "Brother Joe, can I be honest with you?"

Incredulous, he said, "Of course you can. You don't have to ask."

Grace toyed with her napkin—fold, smooth, fold, smooth, unfold, and start over. "I'm confused about something. I've stepped into this life that doesn't belong to me, and I go through the motions, day after day. I've tried to pick up where I left off, but I don't *know* where I left off. All I know is what everyone tells me. I *assume* I like a certain restaurant because that's what I'm told. I assume I like a certain store because that's what I'm told. I assume I like certain things in certain ways because that's what I'm told. I assume I'm right with God because—"

"That's what you're told," Joe finished for her. "Tell me, Grace. What do you think? Do *you* think you're right with God?"

Grace didn't look up from the now tattered napkin. "I can only assume that I am. I don't remember ever making that decision. All I know is that we go to church, and I was as involved as my introverted self would allow me to be. But that doesn't tell me how I really felt. I'm not doubting or anything. I know there's a God, and that Jesus died for our sins and all that. I know the basics. But if you ask me how I know, I honestly can't answer. I don't remember ever going to church before the accident."

Her frustration wasn't lost on Joe. "This is new territory for all of us. We read about things like this, but it never happens to us, right?" She nodded. "Your personal relationship with God isn't something Danny, your kids, or even I can decide for you. All I can do is tell you what I've observed, and what I've seen is a devoted wife and mother who wouldn't hesitate to step in front of a train to save her family. You've always been shy, but you're a worthy adversary when it comes to pulling a prank. This new Grace is different, but in a lot of ways, the same. Now, I can't see into your heart, but if you've asked Jesus in, He's there."

"But how do I know if I have?" Grace pleaded.

"Maybe you're looking at this from the wrong perspective. Maybe you should look at it in the here and now. Forget what you did or didn't do in the past"—he snickered at his unintended pun and Grace rolled her eyes—"and view it from the point of view of someone who is new to the Word. Dive in and pay attention to how you feel, pay attention to what God says to you. You said it yourself, you have the foundation. Build from there. I've said this before, Grace, God has something big planned for you. And I'll say this. When I see you sing at church, the emotion that radiates from you is almost palpable. You can't sing like that and not have a connection with God."

Although Grace didn't get the straight answer she'd hoped for, she felt better having gotten her frustrations off her chest. They thanked the waitress when she brought their salads and refilled their drinks, and Joe asked casually, "What do you plan to sing this week?"

Chewing thoughtfully, Grace replied, "I'm not sure yet, but I've been thinking I want to keep it simple. Nothing grandiose, you know what I mean?"

The preacher nodded. "I think I like where you're going with that. Whatever you're comfortable with is fine."

They chatted throughout the rest of the meal, then went their separate ways. Grace was relieved when she made it to her car without suffering one of his shenanigans. She felt as if a weight had been lifted, and she decided to stop at the market for something special for dinner.

Alone in the kitchen, Grace sang as she added the last of the ingredients to the pot on the stove. She stirred the Tuscan soup, and her stomach growled as the aroma of garlic and spices reached her nostrils. She smiled to herself. The name of the song on her mind was "Hungry." Fitting, because she was starving.

"Hey, that smells great." Danny dropped his briefcase and suit jacket on a barstool and stepped around the counter to kiss her cheek. "I have a great idea. Let's go camping." His smile lit up his face as he gauged her response. He'd caught her off guard.

"Camping?" Grace chewed the corner of her lip. Of all the things Danny could have suggested, camping was the last thing she'd expected. "Do I like camping?" She laughed at her own question.

Danny laughed with her and said, "Yes, you love camping. At least you used to. We haven't been in a while, and since the kids are out of school for fall break, I thought maybe it would be good to get you away from the house. We'll start small, just for one night. I've already mentioned it to the kids and they're on board. Lucy and Daniel have plans with their youth group tomorrow afternoon, but you and I could leave after church. We could hike up Alum Hollow Trail and be at the top within a couple of hours. The kids can ride up with Lizzy and be there before dark."

"Lizzy's going too?" Her interest piqued. She hadn't seen her friend since she'd returned from Michigan and looked forward to spending time with her. "And what is Alum Hollow Trail?"

"Alum Hollow Trail is a local hiking spot that goes up Green Mountain. It's a few miles from here, and beautiful, especially this time of year. There are waterfalls, rock formations, and the view isn't bad either." He looked up at her and grinned. He had been hesitant to spring this on her but was relieved that she was open to a new adventure. "And yes, Lizzy is going with us. She agreed to wait and bring the kids, although they insisted that they're old enough to go without supervision." He held a hand up when her eyes widened. "Don't worry, it's settled, and they're good with it. Now, let's get packed." His plan was coming together.

* * *

Danny held Grace's hand in one of his, rubbing the back of it with his other one. She held tight, trying to draw as much strength from him as she could. She was so nervous and wished she hadn't agreed to sing. She also wished that they could leave for their hike up the mountain right now. It would serve that pastor right if she backed out after that stunt he'd pulled at the FunPark. But of course, she wouldn't. She'd made a promise and she would keep her word. But she'd get him back. She didn't know what the old Grace would have done, but he didn't know the new Grace. Brother Joe's morning greeting from the pulpit brought her out of her reverie.

"... and Grace has graciously agreed to bless us this morning. Grace?"

Taking a deep breath, Grace stood from the pew and walked down the center aisle to the altar, then up three steps and over to the pulpit. Adjusting the microphone attached to the podium, she grimaced when it squealed its resistance. "Whoa, there." She laughed nervously. "I hope my voice isn't that rough on your ears this morning." Muffled laughter rumbled throughout the room. "Let me try that again. God has a sense of humor, doesn't he? He plays jokes on me all the time." More chuckles and nods. "Along with some other people I know." She directed a pointed look at the preacher before continuing. "Um, I agreed to this before taking the time to think about it, mainly because I knew I'd say no. By now, everyone knows about my amnesia and this singing thing. The first sound I heard when I woke up in that dreadful hospital bed was music in my head and an elderly woman singing 'The Lily of the Valley.' Ever since then, I've had *something* inside me that I feel this undeniable *need* to get out. And for some reason, singing is the only way that I know how to do that. I can't explain it, and I don't pretend to understand it. That's what pastors and psychiatrists are for, right?" Even Pastor Joe chuckled at that.

"Please feel free to join me." Grace nodded at the man sitting in the sound room upstairs at the back of the room. She sang the first four lines of "Lord Prepare Me to Be a Sanctuary," thankful when members of the congregation joined in as she repeated the verses. Simple words that held so much power and elicited so much emotion. As they sang the last line, Grace slipped quietly back to her seat, her own smile mirrored on numerous faces in the crowded pews. She knew some had probably expected more, but her mission wasn't to entertain. People came to church to hear God's word, not to hear her sing. Her heart swelled when she met Danny's eyes.

"I'm so proud of you," he whispered, and took her hand in his when she sat beside him. He lifted her hand to his lips and brushed a soft kiss against the back of it. As much as she longed to remember the man she'd known for half her life, she was content in that moment. She didn't have a clue what God was preparing her for, but she was confident the man sitting beside her would be with her every step of the way.

* * *

Following Danny up the wooded trail, Grace was astonished she couldn't remember being here. It was beautiful. Other than the trail they were on, the area was undisturbed. Untouched by development and modernism that impacted the city so close by. Overhead and all around her was a rainbow of fall-colored leaves, turning the forest into a scene no artist could duplicate. The gurgle of nearby water told her they were nearing the spot where Danny planned to stop for a break.

A few minutes later, they topped an incline in the path and a gorgeous waterfall came into view. It wasn't large, but three tiers of natural rock formations allowed water to cascade as if it was flowing down a curving staircase. On the ground and scattered over the rocks were fallen leaves, varying shades of red, orange, yellow, and brown, creating a plush blanket for the cooling autumn ground underneath. Grace couldn't resist pulling out her phone to capture the picturesque scene with Danny in the foreground. He sat on a small boulder, smiling at her. She stepped over stray limbs to join him and accepted the bottle of water and protein bar he offered.

"This is beautiful," she said. "Do we come here often?" Then laughed at her own cliché.

Laughing with her, he replied, "We do. It's one of our favorite spots. We're a little over halfway to the top. You're going to love the view from up there, it's beautiful. We're only a few miles from town, but you'd never know it, would you?" He leaned back against the rock and closed his eyes. "It feels good to be back out here."

They spent a few minutes relaxing and listening to the water cascade over the rocks into small pools. When they were ready to continue their hike, Danny stuffed their empty bottles and wrappers into his backpack and zipped it closed as another hiker came into view on the path. He carried only a small pack on his back, and had a long stick in one hand, poking it into the ground with every other step. As Grace watched him, a chill crawled up her spine. There was something familiar about him. As soon as the thought hit her, she dismissed it. Nothing and no one was familiar to her. She wouldn't allow her fears into every moment of their lives.

Hefting his pack, Danny said, "Come on, let's go see our spot." He pointed out different rock formations and groupings along the way, including one cluster he said looked to him like a family of bearded turtles. When she didn't share his vision, she laughed and said,

"Okay." Moving on, Grace followed Danny up the narrow path, wondering how many times they'd taken this route with their kids or just the two of them.

Soon they reached the top, and not far off the path was their destination. Grace dropped her pack to the ground and slowly turned, taking in her surroundings. Danny had led her to a flattened area of grass about twenty yards from the cliff edge near an outcropping of rock, under which was an area large enough to sit without feeling cramped. They would roll out their sleeping bags under the stars. Danny had brought a tent in case it rained, but the weather was predicted to be perfect. They gathered firewood and set up their little campsite, leaving enough space for Lizzy and the kids. As it got darker, he led her closer to the edge of the cliff so they could watch the sunset. When she looked over the side, she found the drop wasn't as steep as she'd expected, but she still wouldn't want to suffer a fall from that height. Down below was a valley of sorts, with trees surrounding a clearing where she thought she saw movement. Sitting up straighter, she squinted, trying to locate the source.

Danny noticed and asked, "What's wrong?"

"I thought I saw something." She adjusted her position until she was on her knees, straining harder to see as the light faded.

"It was probably a deer. They're all around. I'm surprised we didn't see any on our way up."

Relieved, she let out the breath she'd been holding and sat back, moving a little closer to her husband. He put an arm around her shoulders and chuckled.

"You were right. It's beautiful up here."

"Mm. Told you so."

Grace relaxed and laid her head against Danny's shoulder as the sun sank below the horizon, taking with it the last of its warm glow. "Wow, it's really dark," she said, turning to look behind her at their small campfire for a bit of reassurance. Yet she wasn't ready to move from the security of Danny's arm. Looking back over the valley, she thought how the darkness reminded her of the days immediately after she woke up from her coma. Those days had been dark and scary as well. But like the sun that had just set would rise in the morning, Danny had been her shining light, her beacon to follow out of her darkness.

A flicker of light down below interrupted her thoughts. Grace sat still, wondering if Danny had seen it too. Maybe someone else was camping. There it was again, but further to the right. That was no campfire. A flashlight? Leaning forward, she waited for it again. "Do you see that?" She was on her knees again, trying to figure out what she was seeing. A line of lights had appeared, now to the left of the last flicker. A few seconds later, another line had lit up even further to the left. Rising to her feet, she stood beside Danny, waiting to see what unfolded. Random lines and slants flickered to life, with no rhyme or reason. She had no idea what she was seeing and assumed Danny didn't either, because he was watching as intently as she was.

One by one, new lines appeared, eventually forming letters. Grace gasped as the two words registered in her mind. She shook her head as the beauty of what she was looking at became obvious. Someone had gone to a lot of trouble to arrange strings of lights to spell out a proposal.

MARRY ME

"Danny, look!" she whispered.

"I see it. What do you think she'll say?" Something in his voice caused her to turn to him. Danny had dropped to one knee, and in his outstretched hand, he held a ring.

"Wha—wait. *You* did this?" Grace's legs trembled and her heart raced. "I don't understand. We're already married."

Danny laughed as he got to his feet and stepped toward her. "We are. But remember when I told you we would create new memories?" She nodded. "Well, I decided to *recreate* one. A little over twenty years ago, I proposed to you right here in this spot. Just like this.

And I want you to know that I love you even more today than I did then."

Grace couldn't move, couldn't speak. Tears flowed down her cheeks and she was powerless to stop them. This man. This beautiful, perfect, incredible man belonged to her. How was that even possible? she wondered. She threw herself into his arms. Sobbing into his chest, she gave him the same answer that had changed their lives twenty years ago. "Yes."

She pulled away. "Today is our anniversary? I'm so sorry. I didn't know." With a grin, she said, "I forgot." They both burst out laughing, and he took her in his arms and kissed her.

"Now. May I put this ring back where it belongs?" She held out her left hand and when he slipped it on her finger, she thought her heart would burst. Sliding her hands to the back of his neck, she tugged him closer and said the words he'd been longing to hear for months.

"I love you too."

As they walked hand in hand back to the campsite, Grace asked Danny, "How did we meet?" Even though she couldn't see his face, she could hear the smile in his voice when he answered.

"We met in Atlanta. That's in Georgia, if you don't know," he said hesitantly.

"I know where Atlanta is, Danny." She snickered. "I just don't know *how* I know."

He chuckled, then sat next to Grace on her sleeping bag, and continued. "So, I was in law school at Emory, and you were finishing up your teaching degree. One evening after a late study session at the library, I stopped in this hole in the wall diner to grab a bite to eat. As soon as I walked in, my eye found the most beautiful girl I'd ever seen in my life."

"Awe, me? That's so sweet."

"No, it was this med student who wouldn't give me the time of day. You were her waitress."

At Grace's stunned silence, Danny laughed. "I'm kidding, Babe. Of course it was you. But you wouldn't give me the time of day either. I intentionally sat in your area and when you came over to take my order, I said, 'I'd like to take you out to dinner.' And you said, 'What would you like from the menu, sir?'

"I wasn't giving up. I asked what you'd recommend, and finally, I saw your lips twitch. You almost smiled. Yep, I was breaking that ice. Then you said you'd recommend the special, and that's what I ordered. I sat and watched you hustle around that diner till the cook yelled, 'Grace, order up!' and then you came back with a huge plate of liver and onions and a side of steamed brussels sprouts."

Grace slapped a hand over her mouth. "Gross!"

"Exactly. But I choked down over half the plate before I couldn't take it anymore. I sat there doing my best to keep it down when you arrived at the next table with two orders of bacon burgers and curly fries, announcing 'Two specials for my best customers!' I waved you over and said I thought the special was liver and onions. You replied, 'Oh, they ordered the daily special, sir. You ordered the *jerk* special.' And that's all it took. I fell hard for you right then and there. Hook, line, and wiggly worm. I kept going back, never ordering the special, of course. And eventually, my good looks and charm wore you down. The rest is history."

Grace smiled.

"I found out you liked country music and pizza, you got your degree, and I finished law school. I brought you back to Huntsville with me, and we got married. You taught high school for a couple of years until Daniel came along, then decided you wanted to be a full-time mom. After a while, you missed teaching, and when Daniel started school, you began tutoring part time at the local college. You helped a lot of adults get their GEDs."

Grace put her hand on Danny's and said, "Thanks for not giving up."

As she leaned over to kiss him, Grace jumped at the sound of boots crunching on rocks. "Well, that must be our crew." He smiled and poked at the fire with a stick.

Lizzy's backpack landed with a thud, and she dropped to the ground with it, panting. "I'm too old for this. I hope you said yes."

Grace looked at each of them in turn. "You knew about this? You three were down there with the lights?"

Daniel spoke up. "Yeah, it was us. I still don't get why we had to run back and forth plugging in random strings instead of just one big plug-in." He lay back, using his pack for a pillow.

"Because that's not the way we did it twenty years ago," Danny answered.

"Who's we?" Lucy asked.

"My football team."

Daniel sat up and glared at his father. "Wait. You mean to tell me the three of us about killed ourselves running around in the dark plugging in lights that you strung up all over the place, and when you did it you had the help of a whole football team?"

Danny shrugged and grinned.

"Wow, Dad. You could've recreated that part too." He flopped back down and threw an arm over his face.

They all sat around the campfire for hours, telling their favorite stories. Grace was a bit saddened that she didn't have any memories of her own to share, but she had fun listening and laughing with the others. Lucy, wise in her young age, spoke up. "So, I bet this is a great new memory for you, huh, Mom?"

Grace smiled at her daughter and said, "You read my mind, Lucy. This is a terrific new memory that I'll never forget."

Lucy smiled, satisfied, then said, "Hey, did anyone bring snacks? I'm starving."

Grace tossed her pack to her and said, "Help yourself."

Danny and Grace both lay awake long into the night, each in their own thoughts about the milestones they'd reached, and the ones that lay before them. As her eyes got heavy, she reached for Danny's hand and drifted off to sleep.

Grace's eyes flew open, and she lay still, unsure what had disturbed her. The sky was dark, the sliver of moon barely visible amid the clouds. A rustle of leaves too close for comfort caused her heart rate to race. More rustling and the snap of a twig, then silence. Her nerves were at full attention now. An animal wouldn't be wary of making noise. She inched her hand toward Danny, needing him to be on alert as well. She touched his shoulder, then tapped harder until he stirred. "Danny," she whispered, "there's something in the bushes."

"Probably a raccoon or something," he mumbled.

"I don't think so." She was on edge now, and it must have been obvious in her voice. Danny rolled toward her and listened, hardly breathing. After a full minute of silence, he sat up.

"I don't hear anything. Whatever it was, I think it's gone."

Grace sat up but didn't let go of Danny's shirt sleeve. She couldn't shake the feeling that it was something more than an animal out there. They'd seen other campers on their way up, and a couple had gone by their campsite earlier in the evening on their way around to the other side of the mountain. Finally she lay back down, but not before checking on the kids and Lizzy snoozing peacefully nearby. Danny left his hand within reach, and she slid her own underneath it. When she felt his fingers close around her hand, she closed her eyes and forced herself to relax.

Beyond the glow of the dying campfire, hidden in the shadows, a figure crept along the edge of darkness. Unable to turn on his light, he used the stick in his hand to feel the ground in front of him for unforgiving holes and limbs large enough to trip him. He eased toward the campers, careful not to make a sound. He paused near Danny and poked at the embers of the dying fire with his stick. He held it to the heat long enough for the end of his stick to glow, then moved it toward Danny's face. Pausing at his cheek, he lowered the stick toward his neck, stopping millimeters before making contact with his skin. In a little above a whisper he said, "What do you have that I didn't?" Pulling the stick back, he stepped around the fire and closer to Lizzy and the kids. Lucy's hair lay spread across a sweatshirt she used as a pillow, and the stranger used the black tip of his stick to pull it toward him. He looked at Grace. "You made quite a life for yourself here, didn't you?" He stood there a moment longer, then leaned down close to her. "Maybe I'll catch you on the way down." He smiled and disappeared into the night.

"Rise and shine, sleepyheads," Danny said the following morning. "Who wants breakfast?" They all groaned, but the smell of bacon roused them. Danny had brought ready-cooked bacon and had heated it in a small pan over the fire he'd rekindled. Passing it around, he watched Lucy as she snuggled close to Grace. "Hey, what's that in your hair, Lucy?"

"Where? Is it a spider?" Lucy sat straighter and swiped at her hair, sure Danny had seen a disgusting creepy crawly moving through her strands.

"No, calm down. There on your left," he said.

"Here, let me see," Grace offered. Fingering the blond strands, she brushed at the black powder-like substance that discolored her fingers. "It looks like ashes, Lucy. How did you get it in your hair?"

Relieved, Lucy's shoulders sagged. "I don't know, and I don't care. I'm just glad it wasn't a spider." The thought made her shiver.

"Don't we need to get the lights?" Grace asked as Danny led them down the same path they'd hiked the day before.

"No, my secretary's daughter is getting married next month and was planning on buying a bunch to decorate the venue. I told her she could have them all if she'd take them all down, so she's sending her husband and son to get them."

"Oh, that was nice of you."

"Yeah, Danny, that was nice of you. Always getting someone else to do your hard work," Lizzy teased, and Daniel and Lucy mumbled agreements under their breaths.

"Hey, I heard that. What can I say? I'm very persuasive when— Grace!" Danny shouted as Grace's foot slipped on some leaves at the edge of the narrow path. She slipped over the embankment and rolled.

The world spun as she tumbled. Rocks and sticks jabbed through her clothing. She grabbed at limbs, but none were rooted. Instead of stopping her roll, they rolled with her, tearing at her clothes and scratching her skin. She continued to slide until she slammed against the cold, hard base of a tree, knocking the wind out of her. Groaning, she lay still and performed a mental check of her body parts. Everything seemed to work. A rustle of underbrush spurred her to try and sit up.

"Whoa, don't move until we know nothing is broken," Danny said, leaning over her.

"I thought I heard something over there."

Danny followed her eyes. "Well, my guess is you scared it."

Lizzy stormed over and shoved Danny aside. "Don't move." Starting with her head and neck, she used her hands to examine Grace for broken bones. When she was satisfied Grace was safe, she gave her permission to sit up. "I think your clothes prevented any deep cuts, but you'll probably have some bruises. Did you hit your head?"

"She hit her head?" Daniel skidded to a stop at Lizzy's side like he was sliding into home plate. "Did you get your memory back?"

They all looked at him with confusion on their faces, then a combined "What?"

Daniel tried his best to look serious, but then started laughing and threw a handful of leaves at Lizzy. "I'm kidding. That's the way it happens in the movies."

Grace laughed. "I didn't hit my head. I'm fine. Now help me up."

The crew made their way down without further incident, stopping again at the waterfall to rest and to chat with other hikers they met along the way.

* * *

After making one last entry into a file, Danny logged off the computer and turned it off. Leaning back in his chair, he threw his feet up onto the corner of his desk and rubbed his eyes. He'd been trying to work from home as much as he could, wanting to stay near Grace in hopes that her memory would return. It had been nearly three months now, and his initial optimism was waning. Grace, too, was growing anxious. He could feel it. He leaned his head back. "God, you know our need. Help us hang in there. I'm trying to trust your timing, but it's hard. We need Grace back."

Not wanting to get up yet, he let his eyes roam over the bookshelves lining the walls. In the center of the middle shelf sat a Bose stereo receiver and CD player. He hadn't turned it on in months. On a whim, he picked up the remote and pressed play, wondering what CD he'd last listened to. He smiled when the music began, and Drake White's voice drifted through the speakers.

"Hey," came Grace's soft voice from the doorway, and she stepped toward his desk. Danny thought she looked beautiful, even in her robe, with her hair down and messy from sleep.

"Hey," he returned, and held out his hand as she drew closer. "What are you doing up?"

Grace stepped into his outstretched arm and allowed him to pull her close. "I was wondering the same thing about you." She smiled. "What's this?" she asked, indicating the music.

Danny smiled up at her and replied, "One of your favorite songs." Lowering his feet to the floor, he stood and took her hands, bringing them up around his neck. With his own arms around her waist, he swayed side to side. He smiled down at her, pleased when she followed his lead. Grace let him rest his forehead against hers while they danced, and she laid her head on his chest when she felt his fingers in her hair. They continued to dance as the song played. The room faded around them and they remained silent, needing no words to communicate. Their bodies moved as one; Grace's newfound love for her husband was discovering what her heart had never forgotten. A few minutes without worry, without fear. As the song neared its end, Danny leaned forward, guiding Grace into a slow dip, then raised her back up and kissed her.

13

Secrets

Grace sat down on the edge of the bed to tie her shoes, then stood up to stretch. She had a lot of pent-up energy today and was eager to get started on her walk. She pulled her hair back and secured it with a hair tie as she walked down the stairs. After grabbing a bottle of water from the fridge, she picked up her keys and headed for the door.

As soon as she pulled it open, her breath caught and her heart skidded to a stop. There in the doorway stood her nightmare in the flesh.

Grace stepped back and pushed against the door, but his foot prevented it from closing. He pushed it back open and moved inside, closing the door behind him. The finality of the door clicking closed froze her where she stood, even though her brain was screaming at her to run.

"Hello, Anna, going somewhere?" The gravelly voice sent chills down her spine, and the panic she'd worked so hard to suppress over the last few weeks gripped her chest like a vice.

"M-My name is Grace," she stammered. Her breath was coming in short gasps.

"That's what you call yourself now," he sneered as he stepped closer to her. "But you're definitely my Anna."

She shook her head from side to side. "I'm not your anything. I don't know you."

His laugh sent an icy shiver down her spine. "We were together for too long for you to forget so easily. Maybe I should remind you." He raised his arm and reached for her shoulder. The same shoulder that he'd grabbed in the hospital, and the same one that she'd hurt when he'd shoved her against her car.

That was all it took to release her from the paralysis that glued her to the floor. She flung the bottle of water at him and it connected with his nose. She ran to the kitchen in search of a potential weapon, knowing he wouldn't be far behind. "Where do you think you're going? You can't escape me that easily again." She rounded the kitchen island and lunged for the knife block on the counter. Her fingertips grazed a knife handle as she was jerked backward, landing hard on the floor, nearly knocking the breath out of her. He grabbed a fistful of her hair and was now standing over her as she lay supine on the hard kitchen floor with his boot-clad foot pressing on her shoulder.

"Tell me where it is, Anna." He used the back of his hand to wipe blood from his nose and mouth.

"I told you my name is Grace. And I have no idea what you're talking about." Grace struggled against the weight of his foot and pushed against his leg with her other hand. He didn't budge. He had his right hand on the island top and his other one on the counter to his left and used both for leverage.

"And I told you not to lie to me. I'm tired of playing games." Rage dripped from his words like the blood from his lip. Then his head snapped up at the sound of the garage door opening. "I'll be back, and I *will* get what belongs to me. Remember, Anna. I know your secret and don't think for a second I won't tell your precious little family." And with a final shove of his boot, he left through the back door.

She gasped, not realizing she'd been holding her breath. Pulling herself into a sitting position, she wrapped her arms around her legs and leaned her head on her knees as she sobbed.

"Mom? Mom!" Daniel rushed to his mother and dropped to his knees at her side. "Mom, what's wrong? Are you okay?"

Grace lifted her head and looked at her son with relief. "I'm okay. Call your father." Leaning her head back against the cabinet, she tried to calm her breathing while she waited for him to place the call to Danny.

By the time she heard Danny's tires screech to a stop in the driveway, she'd calmed down some and was sitting in the den sipping on the cup of hot tea Daniel had brought her. Her husband's face was drawn with worry as he burst through the door. "Grace, Daniel! Are you okay? What's going on? Daniel said you were attacked."

Grace tried to reassure him with a nod and motioned him over to the sofa where she sat. "I was on my way out for a walk. When I opened the door, he was standing there, and pushed his way in." Danny grew more agitated and tense as Grace relayed the events, filling in details she hadn't told Daniel. "Thank God he left when he heard the garage door. If Daniel hadn't come home when he did ..." She left what she was thinking unsaid.

Danny spoke then, realizing that his son should be at school. "What *are* you doing home, son? It's the middle of the day."

"Chad threw up on me and I had to come home to change." He grinned.

"Threw up on you?" His question begged for an explanation, which Daniel was all too ready to provide.

"Yeah, we were dissecting pigs in class today and—"

"Okay, I get it," Danny broke in, holding up a hand. "I know all about Chad's weak stomach."

Turning back to Grace, he said, "Do you take your walk at the same time every day?"

She lifted a shoulder and nodded. "Most days, yes. Around ten or so when it's not too chilly but before it gets too warm."

Danny put a hand over hers. "He had to be watching you to know you were here alone."

Grace chewed at her bottom lip. "I've seen him a couple of times watching the house."

"What?! Why haven't you said anything about it?" Danny ran a hand through his hair and tried to maintain control.

"Because I didn't think you would believe me. Just like you didn't believe me when I said I saw him at Dr. Hyatt's office."

"Wait. This was the same guy?"

Nodding, she said, "Yes. You thought I was imagining things, and honestly, I began to think the same thing." Then she told them about her suspicions during previous walks and the feeling she was being followed.

Danny's face betrayed the guilt he felt. "Grace, I'm sorry. There's no excuse for that, and it put both of you in danger." He stood when the doorbell rang. "That must be the police. I called them on my way here."

It was nearly an hour before Danny escorted the two officers out of the house after they'd taken her report and she'd answered countless questions, each asked in at least half a dozen variations. The officers left with a promise to patrol the area at least every hour, explaining that the situation didn't warrant providing continuous surveillance.

Danny returned to the sofa and sat back down beside Grace. "Is there anything at all you may have left out? Anything that you didn't want to say in front of Daniel or to the police?" Daniel had left after the police arrived to go back to school, but not before promising his dad to keep his mouth shut.

"No. I told you and them everything. I have no clue who that guy is or what he wants. And I don't understand why he kept calling me Anna." She paused before continuing. "Is there anything you haven't told *me*, Danny?"

"What do you mean?" Confusion replaced his concern.

"Well, all I know about myself is what you've told me. How do I know you've told me everything? How do I know any of it's the truth?" She immediately felt guilty for saying it. The pain that pinched

Danny's face was real. "Listen, I'm sorry. I didn't mean it like that." Grace reached out to him and placed a hand on his arm.

He pulled away. "Do you think you're the only one struggling? We're going through this with you. This happened to us too. You're my wife, but you aren't the same. I don't know you any more than you know me." He looked at the ceiling and then back at her. "You're right. You have no reason to trust me. But I promise you, Grace. I've never lied to you, and I'm not about to start now." He stood and moved away. "I'm going to make a few calls."

She knew she'd hurt him. But what was she supposed to think? She'd placed her trust, her life, in this man. Frustrated and tired, she rubbed her face with her hands. Somehow, she knew Danny was telling the truth. But if he wasn't lying, who was? That man knew her. But how? And what secret was he referring to?

Danny had closed himself in his office for hours, coming out only when the kids had gotten home from school. Her questions had been insensitive. He knew she'd been shaken up, but her words had stabbed him. She wasn't entirely wrong. He was keeping something from her. Danny moved his mouse to open the email he'd received a few days before Grace's attack. It contained only one line. *How well do you know your wife?* It wasn't uncommon for him to receive the occasional angry email from someone who was upset by how a case turned out. But they had never been threatening or directed toward his family.

He'd tried to reply to the email, but it had bounced back as undeliverable. The VPN had been untraceable. Danny hadn't mentioned the message to Grace and then she'd been attacked; it wouldn't have done any good at that point. But he also hadn't told the police. He knew better than to withhold information. It might have been useful for the investigation. But he hadn't wanted to shed any bad light on Grace. Especially when he didn't know what the email meant. It could be nothing. But he wasn't so sure. Maybe it was time to dig a little deeper into his wife's past. He needed answers.

Grace stood looking out the window, the dark bedroom behind

her. She'd replayed the events of the day over and over in her mind, hoping to find a clue to who the intruder was and what exactly he wanted. She barely knew who she was at the moment, much less prior to meeting Danny. Did she really have a secret that was so deplorable she'd do anything to keep it hidden? She closed her eyes and rested her forehead against the cool glass. What had she done?

She watched as a patrol car crawled past her house, then turned at the next corner. It only provided minimal reassurance for the sixty seconds it took for it to drive by. What about the other fifty-nine minutes of the hour? That left plenty of time for someone to break in and—well, do anything.

She turned her head at the soft knock on the door, then smiled at Lucy when she poked her head in. "Dinner's ready."

"I'm not hungry right now, honey. But I'll be down in a bit, okay?"

"Are you okay? Do you want me to save you a plate?" Lucy sounded worried.

"No, thanks. And yes, I'm fine. Just a little tired." Grace tried to reassure her.

"Okay, then. See you in a few." Lucy closed the door behind her, and Grace sighed.

Conviction and determination moved her away from the window and toward the door. This wasn't right, she thought. She refused to regress back to being timid and afraid, like the woman she was when she'd left the hospital. She had to talk to Danny and attempt to repair the damage she'd done. As she reached for the knob, she yelped in surprise when the door opened and Danny stepped in.

"I'm sorry," both said at the same time.

Danny closed the door, and they moved further into the room. "Danny, I'm sorry about what I said. I was upset. I didn't mean it, I swear."

He took her in his arms and held her tightly against his chest. "I'm sorry too," he whispered into her hair. "I know you didn't mean anything by it. But you were right." He shushed her when she started to speak. "You've had to rely on everyone else to tell you who you are, and we've failed you. We need to do better." He pulled back and looked at her. "Starting now."

Guiding her to a chair near the window, he motioned for her to sit, then knelt on the floor in front of her. Taking both her hands in his, he lowered his head and prayed. "Father, we love you, and we come to you tonight with grateful hearts. We thank you for protecting Grace today and ask that you continue that protection. Surround our family with your loving arms. Help us to remember to lean on you when we struggle and remind us that you have a plan for us. You've brought us so far, Father, and we trust you to guide us to a quick resolution to this difficult and confusing season we're in. In your precious son's holy name, we pray, Amen." He looked up to see Grace smiling down at him. "I love you," he said.

"I love you, too. Thank you." She slid off the chair onto her knees and back into his arms.

* * *

Grace sat in her favorite chair in the den with a book lying open on her lap. She'd thought reading would take her mind off things, but it was useless. Thoughts of the man who'd forced his way into their home consumed her. She played the scene over and over in her mind, searching for any clue to the man's identity. It had to have something to do with her past since he kept calling her Anna. With her elbow on the armrest, she rubbed her forehead with her fingertips. Dim images flashed in her mind's eye, so fleeting she couldn't make them out. A memory was there, just beyond her reach. She tried to rein it in, but as she pulled it toward her the fuzzier it became until it went dark. Frustrated, she closed the book and tossed it aside. If only she could remember! At this point, any memory at all would be a relief. She felt as if she was standing in front of a stone wall that encircled her, a dam blocking out all of her past. If only she could find one stone loose enough for her to pry out, then all her memories could be released.

Her phone buzzed on the table beside her, and she answered Lucy's call. "Mom? I need a favor. I can't find my bracelet and I want to make sure I didn't leave it at home before I panic for no reason."

"Sure, honey. What does it look like and where should I look first?" Grace headed up the stairs to Lucy's room.

"If it's there, it'll be in the jewelry box on my dresser. The one with my initials on top. And it's the gold link bracelet with the silver cross, the one I wear almost every day. By the way, are you okay? Is Dad home?" Although Danny had finally gone back to the office, he had chosen to work from home for the past few days, unwilling to leave Grace or the kids alone in the house.

"Yes, I'm fine. Your dad's working in his office. I'm in your room now, hang on." As soon as Grace lifted the lid to the box, she spotted the familiar bracelet. "Yep, it's right here. Do you need it?"

Lucy's relief was evident in her voice. "No. I was just afraid I'd lost it. I guess I was in a hurry this morning and forgot to put it on. Thanks Mom, gotta go." And then she was gone.

Grace replaced the bracelet and closed the lid. She ran her hand lightly over her daughter's initials, appreciating the craftsmanship of the box. She wondered if it had been a gift from her, something special on her birthday or Christmas. Or if someone else had given it to her for some other occasion. Tears sprang to her eyes as she was once again reminded of how little she knew about herself or her family. After another glance around Lucy's tidy domain, she exited the room and softly closed the door.

14

Unanswered Questions

Grace and Danny sat at a table in the fellowship hall along with parents of other kids wanting to sign up for the upcoming youth trip. Pastor Joe stood at a small podium in the front of the room, the same podium she had cowered behind a couple of weeks before at the WAG meeting. She smiled at the memory, recalling how nervous she'd been.

Pastor Joe waved a handful of papers and whistled to get everyone's attention. "Okay everybody. Listen up. This trip is for the older youth, which is why you don't see any of the younger kids here today. There's a separate trip in the works for them, headed up by the youth pastor. Now, I've been talking with your kids about this for a few weeks and they may have mentioned it. Most of you know that my son attends Elevation Church up in Charlotte, North Carolina. Well, they're hosting a regional youth conference next month and I want to take our older youth. Y'all, it's gonna be awesome!" His voice rose on the last word. "There will be thousands of youths there. Thousands of young Christians, in the same room, all worshiping together." Joe's emotion was contagious. Every youth in the room had turned to a parent to beg for permission to attend. Grace had to admit if she were a teenager, she'd be the first one in line to sign up. He went on to give them official dates and a rough itinerary. By the time he'd gone through all the specifics regarding travel, lodging, and cost, Grace was convinced. This was a terrific opportunity for their kids, and with Daniel going along, she wouldn't worry quite so much about Lucy's safety. With this man on the loose lurking, she worried any time they were out of her sight.

After a quick discussion, Danny agreed and gave his blessing. All he had to do was write a check for half the cost. All the kids had readily agreed to raise the other half, and already had plans for how they would accomplish it.

As Danny and Grace made their way to the door when it was time to leave, the pastor stepped in front of them and pulled them aside. "Hey you guys. Before you say no, hear me out."

"Uh oh," Danny said. "The last time you said that I ended up hanging from the rafters wearing a dinosaur onesie." He looked at Grace. "Don't ask. You don't want to know."

"Just hear me out here. I need you guys to chaperone this trip. We have nine kids signed up. If we drive, it'll cut the cost, and your SUV will hold at least five or six kids. We can throw all the luggage in the back of my truck, three kids in the back seat, and we're good to go." He looked from Danny to Grace and back again, waiting for their agreement.

"And you think I can take off work on a whim?" Danny tried.

"Oh, you can make it work. You're the boss. Thanks! This is gonna be great!" And just like that, he was gone.

Dumbfounded, Grace looked up at Danny and asked, "What just happened?"

Danny shook his head. "Brother Joe happened. Let's get out of here before he comes back and talks me into renting a bus."

* * *

"Yes, all the doors are locked. We'll be fine," Grace said, although she wasn't so sure. "Love you too." She placed the phone back on the cradle and sighed.

Danny had driven to his office for a meeting with a new client and had called to tell her he was running late. He'd be home as soon as he could get away. She didn't like being home alone after dark. Danny didn't leave her often, but at least during the day, she could look out the windows and see that she was safe. But when it was dark outside, she felt exposed. She made sure all the curtains were closed so that no one could see in. Danny's connections with the police department ensured that a patrol car still cruised by several times per shift, but he didn't have enough clout to warrant an officer watching the house full-time. Danny usually tried to plan his schedule so that he'd be home early if Daniel had practice or couldn't be home for some other reason. This was one of those evenings when Daniel wasn't home yet, probably because he was expecting his dad to be there.

She decided to start dinner and called up the stairs for Lucy to come down to the kitchen. "Hey, you. Dad's going to be a little late. If you don't mind, I'd rather you stay close to me until he gets home."

"Okay, sure." Lucy understood her concern and was happy to oblige. They'd all been a little on edge since the break-in, and even more protective of Grace. Lucy slid onto a barstool and watched as her mother stirred sauce for pasta. "So, how do you know how to cook? Do you, like, remember things like that?"

Grace slowed her stirring as she thought about how to respond. "Well, I somehow knew without asking that the pasta has to be boiled, and that we need sauce to put on it. I can't explain it. It's like the simple stuff is there, you know? But I had to look up a recipe for the sauce." She shook her head and chewed on her cheek. "It's kind of like when you get up in the morning and already know how to walk. You don't have to think about it, it's just there, even though you may not remember actually learning how to walk and talk. Does that make sense?"

Lucy thought for a second. "Yeah, I guess it does. You know, we've been talking a lot about career choices in class. I've been thinking about going into psychology." She paused, waiting for her mother's reaction.

Grace smiled and turned the stove down to let the sauce simmer, then looked back at Lucy. "I think that's an excellent choice. And you already have some insight into the mysteries that go on up here." She tapped her own head and Lucy smiled with her. "I think you'd be a wonderful psychologist, or psychiatrist, or brain surgeon, or anything at all you want to be. You might change your mind and decide to pursue your art."

Lucy smiled. "It's just a hobby right now, but you never know. Hey, I finished the painting I was working on. Do you want to see it?"

"Yes, I'd love to!"

Lucy dashed up the stairs and returned with a canvas. When she held it up and turned it toward her mother, Grace's breath caught. A woman was standing in a field, her blond hair blowing in the breeze. The view was from behind her as she walked away. Grace knew without asking that the woman was her, but that wasn't what grabbed her attention. The woman was walking toward a cross. A lone cross standing on top of a hill. It was from a different angle than the one in Dr. Hyatt's office, but Grace was sure it was the same one. She reached toward the canvas.

"Lucy, it's beautiful. I've seen this before. Not this one, but one similar." She described the painting and where she saw it, and Lucy smiled.

"That's the painting I won the award for. The one that was auctioned. So that's who bought it. Cool." Her face grew serious. "Wait. So you felt something when you saw it. Does that mean you remembered it?"

"Maybe I did. At least my subconscious did." She studied the painting again. "Is this place real? Somewhere you've been?"

"Yeah, it's at the Old Place."

"Old place?" Grace cocked her head.

"That's right. It's where Dad grew up. Out in the country. We go there sometimes to hike. Grampa built that cross before he passed away and you insist on going every Easter."

"It really is stunning, Lucy. I love it."

Lucy beamed. She placed the painting on the floor and propped it against a barstool, then picked up a magazine and thumbed through it while Grace set about chopping vegetables for a salad. With the task of preparing dinner done, they set the table and moved to the family room to watch TV while they waited for Danny and Daniel to get home.

The crash of glass breaking near the back door ripped their focus from the movie. Lucy stared at Grace wide-eyed, then they both made a run for the front of the house. "Mom, what do we do?"

"Hide." Avoiding the front door, Grace led Lucy to the closet underneath the stairs and pulled her inside, then pushed her as far to the back of the closet as she could. Her heart sank. She'd left her cell phone on the counter in the kitchen. "Lucy, do you have your cell?"

A moment later, her screen lit up. Relieved, she took it from her and dialed 911. As quietly as she could, she reported the intrusion to the dispatcher and gave her their address. The woman on the other end advised her to stay on the line until officers arrived, but Grace never heard her. She jumped at the sound of the back door breaking in and Lucy slapped her hands over her own mouth to stifle a scream.

They held their breath, expecting to hear footsteps moving through the house. "Where'd they go?" Lucy whispered. Grace shook her head, not thinking that Lucy couldn't see her in the darkness. Muffled voices came from the back of the house, but they couldn't make out the words. Something else crashed, but what? Lucy gripped her tighter at every sound, expecting the door to be yanked open any second. Then a faint "Hey!" The voice got their attention. Was that Daniel? Grace thought.

Grace forgot her fear, and pushed open the door, Lucy on her heels. She tried to push her back into the closet, but Lucy adamantly refused. "No way. I'm going with you." Grace glanced at the golf club clutched in Lucy's hand and reached back to grab one for herself.

They crept toward the back of the house, where they could hear noises coming through the door. Outside, they stepped around the patio table, which had been knocked over on its side. As they peeked around the corner of the house, they could make out figures struggling in the shadows beyond the glow of the security light. When she heard her son's voice, she moved toward the darkness. The tangle of bodies rolling on the ground moved close enough to the light for her to catch a glimpse of a face. Her heart seized. She couldn't breathe. She couldn't let him hurt her son.

Headlights swept across the trees, and she made a run for the driveway with Lucy in tow. She nearly collided with Danny as she rounded the corner of the house. She clutched his shirt. "Danny! It's him! He broke into the house!"

"Dad, we got him!" Daniel shouted, breathless, from atop the back of the man now lying face down on the ground, sitting back-to-back with his friend Chad, who sat on the man's legs.

In a split second, Danny's eyes took in the scene. The change in the air was palpable the moment Danny realized what was going on. The tension on her husband's face morphed into rage. "Daniel!" he called and rushed toward his son.

Before she knew what was happening, he'd grabbed the man's shirt, pulled him from underneath the boys, and flipped him onto his back. Danny was on top of him, pummeling his face. The sickening thud of fist against flesh could be heard amid the wails of pain coming from his target. The man tried to throw his own punches, but they proved ineffective. Danny didn't seem to notice. He released months of stress, anguish, and despair with every strike. He wanted to hurt him, wanted to make him pay for tormenting his family.

Two patrol cars whipped into the driveway, red and blue lights flashing. Two police officers pulled Danny away and were struggling to restrain him while a third officer was placing handcuffs on the now bleeding man on the ground.

A fourth officer approached Grace and Lucy and asked who'd placed the 911 call. Grace gave a quick summary of what had happened, then moved to Danny's side, anxious to get to her son. The officer questioning Daniel was speaking. "Okay, let's back up and try this again. Sir," he said to Danny, "please let me ask the questions here. All right, son, start from the beginning."

Daniel took a deep breath and let it out. "Okay. So, we were hiding in the bushes when we saw this guy sneak into the backyard and go up to the back door."

Danny broke in. "What were you doing in the bushes?"

"Sir! I'm going to ask you one more time. Please."

"All right, all right. Daniel, go on." Danny wasn't accustomed to being told what to do. The lawyer in him wanted to be in charge of the questioning.

"Okay, so he was peeking in the windows, then broke the glass with his elbow, like this." Daniel bent his right arm, bringing his fist to his left cheek, then brought his elbow down and back. "That's when we rushed him from behind. I jumped on his back and Chad went for his legs. He tried to buck me off, but we both fell backward and landed on the table. When it turned over, he broke free and ran off the deck. We ran after him, and Chad tackled him in the yard."

Grace could practically see the smoke coming from Danny's ears.

Danny looked at the cop and said, "My turn yet?" The officer was a smart man and gave him an affirmative nod. Danny turned to Daniel and said as calmly as he could, "Daniel, what were you thinking? You could have been hurt. Or worse." Then pointing at Chad, "And you could have been too. How long have you boys been out here?"

Daniel was undaunted by Danny's barely controlled fury. "We've been out here all evening, watching out for Mom and Lucy. The cops come by once an hour, if that. Anything could happen between one drive by and the next."

Grace was astounded to realize Daniel had feared the very thing she'd worried about, and even more shocked that he'd acted on that fear. Risked getting hurt. Her amazing, precious son.

Danny wasn't convinced. "Don't you understand how dangerous that was? How close you came to—"

"It's okay, Mr. B, we had their backs." One by one, six more boys stepped out of the shadows.

Grace's mouth dropped open at the sight of them.

Daniel said, "We're a team, Dad. We look out for each other. Right?"

Danny shook his head, then grabbed his son by his shirt and pulled him in for a bear hug and a slap on the back. "Don't you ever do that again."

One of the officers interrupted, "Excuse me, but we'll need these boys to come down to the station to give a formal statement." The other patrol car had already left for the police station with an unhappy criminal handcuffed in the back seat.

* * *

The boys didn't seem to notice the discomfort of the hard plastic chairs in the police department lobby. They chattered incessantly about their stakeout of the Bradford home, and each told his own animated version of Chad's tackle which took down the man they now referred to as "The Perp." Undoubtedly the tale would grow as it spread across the student body of the local high school. Danny and Grace requested they keep it off social media as much as possible, but knew it was inevitable. Danny had insisted that each young man call his respective parents to let them know what was going on and that they were okay. He'd also asked them to tell their parents he'd be calling them over the next couple of days to fill in any blanks and clarify details. All he needed was an irate parent on his back demanding to know what kind of household he ran, putting their precious child in danger.

Danny shifted in his chair and rested his elbows on his knees, hands together. "Listen up, guys." His voice was strained, but all eyes were on him. "I want to say something, and I want you all to pay attention. I lost control back at the house, and that's not okay. What I did, jumping on that guy like that, wasn't the right thing to do. I acted on impulse and adrenaline. Let me be clear. Violence is never the right choice. I should've let the authorities handle the situation, and I was wrong. And," he continued, "although I'm proud of what you boys did, taking matters into your own hands wasn't the best decision. Do you understand?"

Joey, a lanky redhead, was the first to speak up. "We get it Mr. B. But you gotta admit, you clobbered that dude."

Danny pulled a hand down his face and hid a grin. "It was wrong."

Grace watched Danny out of the corner of her eye but kept her thoughts to herself. Unwilling to stay behind, she and Lucy had tagged along to the station. She hadn't expected violence from Danny. Since she'd come out of her coma, he'd been gentle and patient. Was there a darker side he was hiding? Grace didn't like where her mind was headed, that she might be living with the very thing she was afraid of. Danny wouldn't have hurt her. And now her attacker was in a cell.

Lucy laid her head on Grace's shoulder, and Grace rested her own head on top of Lucy's. In direct contrast to the boys' adrenaline high, they looked exhausted. Danny draped his arm around Grace so that he could also place his hand on Lucy's shoulder. He was lucky. They had been so blessed. He smiled. God continued to protect them, answering yet another of his prayers.

"Mr. Bradford," said a voice from the doorway.

"Yes," said Danny, standing.

"Looks like we have everything we need, so y'all are free to go. You can get these guys outta here." The young cop didn't look much older that the boys he indicated with his clipboard. "Y'all drive safe now."

"Hold on," Danny said. "Can you tell us anything about the guy? After all, he did try to break into my house."

"Oh yeah. Sorry, sir. I thought the LT had already been in to speak with you." He referred to his clipboard and said, "We ran his prints. Almost had to reload the printer when we got the report." His own chuckle was the only one he was rewarded with, and he cleared his throat. "Name's Vincent Crawley. He was released from prison about four months ago and apparently skipped parole and went on the run. Not sure why he ended up here, but I guess it's as good a place as any. I don't get why he didn't keep goin' if he was runnin', though. Started out from South Florida. He could've been long gone by now." He sniffed and rubbed at his feeble mustache.

Danny's patience was wearing thin. He didn't care about the man's opinion. "Why was he in prison?" he asked pointedly.

The officer obviously was smart enough to read Danny's tone. "Oh. Yes, um, armed robbery," he said, reading his notes. "Also got him for attempted murder, too."

"Murder?" the boys exclaimed in unison. That tale would definitely grow taller knowing they'd subdued a murderer.

"Attempted," corrected Danny.

"That's right," agreed the officer. "Claimed he stabbed the guy in self-defense but it didn't fly with the judge. That, plus the armed robbery and a mile-long list of petty stuff, got him twenty-two in the big house. Couldn't play nice with the other kids in there either, so he couldn't even get early parole. Bad onion, that one." And with that, he turned and left the room.

The report left the boys in a frenzy, and likely scheming their next stakeout. Danny knew he'd need to have another sit-down with them. After they'd gotten over themselves. "Simmer down, Magnum. We'll discuss this later. Right now, we all need to get some rest." Danny ushered the group out the door and into the parking lot. As the boys loaded into Daniel's truck, he heard a muffled "Hey, who's Magnum?" and chuckled to himself as he followed his son out of the lot.

On the drive home, Grace noticed Danny had grown quiet, but attributed his mood to everything that had happened. When they were inside the house and the kids had retreated to their rooms, Grace said, "Something's bothering you. What's wrong?"

He looked up from his phone screen, more alert. He held up the phone. "Yeah. Something was bothering me. I needed to check my work calendar, to be sure. The late appointment I had today was a no-show. The name on my calendar was Vincent."

Grace's eyes widened. "Crawley?"

Danny shook his head. "No, not Crawley. Douglas. But no way that's a coincidence. He wanted me away from the house. And with Daniel's truck parked two blocks behind us at Chad's, he must've bet on you and Lucy being alone. I can't believe I'm saying this, but thank God for Daniel and his bullheaded friends."

Grace sank into a chair. "What have I done?" Her hands trembled. "Somehow, I brought this man into our lives and put us in danger. What if he'd hurt one of the kids? What could he want, Danny? And why did he call me Anna?" She cupped her hands in front of her face. Whatever she'd done, it was bad.

Danny lowered himself to his knees in front of her. "I don't know. I don't get it either. Hopefully, the police will get more information from the authorities in Florida. Tomorrow I'll make some calls and see if I can find out anything."

As she got ready for bed, Grace picked through the cobwebs of her mind for any hint of recognition. She even replayed the distorted memory of her assault, hoping to match her attacker to Crawley. Frustrated, she pulled back the covers and slid between the sheets, praying that sunrise would bring with it some answers.

Downstairs, sitting behind his desk in his office, Danny stared out the window into the night. "God, it seems like all I do is ask for help these days. Now it's time to thank you properly. Thank you for keeping my family safe. And thank you for Daniel. For our stubborn, impetuous, foolish, amazing son. And for his kamikaze friends. You sure know how to test us." Looking up toward the ceiling, he said, "But don't you think it's time for a break?"

After a few more minutes and jotting down notes on a few things he wanted to follow up on, Danny headed upstairs to bed. He was relieved the guy was in custody but was well aware the mystery remained unsolved. They still had to figure out why he had targeted Grace. He'd never questioned anything she'd told him about her past, and even if he wanted to start now, it would be useless. She didn't remember. The only thing he could do now was put his faith in the Lord and trust Him to work it out.

When Grace woke up the following morning, Danny was already in his office on the phone. She could hear his muffled voice through the door as she poured herself a cup of coffee. She hadn't heard him come to bed the night before, and judging by the half-empty pot, he'd been up for a while. She dropped two pieces of toast into the toaster, and no longer hearing his voice, she knocked softly on his door, pushing it open a few inches. Danny sat behind his desk, tapping on the keyboard in front of him. He smiled when he saw her and said, "Good morning."

"Hey. I don't mean to bother you. I was wondering if you want any breakfast."

"No, I'm good, thanks. I've been trying to get information on this Crawley guy. We have his record but not much else. No social media accounts that I can find, no bank accounts, nothing. He has to have another name he operated under before he went to prison. But the thing is, I don't understand why the state of Florida hasn't figured it out before now. Or if they've even tried. It looks like once they had him behind bars, that was it." Danny pushed his chair back and ran his hands through his hair. "Maybe they had it and lost it, I don't know. But what I do know is this guy didn't come from nowhere. He *had* to exist before prison." He looked back at his wife. "I promise, Grace, I'll figure this out. Somehow. As soon as I can get a contact in South Florida, things will start moving forward."

"I trust you, Danny. I'm happy he's back in jail. Do you have his picture?" Danny slid a printed photo across his desk toward her, watching her reaction as she studied the image.

Her eyes narrowed and her forehead wrinkled as she stared at that awful face. If he hadn't been such a horrible man, Grace would've thought he was fairly handsome. She'd been sure that once she got a good look at him, when he wasn't running trying to wrestle himself free, that she would recognize something. Remember something. She shook her head. "I don't have a clue who he is, or why he would come after me. The name Anna keeps haunting me. Maybe I look like someone he knows. If he was in prison for that long, maybe he hasn't seen Anna in a long time and made a mistake." She knew she was grasping at straws, but the man stirred nothing in her. She handed the photo back.

Danny accepted it and stared at the image. "I don't know, Grace. Anything's possible. But we'll figure it out. He can't get to you now."

15

Your Word

"Of course we'll still go. I don't see any reason we shouldn't," Danny reassured the kids. "I think it'll be good for your mom to get away from here for a few days. Besides, we made a commitment, and you know what we say."

"Keep your word, keep your honor," Lucy and Daniel said in unison. They resumed their breakfast, visibly relieved. Danny actually looked forward to the trip and the distraction it would bring. He felt a little better about leaving Grace while he went to work every day, since he'd installed the security cameras at all the doors and linked them directly to his iPhone. But he hadn't received any useful information on how the intruder sitting in the county jail was connected to Grace. And until she got her memory back, *if she got it back*, this nightmare was far from over. The guy still wasn't talking, and they had no way of knowing if he had partners.

"Good morning." Grace smiled as she stepped into the kitchen.

"Morning, hon," Danny replied as he brushed his lips against her temple. "Any plans for today?"

"Not really. Lizzy said she might drop by for a bit."

"Oh, good. You two can have some girl time." He didn't mention how relieved he was that she wouldn't have to be alone all day. "I've gotta run. Call me if you need anything."

Grace turned her attention to Daniel and Lucy as they gathered their backpacks and made for the door as well. "You two be careful, and call me when you get there, please."

"We will, Mom, promise. Chad is picking up Tori and we're meeting them at his house and riding together. His parents are already there and they'll for sure make us call when we get there. I wrote everyone's numbers down, taped them to the fridge, and yes, we have our chargers and clean underwear."

Grace stared back at him, wide-eyed. "Am I that bad?" she asked with a laugh.

"Yes!" they said in unison.

"But in a good way," Lucy was quick to add.

"Well, okay then. Give your mom a hug and be on your way." Both kids readily stepped into her outstretched arms before hurrying out the door. Daniel had been invited to Chad's family's lake house for the weekend and his cousin Tori was Lucy's age, so she was invited as well.

As the kids left, Lizzy breezed in, laden with plastic bags. "I brought lunch ... chicken salad! And a surprise for dessert." She placed the bags onto the granite countertop, and Grace began pulling out containers. When she pulled out a plastic storage container with homemade goodies inside, she looked up at Lizzy with raised brows. Her friend gazed back with a smile and said, "Pound cake. Your recipe."

"Mine? I have my own recipe?" Grace pulled at the lid before Lizzy slapped her hand away.

"You have to finish your lunch first. Rules are rules. Besides, stuff that good is worth the wait." Lizzy sat on the barstool. "Tell me all about the guy they arrested. I want all the details. Do they know who he is, or what he was after?"

Grace joined Lizzy and filled her in on the details of their most recent saga.

"Vincent Crawley. Hmm, sounds a little sinister doesn't it? Maybe a little gangsta?" Lizzy said with a laugh.

They'd just picked up their forks when the doorbell rang. Lizzy offered to get the door and hopped off her stool with a warning from Grace not to open the door unless she knew the visitor. A few seconds later, she returned with a shrug. "It's a man. I don't recognize him."

Grace swallowed her nerves and went to check for herself. On the other side of the door stood a tall, thin man who looked to be in his thirties. He had shoulder-length black hair and wore a white T-shirt with black skinny jeans and black combat boots. A black belt with silver studs and wide black leather bracelets completed his look.

"Sketchy," said Lizzy, as Grace's phone rang.

It was Danny. "Hey, I just got the doorbell alert on my phone. It's Jimmy from around the block. He's a drummer for a local band. He travels a lot and lives with his parents when he's in town. He's harmless. Probably looking for Daniel." Relieved, Grace pulled the door open.

"Hey, what's up, Mrs. B!" drawled Jimmy. "Is Daniel around?"

"Hi. I'm sorry, Jimmy, Daniel's out of town until Sunday." When he didn't seem surprised that she knew his name, she assumed he wasn't aware of her amnesia.

"Oh, man," he said. "I've got a gig down in Savannah, and I was hoping he could feed Snowball for me."

Grace wouldn't have expected him to be a cat guy. More like a bulldog or Rottweiler. He seemed harmless, and before she could stop herself, she blurted, "I'll do it."

"Whoa, really?" Jimmy looked surprised, but relieved. "Are you sure you don't mind?"

She hesitated only a second before she replied, "Sure. What are neighbors for?"

"Man, this is awesome! I'm sorry for the short notice, but I really appreciate it. She's all set with water, you only have to feed her once, between four and four-thirty today. Her food's in the garage. After that she should be good till I get back. She stays in the sunroom. Just make sure you keep the door closed. Sometimes she gets out of her cage and it's hard to find her when she hides in the house."

"I'll bet it is," said Grace, and she thought, less cat hair to clean off the furniture too.

"Give me your digits and I'll text you the alarm code." He pulled his phone out of his back pocket and thumbed in her number, and then her own phone pinged with proof of receipt.

"We'll take care of her, Jimmy. Have a safe trip!"

"We?" Lizzy questioned as she watched Jimmy practically skip down the drive.

"Yes, we. You aren't going to let an amnesiac go to a strange house alone, are you? What if I forget what I'm doing there?"

Lizzy scoffed. "I'm sure you'd figure it out with all the meowing and scratching. I hate cats."

When it was time to feed Snowball, Grace realized she didn't know which house was Jimmy's, and had to call Danny. "Jimmy got a cat? Huh. That's weird. It's the third house on the right over on Lorean. The only house on the street with green shutters and a big frog for a mailbox."

The women decided walking around the block to Jimmy's house would justify all the cake they'd put away. They shared a comfortable silence as they strolled, the sun bathing them in its warmth.

Lizzy interrupted the solitude when she asked, "What's it like, Grace?"

Grace looked at Lizzy with raised brows but didn't break her stride. "What's what like?"

Lizzy lifted a shoulder and considered how to phrase her question. "Living a life you can't remember. I mean, I know it's hard, it has to be. But I can't fathom being in your place."

Grace's focus shifted back to the sidewalk in front of her. "Well, at first it was scary, almost like I'd been kidnapped and held against my will. I wanted to escape, but I had no idea where I wanted to escape to. Does that make sense?"

"It does. And what about now? Do you still want to escape?"

"Now it's like living in my own mystery. I wake up every day wondering what I'm going to discover about myself."

"You'll get your memory back, I'm sure of it." She smiled. "I'm just glad you're okay. It could've been so—" She stopped short. "What in the world ..."

Grace followed her line of sight and gasped. Danny wasn't kidding. A giant green frog sat on top of a wrought-iron pole twisted into the shape of a lily pad. His faded red tongue was sticking out as if waiting for a mammoth fly to land on it. Lizzy, unable to resist, reached out to grab the tongue and pulled. The beast's mouth fell open, revealing the receptacle for mail. "I don't even want to know," she said. "Let's get this over with."

The key was right where Jimmy said it would be. Grace unlocked the door and punched in the code to turn off the alarm. They stepped inside and Grace wrinkled her nose as the stench of stale cigarette smoke hit her nostrils. They crossed the tiled foyer into an open floor plan. In contrast to the odor, the room was a neatly kept, country-style living area. She wasn't sure what she'd been expecting. Black leather, maybe? But this was Jimmy's parents' house, after all.

"It smells like someone is well on their way to emphysema." Lizzy waved a hand in front of her face. "Let's get this done before I need a rescue inhaler."

As they passed through the room, Grace's eyes landed on a chair near the window. Draped across the back was a dark jacket. She reached out to touch the fabric, and as her fingers came into contact with the leather, an image of a man flashed in her mind. She was transported back to her hospital room, face-to-face with the ominous visitor. As his face came into focus, Lizzy said, "Found the garage!" And the image dissolved.

Grace retracted her hand and hurried through the kitchen. The leather jacket would soon be the least of her worries. She joined Lizzy at the door to the garage. Flipping a few switches on the panel by the door, they finally found the correct one and fluorescent lights flickered on to light up the space. A quick visual sweep of the room didn't reveal any bags of cat food, but Grace spotted a walled in space in the corner and headed toward it. After another search for a switch panel, she finally located it and flipped it on. And immediately wanted to flip it back off.

She jumped at Lizzy's voice behind her. "Um, exactly how big is this cat?"

Grace could only shake her head. Sitting on a workbench was a glass aquarium. She would've had no problem with the tank if it had been full of fish. But inside this one ... were mice. Two mice with beady little eyes looking straight at her, noses twitching. She backed away, leaving Lizzy where she stood. "Surely those are pets, Lizzy. Not food. Maybe the food is in the pantry and he forgot. Or he was in such a hurry he said garage by mistake."

"Yeah, maybe," Lizzy replied. "You check the pantry. I'll figure out which room this furball is in." Lizzy headed down the hallway, and Grace opened the pantry door as her phone rang.

"Hey, Mom," Daniel said as soon as she answered. "I just talked to Dad. Where are you?" She put him on speaker and continued her search of the pantry. A quick glance around the small space didn't reveal pet food of any sort.

"Lizzy and I are at Jimmy's. Do you know where he keeps the cat food?"

"That's why I'm calling, Mom. Jimmy doesn't have a cat." An instant later, Lizzy let out a blood-curdling scream.

Grace raced down the hallway and caught Lizzy by the shoulders as she bolted through a door. "No. No, no, no. Uh uh. That," she stammered, pointing into the room she'd just left. "That *thing* is not a cat. How could you agree to this?"

"Lizzy, what are you talking about?" But Lizzy didn't respond. She simply pointed back into the room, and Grace had no choice but to see for herself. She stepped past her friend and through the doorway, then froze. Another glass aquarium took up most of one wall. And Lizzy was right. That was no cat. On the other side of the glass was a snake. A white snake curled up on a rock that had been placed in the corner.

As she stood staring at the tank, she finally heard Daniel's voice calling her name. He was still on the phone. "I'm still here, Daniel. Um, Snowball?"

"I was trying to tell you before you found her. Snowball is a Python. She's harmless, she—"

"Harmless?" Lizzy cut him off. "What do you mean, harmless? I nearly killed myself trying to get away from it!" She shivered.

Daniel stifled a chuckle and continued, "Seriously, she won't bite. All you have to do is drop her food in and close the lid." Lizzy stopped mid-shiver and stared at Grace.

"What food, Daniel?" But Grace already knew the answer.

"A mouse."

Grace was sure she heard muffled giggling in the background. Daniel's phone must have been on speaker as well. She took a deep breath and closed her eyes.

"Does she have other food? Something that doesn't have a pulse?"

"No, ma'am. That's what she eats. She has a strict routine and gets stressed if it changes." Daniel was still trying to control his laughter.

Lizzy piped in. "Did he just say stressed? The snake gets stressed if her routine changes? Are you kidding me?" She turned away with her hands in the air. "And who names a snake Snowball, for crying out loud? There's nothing cuddly about that thing. He should've named it Lucifer. Or Viper. How about Fang? There's a name for ya."

Now who's stressed, Grace thought as Lizzy continued her torrent. "Daniel, just tell me what to do so we can get out of here. Lizzy's gonna need a tranquilizer before this is over." She shook her head with closed eyes as Daniel explained once again that all she had to do was drop a mouse in the tank.

Taking a deep breath, she said, "Lizzy, snap out of it. Let's do this and get out of here."

"So, what now, Einstein?" Lizzy asked.

"Shut up, I'm thinking," Grace snapped back as they both stared into the glass aquarium. In addition to the pair of mice, the tank now held a plastic grocery bag, a dustpan, and a jar with a hunk of cheese in the bottom. Grace had placed the bag in the bottom of the tank, holding on to one of the handles. Instead of crawling into the bag like she'd pictured it in her head, one of the vermin crawled up the outside of the bag, which in turn, had caused Grace to promptly let go of it. Neither woman dared put a hand in to retrieve the bag where the mouse had made himself comfortable. Then Lizzy had found the dustpan and came up with the master plan of scooping up one of the mice. That plan hadn't worked any better than the first one. The mouse had indeed crept curiously onto the pan but didn't stop there. It had scurried up the handle and onto Lizzy's hand, obviously planning its escape up her arm. Nevertheless, the pan and mouse were slung back into the tank where both would remain if it were up to the two women who were close to letting the not so cuddly reptile starve. The jar with the cheese had actually been a good idea. They'd planned to wait until one of the mice crawled inside, then they would pick it up, slap a lid on, and pour it into the snake's tank. It was a beautiful plan. If only the mice would cooperate. They seemed to be only minimally interested in the cheese, but neither were willing to enter the jar to fetch it. So there the jar would stay.

Grace snapped her fingers. "I've got it!" She ran through the door that led into the house and returned moments later wielding her latest mouse-collecting weapon ... tongs. Grace held the tongs toward Lizzy and clacked them in her face. Lizzy, saying nothing, stepped back to allow her room to work. She held little hope this plan would work any better than the others, but what did they have to lose at this point? Eventually, the mice would have enough supplies to build their very own staircase to freedom.

With feigned bravery and confidence, Grace reached into the tank, aimed for her target ... and closed her tongs around a mouse. She pulled back; the rodent squirming in protest. Both women squealed with delight and Lizzy shouted, "You did it! Get it in there! Get it in there!"

Grace rushed into the house and down the hall to the snake's room. "Open the top, Lizzy," she ordered.

Lizzy hesitated but knew it had to be done. She slid the latch and slowly lifted the lid to allow Grace to drop in the mouse. Just as she held the mouse-laden tongs over the opening, the snake moved, her eyes on her snack. In a panic, Grace dropped the mouse in, tongs and all, and backed away. "Close it! Close it!" she shouted, and Lizzy immediately complied. Neither had to voice the need to get out of there as quickly as they could. And neither had the desire to watch as Snowball devoured her meal.

* * *

Danny howled in laughter as Lizzy and Grace recounted their ordeal. "I can't believe you two went through with it," he said, wiping tears from his eyes. "Why didn't you wait and let me do it?"

Lizzy and Grace paused and stared at each other, realizing the thought hadn't even crossed their minds. Grace shook her head and replied, "Believe me, if we'd known what we were getting into, we would've."

Danny looked over at Lizzy and asked, "So, Lizzy, I hear there's a man in your life. Is it getting serious?"

Lizzy grinned in response and wiped at the condensation on her water glass. "I don't know. Maybe. It's hard to work on a relationship when both parties travel a lot with work." She glanced at Grace. "Which is why I accepted the job I told you about."

Grace sat up straighter, excited. "No more traveling? That's great! When do you start?"

"The first of next month. I'm taking a few of weeks off to get some things done around the apartment that I've been putting off."

"Hey," Danny said. "We're going to be going up to North Carolina for a few days next week. Would you mind stopping by here now and then to check on things? After everything that's happened, I'd feel better knowing someone was laying eyes on the house."

"Absolutely. Especially since that creepo is behind bars. I'm having my place painted, so I may stay a night or two if you don't mind."

"Perfect," Grace said. Danny excused himself and retreated to his office as the best friends launched into a discussion on paint colors and fabric patterns for curtains, the leather jacket forgotten.

16

Don't Be Late

The drive to North Carolina took nearly seven hours if they didn't count the meal breaks, bathroom breaks, and the one stop to change seating arrangements to accommodate one car sick teen. When they at last pulled into the hotel parking garage just after one o'clock, they were all ready to stretch their legs. After checking in and assigning rooms, Pastor Joe announced they had a couple of hours before they needed to head to the conference center. He and Danny would room with two boys each in adjoining rooms, Joe's wife would be across the hall sharing a room with three girls, and Grace would be in the room adjoining hers with the remaining two girls. When each had a room key, they separated and scattered to their respective rooms, agreeing on a meeting time in two hours.

Led by their goofy, fearless pastor, the group obediently, albeit impatiently, took their place in the long line of young adults and chaperones waiting to enter the conference center. Grace and Danny stood together and watched with amusement as Pastor Joe darted from one teen to another and back again. As they noticed repeated shakes of the heads as he spoke to them, it soon dawned on Grace that he was up to something. No doubt trying to involve some or all of them in one of his schemes.

Twice she noticed Lucy bending over to pick something up off the ground, then she approached her parents, looking frustrated. "Mom, this earring won't stay in. Can you hold them for me until we get back to the hotel? I don't have pockets."

"Sure." Grace accepted the pair of hoops Lucy held out to her and dropped them into the pocket of her sweater. "Lucy, I see Pastor Joe bouncing around. What's he up to this time?"

With a roll of her eyes, Lucy replied, "He's trying to con us into doing something embarrassing to get us to the front of the line. No one will even let him get as far as telling his plan. He starts with"—Lucy dropped her voice, mimicking the preacher—"'Hey guys, I know how we can get in the building first.' We don't even let him finish. We say no. But we've got something planned for him. Just wait."

"Lord help us. I don't even want to know," Danny said.

Half an hour later, the doors finally opened, and the line began its slow progress toward the entrance. Once inside, the group found seats where they'd have a good view of the stage and were fairly close to the restrooms. They settled in and waited until the host stepped onto the stage and welcomed the crowd to this year's conference.

With a booming voice, he began, "Hello everyone! Welcome to the conference!" He paused to let the applause and whistling die down. "I'm Peter Sofield, your host for this conference. We have an amazing couple of days planned for you guys. We only have about four hours this evening, but tomorrow will be a full day, so be sure and get some rest tonight." He smiled when muted laughter erupted throughout the audience. "We want you all to relax. Don't be overwhelmed by the size of this place or by everything going on around you. Use this time to get up close and personal with God. Let Him speak to you, and most importantly ... listen." He paced from one end of the stage to the other as he spoke, ensuring that he spoke directly to all sides of the room. "I don't care why you came here, it doesn't even matter. I don't care if you're here of your own free will, your parents forced you, or if your pastor, girlfriend, boyfriend, best friend, or secret crush invited you. Doesn't matter. We're glad you're here with us. We're going to worship together and have a great time. Our first band is getting ready to come out and lead us in worship, but first let's pray. Father, we love you. We thank you for allowing us to come together to worship you and praise you. We want to feel you in this place, God. I pray that each and every heart in this building will leave here with your fingerprint on it. Allow us to glorify you, allow us to show your love through our words and our actions. Thank you, God, for sending your precious son to save us. In Jesus's name I pray, Amen." Peter walked off the stage as the band began to play, and that's when Grace realized who was kicking off the conference. Crowder!

All the seats emptied as everyone sprang to their feet to sing along with "Good God Almighty." The band's choice for their opening number was successful in getting everyone pumped up to worship and praise. When they left the stage after three songs, the first speaker approached the podium at the front of the stage and greeted the audience. After acknowledging the opening excitement, he delivered a compelling presentation regarding social media and the potential for young adults to impact the world. Grace was astounded at his ability to hold the attention of so many people at once. She had to admit that he was an amazing speaker and his words sounded nothing like a sermon or a speech.

Crowder returned to the stage for another set followed by another speaker and the host band, and then it was time to go back to the hotel for the night. The group had chosen to walk the short distance from the hotel, so once heads were counted, Daniel and Chad took the lead. All the kids were tired but excited, chattering the whole way about which speaker or words had impacted them most. And of course Crowder had stolen the show, but as one teen pointed out, the entire session was impressive in that nothing was about the names on the stage. It was all about worshiping God and putting Him at center stage, regardless of who else was there. Pastor Joe commended the teens and expressed how proud he was of them for their keen perception.

"That's exactly how this whole conference is planned and I'm so glad y'all realized that not once did they build up any person or band that was coming on stage." He took off running, shouting behind him, "Last man to the top pays for room service!"

Beside her, Danny groaned. "Oh no, I'm not doing that again. I've seen these kids eat." He took off in a sprint after their preacher, easily passing a couple of the boys.

Danny lay across the bed, exhausted. "That man is gonna kill me one day."

Grace laughed as she dropped an empty pizza box into the trash. "At least you didn't have to pay for room service."

"Ha. Neither did he. I don't believe for a second he didn't get an answer when he called down. Pizza was cheaper." The girls sitting on the other bed giggled their agreement.

A moment later there was a knock on the door and Grace opened it to find Joe standing in the hall, his expression unamused. "What's wrong?"

Before he could answer, his phone rang and after a quick glance at the screen, he answered with a swift swipe of his thumb. "No, I don't have any puppies. I have no idea what they look like. You got the wrong number, Pal, sorry." He thumbed the phone off and looked back at Grace, who was struggling to hide a grin. "That's four calls now about some freak puppies. Do I look like have puppies? Anyway, I wanted to warn y'all that when you see a kid with a big L on their forehead in the morning, you'll know who put the Doritos crumbs in my bed. Good night."

Grace barely had the door closed before she started laughing. "I guess the shenanigans have begun."

Danny sat up. "What was that about puppies?"

"Well, there may or may not be flyers posted around the hotel telling folks to call his number for free puppies."

"Don't tell me. I want no part of that." He said good night to his wife and the girls, then headed to his room across the hall.

The next morning, the kids were still pumped from the events of the night before. A few rubbed their eyes, but no one was late getting up and ready. They helped themselves to the breakfast buffet, and all made their way back to the conference center, ready to see what the day would bring. When they found seats and settled in, Pastor Joe announced he was going to find his son, who was working with the sound team.

The morning was filled with speakers and worship leaders. The line-up included a rapper Grace hadn't heard of, at least as far as she could remember, and a Christian comedian who did seem vaguely familiar to her.

Before noon, Peter Sofield returned to the stage and announced they'd have a few hours to grab lunch, freshen up, and rest before starting back at three o'clock. Grace was relieved. The morning's events, especially the loud music, had taken their toll and her head was beginning to pound. She was more than happy to take a break and lie down. Danny held her hand as they walked the two blocks to the hotel, and the group stopped at a sandwich shop on the way for a quick lunch. Afterward, the kids wanted to do some sightseeing, but Grace opted out, choosing instead to go to her room for a nap.

As they neared the hotel entrance where the group would separate, Daniel said, "Hey, Dad! Come take our picture!" The girls were perched on the edge of a bench and the guys had placed themselves behind them on the seat back. Danny pulled out his phone and snapped a few shots, including the obligatory silly face shot.

"I'll text the pics to all of you," he said, then turned when he heard his wife shout.

"You did *what*?!" Grace was certain she'd misunderstood Pastor Joe. There was no way he would do such a thing without asking her. Especially when he knew the answer would be an irrefutable no.

"Now Grace. Just hear me out," the preacher began.

"No, I won't hear you out. Every time you say that I end up in ridiculous situations and you're nowhere to be found. It's like you pull open a giant curtain and leave the rest of us standing in the middle of a stage with an audience expecting a magic show. Except there are no tricks and no props! And how do you do that anyway"—her pointed finger inches from his face—"get us to agree to all your shenanigans and foolery? Do they teach that in seminary or is it a natural talent you were born with and fine-tuned over the years by ambushing every un-suspecting schmo that crosses your altar?" Grace gasped and slapped an open hand over her mouth, wide-eyed. "Oh my. I-I'm—"

She spun and ran inside the hotel. She beelined for the elevators, praying no one would follow her. She punched the button to go up over and over again, desperate to get to the privacy of her room before she completely broke down. What was wrong with her? What had she done? Unable to wait any longer, she made a mad dash for the stairs and climbed the three flights to her floor. Through the blur of tears, she hastily searched her bag for the room card. When her fingers closed around it, she shoved it into the slot and practically fell into the room.

Grace dropped the room key and her bag onto the desk inside the door and stumbled to the bathroom, where she splashed cold water onto her face. Where did that come from? Her head ached. She'd had a few episodes where she'd gotten angry in an instant for no reason, but not to that extent. The things she'd said couldn't have been from memory, but she'd felt as though they were. Maybe her frustration with Joe and his stunts had built over the years and her subconscious finally allowed her to retaliate; something the old Grace would never have done. She didn't understand it, but she also couldn't think straight with the pounding in her head.

Joe paced the lobby floor with his head down until Danny laid a hand on his shoulder. "Danny, I know I should've talked to her first, but I honestly had no idea she'd react that way." Joe paced with his head down until Danny laid a hand on his shoulder.

"I agree, you should've consulted her first. But Joe. Speaking in front of thousands? Really? Come on, now. Do you remember how she reacted the first time you asked her to sing at church?"

"I know, I know. But Danny, she's come so far. And I truly believe God has something great planned for her. I'm sorry, man. I'll go talk to her." Pastor Joe's face was drawn with concern. But Joe's feelings weren't Danny's priority right now.

"No, I'll talk to her. She's had a long day, and it doesn't take much to wear her out sometimes." He called Lucy over and asked for her room key. "You guys go on ahead with Pastor Joe and Tammy. I'm going to up and check on your mom." When she offered to stay instead, he said, "Don't worry, I'm sure she's just tired from the trip."

Lucy nodded, trusting her father. "Call if you need us to come back, okay?"

"I will. Thanks." He gave her a quick hug and turned toward the door.

* * *

With her hands on the counter and her head down, Grace took a deep shuddering breath and let it out slowly. Then again and again, one after the other until she had mostly calmed down. She raised her head and looked into the mirror at her distraught self, eyes red and swollen, face puffy from crying. She had no idea what had overcome her, what had made her say such horrible things. And to her pastor, of all people. It had just been a long day. That long drive, all these people, it was all too much, she thought. She vowed to apologize but had no idea where to start or if she could even bring herself to face him. She was horrified to think about who might have overheard her meltdown. She had to keep it together. This was ridiculous. A shower, then a fresh start, she told herself.

Grace turned on the water as hot as she could stand it, then stripped her clothes and stepped into the shower. As she stood under the water, relishing the heat as it sprayed her face and body, she thought back to one of her sessions with Dr. Hyatt. She'd had many rough days in the beginning, had found herself getting emotional and sometimes even angry for no apparent reason. Dr. Hyatt, as usual, had put her intelligence and experience into graceful advice and instructions. Her voice was both stern and compassionate when she spoke: "Grace, you will have moments of doubt. You'll have moments in which you'll doubt yourself. You'll doubt everything and everyone around you. Including me. You'll question everything anyone has told you since you woke up without your memories. There will be times you'll feel like your mind is imploding and that nothing else can possibly fit inside it. As if there's too much in there and it has to get out. Remember, your brain is healing. Your mind is healing. All the old memories trapped inside are tangling and knotting with the new ones and trying to make sense of each other. Remember the exercises I've taught you. Use them. And if that doesn't work, call me. That's why I'm here and why you have my number." Well, if this wasn't the time to call, she didn't know what was.

Dressed in jeans and a sweater, Grace walked through the hotel room in her bare feet. Toweling her wet hair, she thought through what she'd say to Dr. Hyatt and how she'd explain to her what had happened and how she felt about it. Touching the screen of her phone, she noticed a text that must have come through while she was in the shower.

> Hi, this is Kim from sound. Mr. Stevens gave me your number. We need you on stage for a sound check by 8:00 a.m. Text or call this number if you have any questions. Just remember, we're on a strict time schedule, so whatever you do, DON'T BE LATE.

Her vision blurred. The room spun, the floor shook. Earthquake? No, she thought. Something else. DON'T BE LATE. Images flashed through her mind, some so fast she couldn't process what she was seeing. Her standing at a grave. Her standing in front of a mirror.

Laughing, crying. A room with white walls and that antiseptic smell that's always in a hospital. Someone pounding on a door. She grabbed the sides of her head with both hands. God, her head hurt so bad! And with a gasp, Grace collapsed to the floor.

17

Alone

Kate stood at the edge of the muddy hole, staring at the pair of coffins long after the others had made their way to the long line of cars. She didn't want to leave, yet knew she'd have to. Finally, Van put his arm around her and nudged her away. "The workers need to finish their job." She detected irritation in his voice, but imagined it was because he'd had to come back through the rain to get her.

Kate let him lead her to the car, and she sat unmoving as he buckled her into her seat. Like a child, she thought. But she wasn't a child any- more. She wasn't anyone's child now that her parents were gone. She was alone. No brothers or sisters, no other living relatives that she was aware of. Just her. Well, there was Van, her boyfriend. He would be there for her. He'd rarely left her side since the accident, answering phone calls and replying to messages when she couldn't bring herself to do it. She was in shock, he said. He would handle everything, he said. And he had. He'd made all the arrangements, including choosing the matching coffins that held what was left of her parents. Just shells, she told herself, for she was certain their souls had moved on to the golden city beyond the crystal sea. Just like the song said.

For weeks after the funeral, Van had intercepted guests and phone calls. He'd urged her to eat the food he spooned from the endless casseroles and other dishes left by friends, coworkers, her father's business partners, and other acquaintances she had no desire to remember. He guided her through the motions of showering and dressing, only for her to retreat to her bedroom as quickly as she could. She vaguely recalled speaking with her father's business partners, remembered pieces of conversations with his attorneys. Some days she couldn't remember at all. Finally, though, Van was tired of catering to her depression and forced her out of her bed and out of the house.

"Life goes on, you know?" he said as they ate lunch in a booth at his favorite deli. "You can't mourn them for the rest of your life. Is that what they'd have wanted? No, it's not. And I'm not going to sit back and let you. The first thing we're going to do is sell that house."

Her head snapped up. "What? Sell their house? No. How could you suggest such a thing? I grew up in that house."

Van meticulously wiped his mouth and laid his napkin beside his plate. "All the more reason to sell it. You'll do nothing but mope around and stay depressed. You've had plenty of time to mourn. Get on with your life. Besides, I've already found a condo for us downtown."

She stared at the stranger sitting in front of her. "Have you lost your mind? I'm not selling the house. And what do you mean for *us*? I never agreed to live with you, Van. And if I wanted to find another place to live, I'd do it myself." With that, she pushed her plate away and left. But he'd followed her, pulling her to a halt on the sidewalk.

"Listen, I'm sorry." His anger from moments ago was gone, his voice now pleading. "I'm only doing what I think is best for you. For us," he said, brushing her hair away from her face and tucking it behind her ear. "I've been handling everything for weeks now, I thought this is what you wanted. For us to be together. Come on. Let me take care of you."

Kate's resolve weakened with his touch and gentle words. Maybe it was for the best. Now that she was on her own, maybe it was time to make some changes. As they grew closer in their relationship and spent more and more time together, she assumed they'd eventually marry. Kate supposed Van just wanted to speed things up a little. However, worry still nagged at her, and she wondered if he could afford it. This part of the city wasn't cheap, and she didn't want him stretching his finances, whatever his budget was. She wasn't exactly sure what Van did for a living and each time she'd asked, he'd always responded with, "Oh, boring office stuff, playing with computers. Nothing you'd be interested in." So she'd never pressed further, satisfied with his answer. Certain she'd get the same answer again, she kept her fears to herself.

Reluctantly, she gave in and allowed Van to take her to tour the condo. She had to admit, his taste was impeccable. Kate immediately fell in love with the balcony that overlooked a courtyard. The previous owners had left colorful but tasteful pots and pottery, which held numerous plants and flowers. There was an abundance of greenery she didn't recognize. A small glass-topped table with two comfortable looking chairs occupied a corner of the space.

"See, I knew you'd love it," Van said as Kate's wary expression turned to enchantment. She smiled and stepped into his waiting arms. Maybe this would be good for them after all, she thought.

"Okay," she said. "Let's do it." Van picked her up, swung her around, then deposited her back on the floor. He pulled a set of keys from his pants pocket and dangled them in front of her face.

"It's ours," he said. "I've already put the deposit on it. We can move in whenever we want." Her smile faltered. "I-I don't understand. You already bought it? Without talking to me first? I mean, you can do whatever you want with your money, but I thought ..." She let her words trail off, anger bubbling inside her. He'd made her feel like she'd had a choice in this, like her opinion mattered. What if she hadn't liked it?

"Aw, Babe, come on. I knew you'd love the place. There was another offer on the table, and I had to act fast so I didn't, *we* didn't lose it." He placed his hands on her shoulders and squeezed. "We're going to be happy here. You'll see."

Kate gave him a weak smile and nodded, although if she was honest with herself, she wasn't feeling it. Her life definitely wasn't going according to plan. Living together. What would her mom and dad think about this? Kate knew exactly what they would think, and she shuddered when she thought of what her mother would say ... "Now Kate, there's nothing wrong with being a good girl. You live your life right and you won't ever go wrong. Don't you let those boys tell you anything different." Kate was well aware her mother had been more than a little old-fashioned, and she'd had Kate when she was in her midthirties.

Her eyes blurred with tears as she thought about her parents, the reality that they would never see their only daughter walk down the aisle hitting hard. When Van asked, "Why the sad face?" she tried to explain what she was feeling. She didn't miss the impatience in his voice when he said, "Kate, come on, grow up. It's time to let go and move on. Crying about it won't change a thing." Hurt and slightly humiliated, she turned away with the pretense of needing to use the bathroom. Maybe he was right. Maybe she was acting like an immature child. She was on her own now. A premature adult at twenty. She needed to act like it.

Kate splashed water on her face and dried it as best as she could with a tissue from a box someone had placed on the counter. Facing her reflection, she squared her shoulders, put on a determined face, and returned to the living room.

"Okay. Let's go pack."

The days that followed blurred into weeks and then into months. Kate kept busy packing, moving, and unpacking, arranging all their belongings just right, hoping to transform the new place into a home. As time progressed, she felt as if she were walking in a constant fog. She tried planning for the wedding but had difficulty keeping everything sorted. She showed up for an appointment with the cake decorator and was told the appointment had been rescheduled for the week prior. She sent an order to the printer for invitations only to receive a completely useless bundle of cards. Her name wasn't spelled correctly, the date was wrong, and the color was not the one Kate had chosen. Even the woman at the dress shop had called and canceled her appointment, saying she couldn't continue to accommodate the constant rescheduling. Kate didn't recall any of this and found herself second-guessing nearly every decision she made. When she expressed her concerns to Van, his reassurances did little to alleviate her worries.

"You're just overwhelmed with the move and losing your parents. Take a break and push all the wedding stuff to the back burner. I don't see why we have to have a wedding anyhow. We can find a JP and save a ton of money."

Kate was shocked. "A justice of the peace? Really, Van? A courthouse wedding?" Moving away from him and to the sink to fill the kettle for tea, she took a slow breath. Unbelievable. Did it mean nothing to him? To him, she said, "Honey, we don't have to worry about the money. I can afford it. Besides, I still have the money from Mom and Dad if we ever get into a bind." Kate felt the tension in the air thicken drastically.

"I've already told you. Leave that money where it is. Pretend it's not even there." At that, Van turned and left the kitchen. She knew better than to go after him and shuddered when she allowed herself to remember their last argument, which had actually been their first.

It had been over a month before, but Van had been outraged. Kate had suggested they use some of her inheritance to take a vacation, combine it with their honeymoon. He'd grabbed both of her upper arms and had gotten right in her face. She could still feel the heat of his breath and the smell of his coffee as he ordered her not to mention the money again. That was the first time Kate had felt truly afraid of him. She didn't believe he would hurt her, but his grip had been so tight she'd had bruises for days. He had apologized later, explaining he was under a lot of stress at work. Of course, she'd forgiven him. Wasn't that what she was supposed to do? She couldn't recall her parents ever arguing much. They'd always been respectful toward each other. To-day was the first time Kate had brought up the money since that day and she regretted it already. Van would be in a mood for the rest of the evening. At least he hadn't grabbed her again. She unconsciously rubbed her arms as she waited for the kettle to boil. This wasn't how it was supposed to be. Hearing the front door slam as Van left, she wondered for the first time if she'd made a mistake.

Van stayed gone for the whole weekend, not answering her calls or texts. Kate worried herself sick until he showed up Monday afternoon wearing a huge smile. "Hey, babe. Listen, I'm sorry. I needed to cool off. But forget about that. Something I've been working on finally came through, so we won't have to worry about money anymore."

"Worry?" she asked, confused. "I didn't know we were worried about money. Why didn't you say anything?" Van had always led her to believe he was more than comfortable financially. He'd suggested she take a break from college after the funeral, but she'd had no reason to believe it was due to a shortage of money. At the time, she hadn't been ready to go back, feeling she wouldn't have been able to concentrate on her classes. Van had assured her there was plenty of time for school later and she'd reluctantly agreed, knowing that in only two years she'd have her teaching degree. Looking back over the past few months, she knew she'd have dropped her classes anyway. She couldn't even get her address or her own wedding date right, for crying out loud.

Van huffed. "Not worried, really. I'm not broke or anything. I've just been looking into some other career options, and something finally worked out. Nothing for you to worry about. Hey, let's go out to dinner tonight. I feel like celebrating."

Kate smiled and readily agreed. She felt better than she had in months and would enjoy getting out. As she was brushing her hair in front of the bathroom mirror, she noticed her medicine bottles sitting on the counter. Kate realized with a start that she hadn't taken her meds all weekend, worried as she was about Van. She reached for the bottles, then stopped herself. For the first time in a while, she felt somewhat clear-headed. Silently, Kate wondered if the meds were what was making her feel that way, like she was constantly walking in a tunnel. Making her decision, she pulled her hand back. She'd go a few days without the meds and see how she felt. But she wouldn't tell Van because he frequently asked if she'd taken her meds. She paused as she was about to leave the bathroom, then took three pills out of each bottle and dropped them into the toilet. Just in case he counted them, she thought, and wondered not for the first time when she'd become so paranoid.

"You seem different tonight. Have you been taking your meds?" Van asked later that evening.

Suddenly nervous, Kate had responded maybe a little too quickly, "Of course." Then stammered, "I'm just so relieved you're home. And then I've had this glass of wine." She held up her nearly empty glass.

Van gave her a half smile. "Yeah, it's loosened you up a bit. Let's get out of here." He threw some bills on the table to cover their meal and led her out of the restaurant, leaving no doubt what was on his mind.

Kate continued to flush her meds, making sure she didn't act too chipper in front of Van until she was sure she'd be okay without them. Not that he'd notice, he was always busy with his new "endeavor" as he liked to call it. He often stayed away overnight when he was working further away from home, so Kate was frequently left alone. She found she actually enjoyed it and began reading more, and even bought a few how-to books on furniture refinishing. She was ready to get started on her first project when she woke up one morning with a nasty virus. It came out of nowhere. One minute she was fine and the next she was hugging the toilet. After several near miss trips to the bathroom, she relented and lay down on the cool tile, where Van found her.

"What're you doing in here?" he barked.

"I have a stomach virus. How about a little sympathy?" Kate groaned.

"I don't want to catch whatever it is you have," he snapped, then backed out of the bathroom. "I'm headed out." As if seeming to catch himself, he added, "You need anything?"

"No," she threw back. "I'll manage." Kate rolled her eyes as he turned and left. Finally, she pulled herself up. After rinsing her mouth and washing her face, she went to the kitchen. As she sipped her tea and nibbled on a piece of dry toast, Kate thought about the pills she had been flushing and wondered if that's what had made her sick. But she brushed that thought aside, feeling the meds had had plenty of time to get out of her system. Now that she was able to think more clearly without that medication fog, Kate had wondered what the meds were. Van had begun giving them to her after her parents' funeral and had consistently made sure they were filled. She hadn't questioned them. But why? Why wouldn't she question what she was being given? And who had prescribed them? Kate retraced her steps to the bathroom and retrieved the pill bottles. Sitting at her desk, she opened her laptop and accessed the internet browser. One by one, she entered the prescription names, searching their uses and side effects. Four pills in all. The first three were anti-depressants, sedatives, and sleeping pills, which were bad enough. But the fourth one was the most horrifying. Birth control. Why had Van allowed someone to give her birth control? Surely he knew. And she hadn't asked for it. She wasn't ready for children, but she knew Van was always careful. Lately he hadn't even been home much, but ... Oh, God ... that night. The day he came home in such a good mood after their fight ... She couldn't be. Kate lowered the lid of her laptop, a million thoughts scrambling in her mind. Sick. She was gonna be sick. Kate rushed to the bathroom, barely making it before her tea and toast came back up.

Kate lay on the bed, a cool washcloth across her forehead. The tears had finally ceased along with the nausea. Now her head throbbed, but she was too exhausted to go into the kitchen for Tylenol. Was Tylenol even safe to take during pregnancy? She had questioned her self-diagnosis, but a look at the calendar had confirmed her suspicion. She was definitely pregnant. She jumped at Van's voice, she hadn't heard him come in.

"You still sick?" He stood in the doorway, beer in hand. "What's for dinner?"

With a silent groan, Kate rolled herself over and sat on the edge of the bed. "I haven't felt like making any dinner. Soup and sandwich?" she suggested.

Van snorted. "Chinese it is. Call for takeout. Get me a number seven, extra shrimp. I'm getting a shower."

When had he become such a jerk? Kate reached for her phone and tapped in the number.

Kate sat on the floor of the bathroom, leaning against the side of the tub. As soon as Van had opened up the meal boxes, the aroma had triggered another bout of vomiting. Van had continued to eat his dinner, not even bothering to check on her until he was done. "How long's this gonna last?"

She took a deep breath. No time like the present, she thought. "Oh, about nine months," she said, and waited for the eruption.

"What the hell are you talking about?" Van growled.

Here it was. She had to just get it over with. "I'm talking about morning sickness, Van. I'm pregnant."

His bored expression morphed into cold, hard stone. "That's impossible. And you need to sleep on the couch tonight. I don't want to catch whatever it is you have."

Kate sighed and closed her eyes as he left. A moment later she heard the rattle of glass on glass as he fetched another bottle of beer from the fridge. Maybe he's right. Could it just be a virus? With another sigh, Kate pushed herself up off the floor. Only one way to find out. After washing her face and pulling on a light sweater, she grabbed her purse and keys. She didn't wait for a response when she announced over her shoulder she was going to the pharmacy for meds and ginger ale. And a home pregnancy test.

Back at home, locked in the bathroom alone, Kate read the instructions on the package. She'd had no idea there'd be so many to choose from, so she'd chosen one that seemed simple to perform. Anxious to get it over with, she grabbed the small plastic cup, filled it to the indicated line, placed the dipstick in, and waited.

Her heart sank when she saw the result. Even though she'd been expecting it, a part of her had hoped she was wrong. With a shaky breath, she exited the bathroom.

Van looked at the tiny blue lines that had formed a plus sign without taking it from Kate's outstretched hand. She watched his jaw muscles tighten, then backed up as he rose from his chair. She instantly regretted her choice to show him the results. Her nerves tingled and her chest tightened. She'd never seen him so angry. Kate could practically see bold letters as he enunciated each word. "HOW. DID. THIS. HAPPEN?."

Kate continued to back away from him as he stepped closer to her. When her back reached the wall, she slid to her left toward the kitchen. "Van, please," she began, hating the fear in her voice.

"Shut up. I want to know how this happened! Haven't you been taking your pills?" He was shouting now.

"Van, please don't shout. The neighbors—"

"Screw the neighbors, I said shut up." He was still shouting, however the mention of neighbors must have reached his common sense through his anger, as he dropped his voice a few decibels. He stomped toward her. "What. About. Your. Pills," he demanded.

A small ribbon of rebellion and anger of her own crept around her fear. "I had no idea what I was taking, Van. I trusted that you were doing what was best for me. I assumed those pills were for my depression, and I can't believe I didn't question them. But then again, how could I when you had me drugged into a stupor! How was I supposed to know you were giving me birth control? Besides, you always wore protection." She paused. "Except that one time."

Kate cringed as Van's beer bottle shattered against the counter she now found herself trapped against. "You stupid b—" He gripped the bottle's neck and raised the jagged edges to her throat. His voice now dropped to a low snarl. "Don't ever question me. We're not having kids." He threw the remaining bottle across the room and left, slamming the door behind him.

Kate slid to the floor, sobbing and gasping. "Dear God, what have I gotten myself into? How did it come to this?" Curling herself into a fetal position, she lay on the floor and cried until there were no tears left to shed. Only then did she force herself to move, knowing the shards of glass needed to be cleaned before Van returned.

Bright rays of sunlight peeked through the blinds and coaxed Kate awake the next morning. A glance at the clock told her she'd slept until nearly ten o'clock. She hadn't heard Van come in during the night and his side of the bed hadn't been disturbed. Relieved she was alone, she made her way to the bathroom and washed her face. Her eyes were puffy from all the crying. She pulled off the band aid and checked the cut underneath where Van had nicked her skin with the broken beer bottle. It was only superficial, but she knew full well he could've done so much more damage. Since she wasn't nauseated yet, she decided to have a cup of tea and some toast before a shower. Maybe the nausea would stay away today.

After her shower, she dressed and heard the front door. He was back. Maybe she could stay in there and he'd go away. She did not want a repeat of last night. But surely he had a chance to calm down.

Cautiously, she stepped out of the bedroom and crept up the hallway to the living room. Van sat in his chair with a newspaper in hand.

"Morning," she tried not to sound nervous and walked toward the kitchen so she could busy herself with making another cup of tea.

"I called a doctor's office. They can get you in next Tuesday at one," he said conclusively, and didn't look up.

She wondered if he'd had a change of heart after having a night to think it through. After all, he'd been drinking last night. Surely he'd only overreacted because of the alcohol. She hesitated, unsure, then softly said, "Okay." Afraid he might be taking her to someone for more of those pills, she asked, "What kind of doctor?"

Kate noticed he stiffened slightly, but he looked up at her, then nodded toward her belly. "For that."

That? Well, at least it was a start. Pick your battles, she thought. "Thank you," she said. When he didn't reply, she continued with her tea, feeling slightly better about her current situation.

The next several days were fairly uneventful. Van didn't mention the baby anymore, and Kate was hesitant to broach the subject. She'd decided to let him come around in his own time. Though she was still scared, she used her phone to peruse different baby clothes sites. She'd even allowed herself to ponder names. Maybe when Van was more comfortable with the idea of a baby, he'd help her pick one out.

Finally, the day of her appointment arrived. She had secretly purchased an online version of *What to Expect When You're Expecting* and was sure they'd be doing an ultrasound today. She could hardly believe she'd be seeing a live image of her little butter bean today and hearing his heartbeat. Or hers. It didn't matter to her. So she dressed in comfortable leggings and an oversized top that would allow easy access to her abdomen. After slipping into a pair of flats, she announced she was ready to go.

Van smiled at her for the first time in days. "Everything's going to be fine," he said. "Here, I made you some tea."

Wow. He really was coming around. Maybe after he saw his baby on the screen, he'd be ready to discuss names, even do a little shopping, she thought. Kate drank the bitter tea, grateful for the gesture. She made a mental note not to let him make it in the future. She'd make the tea and he could be in charge of the coffee.

Kate noticed several cars as Van pulled into the parking lot. The building was two stories and had a one-story building attached by a canopy where cars could drive through to drop off and pick up patients. "Hmm, surely they deliver babies in the hospital. That must be where they do procedures."

Van cast her a sideways glance. "You think?"

Kate thought she heard a hint of sarcasm in his comment but decided to ignore it. She didn't want to ruin the day. She was feeling lightheaded but wasn't worried, as she'd read that this was normal in early pregnancy. Van let her take his hand, and as a pair they walked in. Kate noticed a tiered brochure holder which contained pamphlets on several topics. She recognized cervical cancer, as well as HPV, HSV, and other STDs. Naturally, they would explain and simplify diagnoses and treatment options for patients. A few more titled *Your Body, Your Choice*; *You Have a Choice*; *Plan B*; and many others. But no information booklets or leaflets on pregnancy, what to expect in the different trimesters, or how to care for yourself during pregnancy. Kate stopped in her tracks and covered her mouth. She swayed a little and placed a hand on the wall to support herself.

"What are you doing?" Van snapped. "You can look at those on the way out." He tugged at her hand, but she pulled away.

"Van. This ... this is an abortion clinic!" The bile rose in her throat.

"What did you think it was, a daycare?" he retorted, his irritation building.

"But I thought ... I thought you were taking me for my first OB appointment. To have an ultrasound." Kate was trembling and her knees were weak.

"What gave you that idea?" Van sneered.

"You said you made an appointment and everything would be okay." Kate sobbed.

"Yeah, I did. And it will ... as soon as this is over. Now come on." He had grabbed her upper arm and tugged, but she pulled away again.

"No! I'm not having an abortion, Van."

Barely keeping his temper curbed, Van turned toward her and lowered his voice. "Babe. You know now's not a good time for a baby. We need time together, for us." His hands cupped her face, his voice gentle. "I want you all to myself for a while."

"Van, it's wrong. I can't," she whispered, her cheeks wet. A tiredness ate at her.

He tried another approach. "What will everyone think, Anna? What would your parents think?"

Her stomach churned as she recalled the creepy old neighbor from her childhood. "Anna Banana plays the piana!" he'd taunt from his driveway when she played outside.

"Stop calling me Anna! You know I don't like it. Please. I—"

Van cut her off. "Fine. Kate. Do you know anything at all about taking care of a baby? And I thought you wanted to go back to school, finish your degree. How're you gonna do that?"

"I do, but, you said—"

"Yeah, I know. But hey, that's just because I wanted you all to myself. I still do." He was talking faster, getting anxious. "Listen, I love you ... Kate." He kissed her forehead. "I thought you loved me too."

"I-I do, but ..." Kate was confused, weaker now. Her legs trembled. The fog had returned. She did love him. But he'd been drugging her! Maybe he thought he was doing what was best for her. He called her Kate. Did that mean he was being real?

Van made one last attempt. "If you don't do this"—he pointed down the hallway—"we're done. I don't want a baby now, Kate."

"You'd leave me?" Kate whimpered. "Please, Van, don't."

"Then let's go." He tugged at her arm and she let him lead her down the hall.

She stumbled a couple of times, getting weaker by the second. The realization that Van had put something in her tea came too late. Her thoughts had become a jumble of nonsense, her mouth was dry, and she felt like she was walking through darkness.

Moments later, she found herself sitting on a stretcher. A nurse entered the room carrying a hospital gown, which she helped her change into. She left the room and returned a minute later with supplies to insert an IV into her arm, then connected plastic tubing to a bag of fluid hanging above the bed. She looked over at Van, sitting in a chair in the corner, and he gave her a wink. Kate wanted to beg him to change his mind, but the words wouldn't come.

She'd failed. She'd failed herself, her parents, her unborn baby. Kate didn't have the strength to move, and knew if she tried, Van would easily stop her. And if he didn't, she'd be alone anyway. Kate lay on the stretcher, her despair taking over. She was backed into a corner with no way out. No support. After the funeral, her friends had slowly stopped coming around, and eventually even the random phone calls had ceased. Van was probably behind that, too, she thought. He'd ruined her life, and she'd let him. She knew he didn't love her. Now she was just numb and wanted it to be over. She didn't even care if she lived through it. She didn't fight when the nurse came in to inject medication into her IV. Maybe something would go wrong and she wouldn't wake up. Maybe her heart would stop and she'd be with Mom and Dad again. That thought brought on a new fear. Or what if she wasn't? What if doing this awful thing prevented her from joining them in the afterlife? Oh, God ... and then everything went black.

* * *

Kate woke to someone shaking her arm. "Anna, wake up." She forced her eyes open only to see Van standing over her. She groaned and closed them again, but he was relentless. "Come on. The sooner you wake up, the sooner we can leave." Gone was the fake sweetness, replaced by the coldness she'd grown accustomed to. Van coaxed her to sit up, then helped her back into the clothes she'd taken off a short while before. As soon as the discharge papers were signed, he ushered her out to the car, opened the door, then closed it behind her, leaving her to buckle herself in. She was still somewhat groggy, but she felt that whatever he'd put in her tea had, for the most part, found its way out of her system. She leaned her head back on the headrest and stared out the window while he drove them home. The spring colors were muted, the grass no longer seemed green, the sky gray. Everything looked like it was hidden behind a dust caked screen.

"Now that's over with, we can get on with our lives," Van said, breaking the silence. Kate just closed her eyes, refusing to acknowledge him. What life? Life as she knew it was over. Kate fought to hold back the tears that would only trigger another lecture from Van. Her only desire at the moment was sleep. A sleep so deep she wouldn't remember anything when she woke. She wanted to forget. Forget losing her parents, forget Van, forget what she'd just done. How would she go through life like this? Knowing she'd ended a life. The magnitude of what she'd done crashed down her so fast and so hard she couldn't breathe. Her chest burned, acid rising like lava from a volcano. Her eyes flew open and she shouted, "Pull over, pull over!" She unbuckled her seatbelt, and before Van could fully stop the car, she had her door open and was emptying her stomach's contents onto the grassy shoulder.

When they arrived back at the condo, Van walked around to her side of the car and opened the door. Kate pushed his hand away as he reached inside to help her out. "I can do it myself."

"I'm just trying to help, Anna. Let's get you inside so you can rest."

"I think you've done enough," she retorted. "And my name is Kate."

His faked concern evaporated. "Whatever, Anna Katherine," he sneered. "You don't want my help, fine." And with that, he walked away.

A cramp bent Kate in half. She followed Van inside as it subsided and headed straight to the bedroom. After plugging in the heating pad, she lay down on the bed and placed it over her lower abdomen. She closed her eyes, took a deep breath, and let it out slowly, praying the cramping wouldn't last long. Before she could finish even the beginning of a prayer, she thought she deserved this pain. What she didn't deserve was to pray to God when she'd failed Him in the worst possible way. An unexpected memory of her mother triggered a different kind of pain. A memory of her mother sitting by her bed singing her to sleep. Kate had often wished she'd inherited her mother's angelic voice. As Kate hummed her mother's favorite song, a new wave of tears overcame her, and she sobbed quietly until she had nothing left.

"I'm not hungry," she told Van when he brought her a plate of pasta. He'd probably laced it with more sedatives, she thought. In a rare moment of good judgment, Van backed out of the room and closed the door.

Kate rolled to her side and closed her eyes, not wanting to see, hear, or even think of Van. Her life with him was over. She knew that for sure now. In fact, she felt as if her whole life was over. Unable to see herself moving forward, she thought about the remaining pills and wondered where Van had put them. How many would it take to end it all?

* * *

Kate sat in front of the bank manager, waiting as he tapped on his keyboard and rechecked the information on his screen. "You no longer have a checking or savings account here."

"How is that possible? I have a debit card with my name on it that I used just this morning for gas."

"May I see the card?" He took the card she offered and moved his fingers across the keyboard. A moment later, he handed the card back. "This account doesn't belong to you. You're merely the authorized user of that specific card."

"That doesn't make any sense. What's the balance on that account?" Her voice was rising along with her heart rate.

"I'm not authorized to give you that information, Ms. Jennings. You aren't listed as an owner of the account, only as an authorized user of that card." He pointed to the card he'd returned to her. "As I said, you closed your own accounts three months ago."

Three months. Her parents had been gone just over four months.

"Mr. Thames, I'm telling you, I didn't close those accounts. My inheritance went to my savings when my parents died, and I haven't touched it."

The banker turned his computer monitor toward Kate and said, "Is this your signature?"

Kate recognized her own handwriting. "Yes, but I'm telling you, I did not close those accounts."

"Ms. Jennings, I was here the day you and your fiancé came in. All transactions of that magnitude must be handled by me personally. You were still very distraught over the death of your parents, and I recall questioning your decision, but you insisted on moving the entire balance to another bank."

"He took everything," she said, barely above a whisper, leaning back and running her hands through her hair.

"I'm sorry?" the man said.

"I was drugged. He gave me pills and brought me here, to steal my money."

He returned the monitor to its original position and picked up a pen. He tapped the point on his desk, then leaned toward her. "Ms. Jennings, can you prove any of this? We can pull the security video, but I'm certain it will show both you and your fiancé, and you signing the paperwork just as I said."

Of course she couldn't prove anything. Van had known exactly what he was doing. She could barely remember anything of the first few weeks after her parents' death. Van had acted so concerned about her well-being, had even urged her out of the house at one point. The whole time, it was all a lie. All he did was decrease the dose so she could function, but he kept giving her those damn pills so she couldn't think clearly enough to question anything. She was such an idiot!

Kate picked up her purse from where it had fallen from her lap to the floor. "It's hot in here. I-I need some air," she stammered. Making her way out of his office and toward the exit, she ignored the man calling after her. Once outside, she rushed around the corner and crumbled to the sidewalk, her back against the brick wall. She forced herself to slow her breathing to keep from hyperventilating. What was she going to do now? She had nowhere to go. Kate dismissed the fleeting thought of calling any of her old friends. Van was responsible for alienating them. She knew that now for sure. Recalling the issue she'd had with the wedding invitations, she wondered why she'd ever thought any of them would attend. But she knew it was because she was given pills to keep her under his control. He probably made all those changes to screw up the invitations. And she fell for it. All of it. She couldn't bring herself to even think about calling any of them to ask for help. How could she tell anyone what she'd fallen for and what she'd done? It was hopeless.

She could leave now, but as soon as Van realized she was gone, he'd cancel the card. The card! She jumped up and ran back around the corner to the front of the building where the ATM was located. Sliding the card in, she punched in her PIN and tapped the selection to check the balance. Unauthorized. Frustrated, she selected the withdrawal option. Withdrawals not authorized. Defeated, Kate took the card when the machine spit it out and plodded to her car.

Anger boiled as Kate drove home, pushing past the weakness and desperation she'd felt earlier. All she'd wanted to do was leave. To get as far away from Van as possible. But no. He'd taken that away from her too. Well, he wouldn't get away with it. She'd make him give it back. She wouldn't give him a choice.

Slamming the door behind her, Kate stormed into the living room. She stopped in front of Van, who sat in his recliner eating peanut butter straight from the jar, blocking his view of the television. "Where's my money, Van?" Kate was seething now.

Van didn't react, only proceeded to scoop another spoonful of his snack. "Where've you been?"

"I just left the bank, Van. You've taken all my money. And *this*"— she held up the useless debit card—"this isn't my account. It's yours, and practically useless to me."

Van snorted, licked the last of the peanut butter from his spoon and inspected it. "It's not useless, Anna. Haven't you been buying gas and groceries? You've picked up take out, you've been to the pharmacy, even bought some personal items recently. Not to mention those pillows on the couch." He pointed with his spoon. "Am I wrong?"

Through clenched teeth, she said, "I couldn't make a withdrawal, couldn't even check the balance in the account. Where is my money?"

Van lowered the foot of his recliner and stood. Slowly, he said, "What money, Anna?"

She was trembling now. "You know what money, Van. The money my parents left me. The money you got mad about every time I mentioned using it."

He snickered. "Oh, that. You were such a mess after the funeral. You couldn't think straight, fell into depression, you couldn't do anything. I had to step in and take care of all the arrangements, you even asked me to manage your finances until you got better."

She shook her head. "No. I would never give anyone control of my finances," Kate said. "Never. What did you do with my money?"

"Don't you remember insisting on buying this condo?" he said, spreading his arms wide.

"I've seen the papers, Van. This condo is in your name. Not mi—" She stopped midsentence as the realization hit her. "No."

Satisfied she was getting the picture, Van smiled, walked into the kitchen, and tossed his spoon into the sink. "Keep the debit card, Anna. Use it for necessities. But if you get any ideas about leaving, I'll block it just like that," he said, snapping his fingers.

"You can't make me stay here," she said, feeling trapped.

"Then leave," Van retorted. "See how far you get. I know, maybe you could stay with a friend. Oh, wait, they're all gone too. And if you did find one out there, I wonder what they'd think when they found what you did. And after I begged you not to." He shook his head with a cockeyed grin and walked out.

Kate crumpled to the floor, defeated. He'd been watching everything she did. Everywhere she went. Now that her mind was clear, she couldn't believe she hadn't questioned anything before. She never had cash or questioned the need for any. She was trapped. A prisoner, and Van was the warden. She was free to go, but circumstances forced her to choose prison over freedom. She was a captive here. Her cell wasn't locked, but she was chained here by her sins. Her quiet sobs turned into deep gulping heaves. She felt as though she was being smothered, but she didn't care. She no longer cared about anything. Eventually she reached a point where she couldn't cry anymore and she lay there until her body gave up on her and slept.

* * *

It had been days since she'd eaten a decent meal, refusing to eat anything prepared by Van. She drank only from containers that she opened herself, or water from the faucet. Van would laugh at her and lift his own glass in a mock toast. Finally, having had enough of her pity party, he demanded she go to the market for some groceries. "Get whatever you want, Kate, but get something you'll eat. You've lost so much weight, you look like an addict. The neighbors are gonna think you're on drugs." And then he'd laughed at his own joke.

"Hilarious," she muttered under her breath. But she did as he said and obediently headed out to the market. She meandered through the aisles, putting items in the cart she knew he'd expect. For herself, she chose foods that required little effort. For the days Van didn't come home. Nothing appealed to her, she had no appetite for anything. Besides, she didn't care if she wasted away. What was left for her in this life? She laid the last of her items on the conveyor belt and watched indifferently as they moved along toward the scanner.

"Miss?" the cashier said, apparently not for the first time.

"Oh, uh, I'm sorry. How much?" Kate asked.

The cashier repeated the amount, and after Kate inserted the debit card, she asked, "Cash back?"

"No," Kate answered. She thought, I'm not allowed. But, wait. Cash back? Would it work? Would Van find out if she tried? "Wait, I changed my mind." Reading her options on the small screen, she decided to test her luck with forty dollars. She tapped her selection, then held her breath, waiting for the denial.

The cash drawer popped open and the young girl pulled out two twenties. "Here you go," she said, handing them over. "Have a great day!"

"Thank you, you too," Kate replied, stunned. She rushed to her car and threw the bags from her cart into the trunk, nearly tripping when she pushed the cart into the return slot. Back in the driver's seat, she let out a breath and pulled the cash from her pocket. She held the bills to her chest, thinking about what this meant. She knew she wouldn't be able to pull this off often, but it was something.

As the weeks turned into months, Van became more and more aggressive. He did what he wanted and often took what he wanted. He drank more and invited his "friends" over to watch games, play cards, or sometimes just sit around "shooting the bull" as they called it. Those were the nights she stayed hidden, not liking the way they looked at her. She'd lock the bedroom door and stay there until the visitors left. Kate promised herself it wouldn't be long and took comfort knowing her small stash of "escape money" was growing, albeit slowly. She'd fashioned a secret panel in the bottom of a small overnight bag that she'd pushed to the back of her closet.

One evening when Van was in a particularly bad mood, he insisted she clean the place up. A special client was coming over for dinner the next day, and he planned to grill steaks. He'd already picked up beer and a bottle of wine. "Spoof this place up and make a salad. You need to be on your best behavior and keep the beer coming," he ordered. Kate knew better than to argue.

When Lenny arrived the following evening, Kate did her best to put on a pleasant face and act like the perfect host. Even Van seemed pleased with her performance and periodically touched her arm or smiled her way. No doubt it was all an act to impress his guest, but Kate wanted to keep him in a good mood. Life was easier that way.

Kate never knew where things turned bad that evening. One minute she was sitting at the dinner table pushing pieces of steak she had no intention of eating around on her plate, the next Van and his guest were screaming at each other. She recalled words like "product" and "rocks." They yelled about deals and promises. Kate backed away when Van broke the wine bottle against the table. The sound sickened her, reminding her of that awful day when he'd held a broken beer bottle against her neck. Lenny lunged at Van, grabbing hold of the arm holding the bottle. Somehow, Lenny twisted Van's arm and slammed his hand against the table. Crying out, Van dropped the bottle and received a left hook to the face. Stunned, Van wiped his mouth with the back of a hand. He spit blood to the side and pounced on Lenny, both landing with a crash on the table. Van straddled Lenny's legs and threw a punch of his own that landed with a sickening crunch on Lenny's nose. Lenny tried to fight back but was no match for Van's size and strength. He reached a hand inside his jacket where he was likely packing a pistol, but Van didn't miss the move. With an animal-like howl, he raised a steak knife and brought it down, sinking it into Lenny's gut.

Until Van slapped her, Kate didn't realize she'd been screaming.

"Shut up, Anna!" he roared.

"Van. Wh-what have you done?" Kate sobbed, one hand covering her stinging cheek.

That's when the pounding began, followed by shouts ... "Police! Open up!"

Van put his hands on top of his head and cursed. "Agh!" He pointed a finger in her face as a warning and said, "He attacked *me*. Remember that."

Pausing in front of the door, Van transformed himself from monster to victim in an instant. "Oh, thank God you're here!" His ability to cry on demand was impressive. "We were having dinner and he just jumped me for no reason."

The rest was a blur. Kate was in shock, barely registering the EMTs that carried a bleeding but still breathing Lenny away on a stretcher. She felt herself being led to a squad car and then taken to the police station, where she was questioned for hours. Somehow, she told them her version of the events, which didn't include Van's claim of self-defense.

By the time an officer delivered her back to the condo, an exhausted Kate had made her decision. It was time.

In her bedroom, Kate pulled the overnight bag from its place in the back corner of her closet, and after ensuring the roll of bills was still there, she began stuffing in clothes. Shirts, jeans, underwear. An extra pair of shoes, a sweater, and it was full. Needing something for her toiletries, she slid open the door to Van's closet. Perfect. Kate reached for the black duffel on the top shelf and tossed it onto the bed.

She hurried to the bathroom and gathered the few items she had and dropped them on the bed beside the duffel. Turning back to her dresser, she picked up a wooden jewelry box. Van had given it to her early in their relationship. She'd thought it was beautiful and loved the intricate carvings that covered the top and sides. Inside were the few pieces of jewelry she owned. They weren't worth much, but they were all she had left of her mom. Kate thought about just leaving the box and taking her jewelry, but decided to take it and unzipped the bag. Inside was a shoebox that still held the shoes judging by its weight. Kate tossed it aside, replacing it with the jewelry box and toiletries. Having some extra room, she grabbed another pair of shoes and a jacket. As she zipped the bag, she took one last look around the room in case there was anything else she'd need.

She noticed that when the shoebox landed on its side on the floor, the lid had come off. Inside there was another box. She walked over and picked up the box and laid it on the bed. Kate gasped when she took the lid off. Inside, in neat stacks, were several bundles of bills. She had to remind herself to take a breath and then let it out. She stared into the box unmoving for several moments, taken aback by the sudden turn of the cards. No idea how much was there, no time to second guess, she replaced the lid and stuffed the box into the duffel bag. Less than two minutes later, she was driving toward the interstate.

Kate drove for hours, at first on pure adrenaline, stopping only for gas, coffee, and bathroom breaks. In the early morning hours, when she could no longer fight the exhaustion, she pulled into a roadside motel and checked in. Kate double locked the door, put a chair under the knob for good measure, pulled the covers back and collapsed.

Sunlight peeked through a gap in the curtains as Kate opened her eyes. It took her a few moments to recall where she was and how she'd gotten there. With a mixture of moan and sigh, Kate pushed herself up. A glance at her phone told her it was nearing ten in the morning. First a shower, then food, she told herself. The hot water was like a medicinal treatment to her tired body. She opened the duffel to retrieve her toothbrush and deodorant and remembered the box containing the stacks of bills. Taking a quick look at the door to ensure it was still secure, she opened the box and counted.

Kate lay back on the pillow and stared at the ceiling, dumbfounded. In addition to the small stash she'd accumulated, she had nearly sixty thousand dollars in her possession. Her parents had left her close to three hundred thousand, which included what she had gotten from the sale of their house. Their house. Kate's stomach churned at the thought of everything her relationship had cost her. He'd fooled her. She briefly wondered if this was money from her inheritance or if Van was involved in something illegal. Kate also wondered if there was any way to get into Van's accounts now that he was in jail, but she dismissed the idea. She had no plans to go anywhere near him or that town ever again. Discarding the box, Kate placed the money underneath the panel in her bag, along with her own stash. This was more than enough to keep her going until she figured out what she was going to do.

* * *

Seven months later.

Tucking a wayward tendril of hair behind her ear, Kate wiped crumbs and ketchup from the table with a washcloth, then returned the salt, pepper, and ketchup to their proper places. The jingle of the bell above the door invited yet another customer into the diner. She had just one hour left. Maybe he'll sit in Traci's area, she thought.

It had been a tough day. Her laptop had crashed, and she had to re-write a nearly completed essay. And since she'd started her shift this evening, it seemed like every customer had something to complain about. Turning around, she found the customer sitting in a booth perusing a menu. Of course he sat in her area. Groaning inwardly, she headed over with a glass of water and clean silverware wrapped in a napkin.

Pulling out her pen and pad and pasting on the best smile she could muster, she said, "What would like, sir?"

He looked up at her with a big toothy smile and replied, "I'd like to take you out to dinner."

Kate cringed. Another guy who thought he was God's gift. She wasn't in the mood for this. She was too tired. "What would you like from the *menu*, sir?" She tapped her pen against her pad.

"What do you recommend?" he asked, still smiling that goofy smile.

Kate suppressed a smile. "I'd recommend the special."

"Great! The special it is."

"Excellent choice," Kate said, and headed to turn in his order.

For the next ten minutes, she went from table to table, filling water glasses, taking orders, and wrapping silverware. She smiled to herself when the cook called, "Grace, order up!"

18

Unforgiveable

Danny's heart stopped. Grace lay on the floor, not moving. "Grace!" In an instant, he was on the floor beside her. "Baby, please be okay," he choked. He'd almost lost her once. He couldn't let her go. His hand shook as he searched for a pulse. After a lifetime, he felt a steady throb beneath his fingers.

He leaned over her and sobbed when he felt her breath on his face. "Oh, thank God." She moaned when he called her name again.

Grace opened her eyes and saw his face close to hers. Even drawn and twisted with fear, he was still handsome. "Danny," she whispered as she laid her palm against his cheek.

"I'm here, baby. What happened?" his voice choked with emotion. "Are you hurt?"

She shook her head and moved to sit up. Danny gently helped her into a sitting position. "My head hurts, but it's better than it was. I had this horrific"—she held a hand near each side of her head, fingers splayed—"explosion, or at least that's what it felt like, and then I guess I passed out." She looked at him once again and said, "Can you help me to the bed?" Danny gently helped her to her feet and guided her to the bed so she could lie down, then went to the small kitchenette to get her a glass of water. Grace eagerly accepted the glass and sipped. "Thanks," she sighed, and closed her eyes. "I'm feeling a little better. I'm sorry if I scared you."

Danny smoothed her hair with his hand. "Do you need a doctor? There's a hospital a few blocks from here. We can go to the ER."

"No! No, I-we don't need to do that. We should probably call Dr. Hyatt." She laid her hand on his wrist. "But first we need to talk."

Grace painfully recounted the details of the past she'd tried so hard to forget. When the dam opened, the words gushed; but the more she talked, the more Danny withdrew. As she told him about her darkest moments, her heart raced and her breathing shallowed. When Danny moved away from her to stand by the window, she shifted her position to sit on the edge of the bed. She was losing him. But she had to keep going. He had to know everything.

"So, I legally changed my name from Anna Katherine Jennings to Grace Lawson. Then I used the money to enroll in college, and for the most part, never looked back. I kept up with the trial, went back once to be sure I wouldn't have to testify. As soon as they told me about his record and that they had enough evidence to put him away, I was out of there for good."

As he listened, Danny stared out the window. He didn't say a word, didn't interrupt, as Grace recounted her tale of loss, abuse, and failures.

"And that's when I met you. I didn't want to love you, Danny. I didn't think I'd ever be able to give you what you deserved. And you deserved all of me. So many times I thought about telling you. Not at first, but when I realized I was falling in love with you. I knew you deserved the truth. But as our relationship grew, I was afraid you'd hate me and leave. And I couldn't bear that." Her breath caught on a sob. "I'm so sorry, Danny."

He didn't speak for an eternity. When he turned to her, his face was tired. It was over. She'd lost him. Would she lose her children too? Lizzy? She'd be shunned by the church. The pain of that life, that girl she no longer was rushed back to her. Her life would be as lonely as the day she woke in that hospital and remembered no one. She'd have no one. Again.

"Twenty-two years." The lack of emotion in his voice terrified her. "After all we've been through, you never once thought you could trust me with the truth."

"Danny, I—"

"I've loved you unconditionally. And that meant nothing to you."

She dropped her head and didn't respond. He wasn't asking. She deserved his anger. His hatred.

She didn't hear him approach. "Do you see this?" Grace looked up to see Danny holding his phone in front of her. On the screen was an open email. Her eyes widened when she read the words.

"When did you get that?"

"A few days before you were attacked."

"I don't understand. Why are you showing me now?"

"Because when I read this, I doubted you for the first time in our marriage. I even considered hiring someone to look into your past."

"What?"

"Instead, I went to Joe and talked to him about it. He asked me one question. 'Would anything you found out about Grace then, change how you feel about her now?'"

She swallowed. "And what was your answer?"

Danny knelt in front of her and held the phone up. "Look again. This message is in the deleted folder. My answer was no. Your past doesn't change how I feel about you. What hurts is that you didn't have faith in me."

Danny hadn't looked into her past. Did that mean they would be okay? She didn't deserve this man. Grace looked away, not wanting him to see her own pain. "I couldn't. I didn't want you to ever know what I'd done. I was embarrassed, still am. For a long time, I hated myself and felt like no one could ever love someone who did what I'd done. When you found me, I'd just started counseling, and it was beginning to help. I still struggle with it. I've just been hiding it. I've never been fully able to believe that God could forgive me." She looked up at him. "I thought as long as I led our children in the right direction, helped guide them into adulthood with a strong foundation, with the right values," Grace paused, "then it would be enough. As long as they were okay, then it didn't matter if God ever forgave me. I've never felt worthy of forgiveness, and I never want our children to feel that way."

Danny pulled her into his arms. His heart was broken. For her, for everything she'd been through. He whispered, "If anyone is worthy, Grace, it would be you. This doesn't change anything. You know I love you and nothing could ever change that. We've got some things to figure out. But I'm willing to try if you are." He pulled back and offered a sad smile. "So you think Van and this Vincent guy are one and the same?" Danny asked.

"I know it's him, Danny. He's aged some, but I'd never forget that face."

She chuckled when Danny cast her a look that said "Really?"

"Well, except that one time," she said, and they both laughed weakly; one humbled, the other dumbfounded.

"Do you think it's the money he was after?"

"I don't know what else it could be," she said with a shrug. "He must be desperate. Surely he doesn't think I've kept the money hidden in a box all this time, just waiting for him to come and claim it."

"Who knows what goes through the mind of a lunatic."

Grace took a deep breath and blew it out. "I need to talk to Joe."

Joe Stevens removed his cap and rubbed his bald head as Grace finished her story for the second time that day. A myriad of emotions flooded his face. It was one of the things Grace loved about their pastor. He was transparent about what he thought and how he felt. With tears in his eyes and his voice choked with emotion, he said, "You've been carrying this around for over *twenty* years." It was a statement, not a question. "Grace, I wish you'd felt like you could've shared this with me sooner. But I really do understand because I've felt that way before." He nodded when Grace looked at him with raised eyebrows. "The enemy tries to make you hide and keep all your pain inside. He tries to make us think that no one will understand. That's a lie and I can prove it to you! Our meeting today shows that your heavenly Father is reaching out to you. He wants you to *know* that He understands! Essentially, He wants to say through me"—Joe placed a fist on his own chest—"Grace, my child, it's time to leave your fear behind. It's time to let go of it! It's time to walk away from your shame and walk toward all the wonderful things I have in store for you." He paused to let that sink in. "All the bad things that have happened to you were not His plans. That was the enemy trying to kill your dreams and destroy your hope. You can read that in John 10:10. Jesus wants you to have an abundant life. And all the things you feel such shame over, they do NOT define you. They are things you *did*, not who you *are.*" Suddenly the tears in her eyes became a window through which Joe could see her soul. He could tell her heart was already beginning to heal. With a soft, caring voice, he asked, "Does any of that make sense to you?"

She wiped her eyes and looked at the ceiling. "I think so?"

"I don't want you to doubt any longer, so let me put it another way. You know that my wife and I adopted a son years ago. The day his adoption became legal, he took our name and became our child for all time! When you accepted Jesus as your Lord and savior, the Bible says in Romans 8:15-16 that you became the adopted daughter of Almighty God himself. It also says that as His child you don't have to be afraid anymore!" Then Joe placed his hand on her shoulder and prayed that her heavenly Father would walk with her out of the dark valley she'd been in for so long, and into the bright future that He had planned for her long ago.

"Listen, you don't have to speak tomorrow. I'm sure they'll understand. I'll even get up there in your place if I have to. My Michael Jackson impersonation would knock their socks off!"

"It might knock a *hip* out." She laughed. "It's okay. Even though I was ready to strangle you, I've decided to go through with it." Then as a new thought bubbled to the surface, Grace paled. "Are they expecting me to sing? I don't even know if I still can."

"So, try," Joe said, as if the answer was obvious.

"No, not now. Maybe when I'm alone. I don't know if I even want to know. It's not me. Do you understand what I mean?" He acknowledged with a nod. "Listen, do me a favor and don't say anything to the kids yet, okay? I want to tell them myself. Give me a chance to figure out what I'm going to say. The first thing they'll want to know is if I can still sing."

Excited, Joe rubbed his hands together. "You trust me with a secret? Yes!" he said as he threw a fist into the air. Grace knew he was trying to lighten her mood.

"Calm down, Killa. I'm not on stage yet. Let's pray I don't pass out. You know this isn't my thing."

"Oh, that reminds me." Joe pulled a square of paper from his pocket and unfolded it. "I bet this is your thing." He handed the flyer to Grace. "What exactly is an Australian Jack Schnoodledor?"

"Oh, you've never heard of that breed? They're really cute. But from what I hear, they're super hyper. And dumb." Grace put a finger to her chin. "Kind of like someone I know."

"Really? We just had the most serious conversation of your life and you choose now to insult me? Yes, ladies and gentlemen, she's back." He nudged her with his shoulder. "I told ya He had a plan. And you didn't even have to work for it."

Grace skipped the rest of the evening's sessions, with the pretense of working on her speech. In truth, she stood in front of the mirror and stared at her reflection for a long time. The memories poured in, flooding her mind with the devastating weight of a past she had chosen to bury. They'd always been there, lurking in the shadows, but Grace had fooled herself into thinking she'd forgotten. Except she hadn't. As she recalled one of her darkest moments from that long ago life, she began to weep. Her relentless mind forced her back to that aw-ful day. The day she'd wished her life was over. When it hadn't ended, she'd wanted to forget. Not only forget her sin, but everything else.

God, why did you wait twenty-two years to answer that prayer? she thought. She had prayed so hard to get her memory back and had been afraid it was lost forever. She'd been scared during that time, but now that she could remember, she realized it had been bliss. She hadn't had to think about her mom and dad, Van, or ... her baby. Her soft weep-ing turned into chest-heaving sobs. Grace didn't have any prayers left in her. All she could whisper was a desperate "Please."

* * *

Danny pulled Daniel and Lucy aside as the group gathered for break-fast before they made the short trek back to the conference center. "Your mom and I need to talk to you for a minute. Joe and the others will wait in the lobby." Exchanging looks of confusion and concern, they followed their father without question back to Grace's room, where she waited.

"Hey guys, come sit. I'll make this quick, so you can go. First of all, do you remember the time you two tried to do laundry, and we'd run out of detergent? Then one of you geniuses came up with the idea to use a cup of dish soap instead?"

Lucy and Daniel exchanged more confused expressions. Daniel said, "Didn't we already pay the price for that way back then? Why do you—" His eyes widened. "Wait ... you remember that? Like, for real, remember it?"

Raising her eyebrows, Grace smiled back. Lucy squealed and threw herself into her mother's arms. "Yes!" Daniel said and gave his dad a fist bump. "So, you remember everything? How did it happen? Did you hit your head again? Can you still sing?"

Grace held her hands up. "Slow down. I knew you'd ask that, but it's not important right now," she answered as her smile faded. "Listen, you guys, we'll talk more about this later, okay? I wanted you two to know before my speech today. I don't know exactly what I'll be speaking about, I don't have a plan. But there are some things I need to tell you about my past. Before I met your dad." She glanced at Danny, who gave her an encouraging nod. "We'll talk, just not right now. I need to get through today first. I'm depending on God to lead me through this, and I want to allow Him to speak through me. But I want you to be prepared if He chooses to use things from my past. Things that may be very emotional or unsettling. If that happens, I'm asking you both to hang in there and trust me when I say we'll talk about it, and I'll explain everything. I just don't want you to be completely blindsided, okay?"

They both nodded, then Daniel asked, "Were you in prison?"

Danny rolled his eyes and said, "Son, no!"

Lucy asked, "Does it have something to do with that guy who broke into our house?"

Grace bobbed her head. "Yes, honey, it does. I'll explain everything later. I promise. Now go get some breakfast and head out with the others. Dad and I'll be right behind you. And text me to let me know where you're sitting. I love you!"

"Love you too," they chimed, and then they were gone.

"You don't have to do this, you know," Danny said as Grace brushed her hair.

"Actually, I kind of do." Grace offered him a slight smile.

"Do they want you to sing?"

"At the sound check this morning, I got the impression they're expecting me to, but I don't know. I'm gonna wing it."

Danny kept quiet, concerned for his wife. It was bad enough worrying about her up on the stage alone in front of thousands. He had no idea how she'd react if she tried to sing and couldn't. Instead of voicing his concerns, he pulled her into his arms and said, "You're amazing, Grace Bradford. We would've gladly kept the amnesia Grace around, but you have no idea how happy I am to have you back. Although"—he dragged the word out—"it was kind of like having a new girlfriend. Ooph!" He recoiled from her poke in his ribs and laughed.

Serious again, Danny said, "They're good kids, Grace. They'll be fine, no matter what you say up there. Come on, let's pray before we go."

19

Song Worth Singing

Grace fitted the small earpiece into her left ear and adjusted it until it was comfortable. A small microphone protruded from it and rested near her cheek. The tech had shown her how to mute herself and assured her the knocking of her knees wouldn't interfere with the transmission.

"Remember to watch the timer," the tech said. "It'll display in big red numbers that you'll be able to see from three different angles. You can have Dr. Sutherland's full one-hour slot, but if you don't need that much time, we can fill gaps with music. Got it?"

Grace nodded, but what she wanted to do was to run to the bathroom and lock herself in a stall. She looked from their roped-off section in front of the stage on the far left up to the second-level balcony, where the rest of their group and her children were seated.

"Okay, you're up next. I need you to move to the stage and stand behind that portable screen." The tech indicated the spot with his finger.

Danny squeezed her hand for encouragement, and she rose from her chair and headed for the stage, her stomach churning.

Grace took a deep breath as she stepped up to the podium. "Thank you, Peter," she said as he left the stage. "Wow, good morning!" she addressed the audience. A rumble echoed her own greeting as she looked from one side of the arena to the other. "I didn't realize how intimidating this would be. This is a big crowd." With a nervous laugh, she said, "It looks even bigger from here on the stage. So, a little about me. Basically, I'm a nobody. I'm a wife, mother, and teacher-slash-homemaker. I don't have a big fancy degree or an alphabet behind my name like Dr. Sutherland." Then in a mock stage whisper with a cupped hand beside her mouth, she said, "Who is watching!" And just like when she was back home in church, speaking to strangers, the crowd's laughter broke the ice. She began to relax.

"Nothing I say will compare to Dr. Sutherland's experience and expertise, and I won't even try. Now, the original plan was to talk about something that happened to me recently, as Peter said. And I will tell you a little bit about that." Grace moved away from the comfort of the podium and slowly walked toward the right side of the stage, not taking her eyes from the audience. "Back home, in Huntsville, Alabama, I'm known as the 'Amnesia lady,'" she said, with a roll of her eyes. "Several months ago, I had what I'm going to refer to as an accident. I suffered a head injury that put me into a coma"—she held up four fingers briefly—"for four days." Grace wasn't surprised by the gasps she heard. "But that's not the crazy part. The crazy part is, when I woke up, my head was filled with music." She splayed both hands by her head. "Music that I had to get out. And the only way I could do it was by singing. I know, how is that crazy? People sing all the time, right? Wrong."

Reaching the edge of the stage, she turned and made her way to the opposite side. "Some people simply can't sing." She raised her hand high as if she was sitting in class. "I'm one of those people. In fact, sometime during the first days of my recovery, my son"—she pointed to the section where her children sat—"he's sitting right there. He told me that before the accident I sounded like a goat." She paused to allow the laughter to die down. "Oh, and not just any goat. A goat on crack, he said." More laughter erupted from the crowd. "Rude, right? But that's okay, we teach our kids to be honest.

"So, when we got here, my pastor signed me up to speak today with the intention of me talking about my experience, and how God helped my family and me through those first days. How we adjusted, leaned on God for strength and guidance, and how God uses trying times for good and all that." Again, reaching the edge of the stage, she turned and headed back to the other side, pausing at the podium. "But ... he did this without consulting me first. Oh, and was I angry. Not just angry, I was furious! And I let him know it. Fortunately, we have a very forgiving pastor. Now, here's where I can prove to you that God uses bad for good." Grace entered teacher mode now, comfortable in her classroom. "As a result of Brother Joe's actions, I received a text regarding the speech I had absolutely no intention of giving. Just a simple text with instructions. And the last three words of that text were exactly what my brain needed to open a door that it had sealed shut. I won't take the time right now to describe it, but that trigger gave me my memory back yesterday."

The crowd simultaneously gasped, applauded, whistled, and shouted their praise. She stood in silence, waiting for the noise to die down. Once the arena was quiet, she said, "And that's how God made something good out of what I thought was something bad.

"Now, that being said, I had no idea what I was going to say today, didn't rehearse anything, assumed I would come up here, talk about amnesia, and get off." She paused and looked across the crowd. "But God had a plan. He chose the time to give back my memories. And with those memories came the conviction to face some things from my past. Things I'd hidden and tucked away. You see, we all have struggles. Even those around you who appear to have perfect lives. You never know what battle someone is really fighting. Excuse me." Grace paused to clear her throat and take a sip of the bottled water that had been placed on the podium for her. "So today, I want to talk about choices. We all make dozens of choices every day, right? We choose whether to get out of bed or sleep in, what we're gonna wear, whether or not to go to class, if we're gonna eat or skip breakfast ... the list goes on. And with every choice, there's a consequence. If we sleep in, we miss class. If we miss class, we miss important information. If we choose to wear shorts, we may get cold. If we choose a sweatshirt, we may get hot. If we don't eat, we get hungry."

She took a few silent steps. "Then there are bigger decisions we have to make. Bigger decisions, with bigger consequences. For example, which college do I choose? What do I want to major in? Some of you will pick a college close to home, while others choose to leave the area, and your reasons will vary." Grace raised her hand and counted off examples with her fingers. "You get a scholarship, a grant, that's where your parents went, that's where your bestie is going. Some will choose a major based on potential salary, while others will follow what they love and enjoy. Doesn't matter, these are your choices to make. Just remember, every choice has a consequence, and those consequences aren't necessarily the same for everyone. Your circumstances can affect your consequences. Can we all agree on that?"

Grace paused to look around, making sure she wasn't losing anyone. She felt as if she had a small stone sitting in her gut that was growing by the minute. It wasn't the size of the audience that bothered her, it was that she had a suspicion where God was taking her and she wasn't ready to go there. Not yet.

Trust me.

Grace nearly turned around to see who'd spoken to her. *I'm afraid*, she almost cried out loud. She placed a hand on each side of the podium to steady herself. Grace glanced toward Danny and saw him nod, urging her to go on. With a swallow, she pushed forward.

"Solomon tells us in Proverbs 3 verse five: *Trust in the LORD with all thine heart*; then in verse six he says: *And he shall direct thy paths*. Any time you're faced with a decision, you should ask His advice," Grace said, pointing a finger toward the heavens. "Now, let's go a step further and talk about life choices." She smiled at the expected groans.

"Oh, but we have to!" She laughed. "I'm in a room with nine thousand young adults. You don't really expect me to pass up this opportunity, do you?" With renewed energy, she left her post and walked again, seeming to catch every eye in the arena.

"I'm sure most of you have dated to some extent. Maybe you're in a serious relationship, maybe you want to be, maybe you aren't ready for that. We're not going to try to list every single one, but can we all agree that with relationships come ..." She paused and circled a hand in the air to let the audience fill in the proverbial blank. "Choices! Great, you've been listening! We all know there are many stages in a relationship. You go from interested, to liking, to talking, to hanging out, to actual dating. Or at least that's how it was back in my day. These days y'all go from liking a comment on Facebook to dating in six hours or less." Amid the laughter, she said, "I'm kidding, I'm kidding." Grace continued her slow pace across the stage. "But what about once the dating phase begins? When things start to progress. When we go from liking to really liking, to really, *really* liking, then on to the *love* stage." Grace dragged out 'love' like an actress in a '70s TV show.

Then she turned serious. "I get it. Things happen, okay? We're human. In today's society, we're pressured to question the values our parents try to teach us. Society sets the standard on what's cool or what's accepted. And we're pressured by our own peers. Many times, because of these outside pressures, we don't always make the right choice. Pastor Joe once said in a sermon, 'Your attitude and actions show you are more affected by the world than you are by the Word.' Think about that. Makes sense, right? Sometimes, we know the right answer, we know what we should or shouldn't do, and we still take the wrong path. Peer pressure is a real thing. We choose the flesh, not the spirit." Her voice softened. "And that's when you get slapped in the face with a consequence. Now you listen to me," she said, looking pointedly around the huge room, "I'm not here to judge anyone. We're just talking about facts right now. When I say God had a plan for today, He had a plan. He *has* a plan. Because believe you me, I did *not* plan on standing up here talking about this. I've spent years trying to suppress the reality of my own choices. Chances are, there's someone in this room who needs to hear this, maybe more. Maybe it's for someone you know who isn't here today. Take a look around you for a second. The person next to you may be facing something out of their control. Remember, just because someone is smiling doesn't mean they aren't crying on the inside. Just because she's wearing makeup doesn't mean there aren't scars underneath. Just because he's the best or toughest player on the field doesn't mean he's the best at handling or expressing his feelings. You never know what someone may be dealing with and how God might use you to help.

"I've made mistakes. Big ones. One in particular nearly cost me my life. I was in a relationship with a guy that I'd planned on being with forever. I'm not going into details, but several bad choices later, I found myself unmarried and pregnant." Grace felt the now familiar sensation of her throat tightening. What had she done? All she could think about was Lucy and Daniel, what they must be thinking. She hadn't intended to tell them this way. Hot tears spilled over and ran down her cheeks. She knew she couldn't stop now, no matter what it cost her; so with a glance toward Heaven, she took a settling breath and continued, her voice trembling. "I was terrified. I was ashamed and alone, completely broken. My parents had died, I had no friends left, and my boyfriend told me, 'The only solution is to end it.'" *God, help me, she thought.*

Trust me.

Again, Grace felt that invisible nudge that pushed her forward. "With no one to turn to, I felt like I was backed into a corner with no way out. So I did the unthinkable. I crossed that line, and no matter how badly I wanted to, I couldn't take it back." Tears continued to stream down her face. She paused again to collect herself. When Grace looked up, she saw her children leaving their seats. She couldn't blame them. She'd gone too far. She'd hurt and embarrassed them in front of everyone. Why had she risked everything? It was too late now, she was in too far.

"I'm not trying to shock you. This is real life, people. It happens. It happened to me." Grace pointed to her own chest. Tried to swallow the lump closing her throat. "So yes, it can happen to anyone. But I stand here before you today, as living proof that you can go on. Your life is *not* over. You are worthy of forgiveness. Now, can you erase it from your mind forever? No. But I was in your shoes. I was where you are right now. I wanted my life to end. I buried myself so deep in my own guilt that I'd practically dug my own grave. But God had other plans for me. There is no hole so deep that God can't pull you out." Without turning her head, she pointed to where her friend and preacher sat. "Pastor Joe told me recently, 'God has big plans for you, Grace.' I didn't see it. I had no idea what those plans were. Today I do. God took something bad, and today, He used it for good. Make good choices today, so you don't have to pay the price for the bad ones tomorrow. Choose God."

Grace walked slowly toward the podium at the center of the stage. "Allow God to love and heal you. Jesus already took our punishment. He took it on the cross. So stop punishing yourself. Let's pray ..."

Grace closed her eyes and bowed her head as Elevation Worship grabbed their instruments behind her and softly played the music to Graves into Gardens.

"Lord, I come to you, humbled and thankful, for your amazing grace and forgiveness. Thank you for always being on time. I pray you will take me and use me for your glory. Amen."

Grace felt a soft touch on her arm. She opened her eyes to see Danny standing beside her with Daniel and Lucy on the other. They hadn't left her. She muted her mic, and wrapped them in a hug. "I love you guys," she whispered.

She faced the crowd again and wiped the tears from her eyes. Unmuting the mic, she said, "Thank you. And don't forget to forgive yourselves ... today, right now." She smiled and reached for Danny's hand, following her children off stage as Elevation Worship sang the opening words to the song.

Offstage, Danny turned to her and she fell into him with a shuddering exhale and held on as if he was a life raft in an angry ocean. "Baby, I'm so proud of you," Danny whispered into her ear. "Are you okay?"

Grace nodded into his chest, unable to speak for a moment. "I'm okay. I just need a minute." She pulled away and looked up into his eyes, saw the same unconditional love she held for him. Then she turned and brought their children into their arms once again. No words were necessary now; this was all she needed.

She felt Danny's lips on her forehead, then he said, "Do you want to sit?"

Wiping her face, she said with a smile, "No, I think I'll hang out here for a bit." Danny's eyes widened slightly, and his eyebrows rose as his initial confusion turned to realization as Grace stepped away. As she aimed her steps toward center stage, Grace put a hand to her ear and she met the lead singer's eyes. Giving him a nearly imperceptible nod, she took the lead after the chorus. Daniel and Lucy watched with pride as their mother sang her heart out on the stage, her arms held high in praise. With Elevation Worship! Each had questions but knew those questions could wait until they were home. Daniel draped an arm around his sister's shoulders in a rare moment of public brotherly affection, and without hesitation Lucy snaked her own arm around her older brother's waist as they sang along with nine thousand other young adults.

Grace sang with confidence and pride, her voice strong and her hands lifted. Her fear was gone. It was a testament of where'd she'd been and how far she'd come. Her voice was a way for her heart to share her love for the God who'd stayed by her side and loved her regardless of her faults and failures. He'd turned her weaknesses into strengths. The same God had loved her through highs and lows, through good and bad. He'd pulled her from the grave of her past and led her into a beautiful garden.

20

Praise

By one o'clock that afternoon, the four adults were packed and on the road, headed south with nine exhausted teens. As Danny drove and the teens napped in their seats behind them, Grace gazed out the window with renewed appreciation for what she saw. She was finally free. Free from a past she'd fooled herself into believing was behind her, when all along it had hindered her future. Released from the confines of her own mind that had sentenced her to a future without a past, to be forever tortured by a past she couldn't remember. Eyes heavy, she finally succumbed to sleep, to a peace in her heart she hadn't known was missing.

Grace found herself walking down a sterile hallway. Familiar sounds—cardiac monitors beeping, someone crying, muffled voices from a TV show she couldn't place—drifted from inside open doors that lined both sides of the hall. A voice spoke over the intercom, but she couldn't make out the words. A small woman stepped through one of the doors. She had silver hair pulled back into a bun, and in her hand was ... a staff. No, a broom. She was humming "The Lily of the Valley" and when she saw Grace, she stopped, her smile widening.

"Hello, child. It's good to see you again."

"*Ms. Eva? It's good to see you too,*" Grace replied, hesitantly. "*But I don't remember how I got here. Am I dreaming?*"

The woman made a tsk and said, "You don't remember what I told you?"

"*You always talk in riddles. I don't understand.*"

Eva smiled and shook her head. "If you've had the answer all along, the question isn't really a question, is it?"

Grace pleaded, "Please, Ms. Eva, tell me what you mean!"

Again, the woman smiled. "I told you songs aren't dreams. But dreams can be songs, dear. A song from your heart to praise the Lord. What else did I tell you?"

Grace struggled to remember the woman's words in her hospital room that day, then in her mind the message came back to her clearly. "You said, 'There's a reason for every song worth singing.'"

The old woman stood straighter and said, "That's right. Your heart found a song worth singing. And you sang it with praise. Your heart found healing in praising the Lord."

Confusion morphed into understanding as Grace finally comprehended the words that had haunted her for months. "I get it now."

Pressure on her arm called her from sleep. "Grace, honey?" Danny was saying. "What are you talking about?"

"What?" Grace asked, disoriented for a moment. "Oh, I guess I was dreaming. But I get it now."

"Get what?" he asked, confused.

She smiled and squeezed his hand. "Nothing."

When they'd delivered the last passenger to eager parents, Danny and Grace beelined it for home with their kids in tow.

Happy to be home, Daniel and Lucy headed for their rooms. They'd all agreed to talk about the events of the last few days once everyone had rested. Grace knew, now truly knew, that Daniel would head straight to his bed for a late nap, while Lucy would want a shower first. Grace walked slowly through the house, no longer feeling like a stranger in her own home. She made her way upstairs, and Danny followed with their bags. Grace shrugged out of her sweater and laid it on the back of a chair near the window.

"It's good to be home," Grace said.

"Mm," Danny agreed. He stepped up behind her and placed his hands on her shoulders. "Physically or mentally?" he teased.

"Both." She laughed and turned to him. "I can't explain how strange it felt to not know you. And these past few days have been ... exhausting, you know?"

"Let's rest this evening. No cooking. I'll order pizza and we'll hang out with the kids and talk about everything."

"Sounds good to me," she agreed, letting out a breath.

But Danny could sense her uncertainty. "Hey, look at me," he said, turning her to face his. "It'll be fine. Our children understand that people make mistakes. Even their parents."

"You're right. I can do this. I'm going to take a shower and lie down for a bit. Let me know when the pizza is here, okay?"

A couple of hours later, Grace wiped her mouth and tossed her napkin into the empty pizza box. "So, any more questions?" Their transparent family talk had been easier than she'd expected. They'd asked some tough questions, but she'd been as truthful as possible. As painful as it had been, she prayed her children would use her trials as inspiration to make choices based on a foundation of prayer, openness, and trust.

Daniel and Lucy were quiet as they finished their own slices. Lucy was the first to speak. "So we would've had an older brother or sister?"

Slightly surprised by the question, Grace nodded. "Yes, but who knows how things would've turned out if I'd made a different choice back then. I may never have left Miami.

"Then you wouldn't have met Dad," Daniel interjected.

"That's right, son. And if we hadn't met, you two wouldn't be here." Danny added.

"Wow," said Lucy. "That's a lot to process." She paused as she thought about it. "But we'll see him, or her, in Heaven, right?"

Tears welling, Grace smiled. "Absolutely."

21

What's Still Hidden

With the kids in school and Danny at work the following day, Grace was able to catch up on the mountain of laundry they'd brought home from the trip. Lizzy was on her way over. Grace hadn't told her about her good news, only that she had a surprise for her, wanting to tell her in person. The doorbell rang as she placed the last folded shirt on top of the pile in the basket.

"Hey, bestie!" Grace said cheerfully as she opened the door. Her smile fell as soon as she saw Lizzy's tear-stained face. "What's wrong, Lizzy, has something happened?" asked Grace, ushering her inside.

"I think you need to sit down for this," said Lizzy, and turned to the kitchen. "You want some coffee?" She didn't wait for an answer, instead flitted about the kitchen putting a pot on.

Grace found her usual seat at the bar and waited for Lizzy to join her. When Lizzy sat, she said, "Okay, do you want my news first, or do you want to tell me yours?" It was just like Lizzy to get straight to the point, but she was trembling.

"Well, you seem pretty upset. Why don't you go first?" Grace suggested. She watched patiently as her friend took a deep breath, gathering her thoughts.

"Well, I stopped by the coffee shop on my way here to get us some of the good stuff. You know, flavors and such. While I was waiting for our order, I flipped through a newspaper someone had left on one of the tables, and there was a mugshot of that guy who broke into your house."

Lizzy pulled a rolled-up newspaper from her bag. Grace paled, the memories of the previous few weeks flooding her mind. She shook it off and motioned for Lizzy to continue.

"Well, you know I rarely watch the news or read the paper. I knew the guy's name, of course, you guys told me." She jabbed the photo with her finger. "But when I saw this, I had a face to go with the name." She put her elbows on the counter and her forehead into her hands, then ran her hands through her hair. "Oh God, Grace, I can't believe this." Her knees gave out and she slid to the floor, her sobs escaping in chest-heaving cries.

Grace was around the counter in a flash. She dropped to her knees in front of Lizzy and pulled her into her arms. Lizzy clutched Grace's shirt in her fists and cried into her chest. Grace held her until she had quieted, then reached for the hand towel hanging on the oven door and offered it to Lizzy. "Talk to me. What's happened?"

Lizzy sniffled and used the towel to wipe her face. "The man in the photo. It's Vince. *My* Vince. Except he told me his last name was Douglas. As soon as I realized it, I came straight here. I didn't even wait for the coffee." A shudder went through her body.

Grace leaned back and stared at Lizzy open-mouthed. "Your Vince? What are you saying?" She couldn't believe what she was hearing. Van, Vincent Crawley, had been dating her friend. Had been alone with her. What if he'd hurt her?

"Aren't you listening? It's him. Vince, my Vince, is Vincent Crawley. That means my Vince broke into your house. I thought about it all the way here. We met right after your accident and he's been MIA since the break-in. He asked a lot of questions about you and Danny, but I thought he was interested because you're my friend, you know?"

Her chest heaved again. "I trusted him. Quit my job to settle down with him." Fresh tears streamed down her face. "I guess this explains why he always seemed to get called out of town when I'd try to plan dinner for you all to meet. But why? I don't understand what's going on. I'm sorry I brought him into your life. When I think about what he could've done—" She choked on a sob.

"Whoa. Slow down." Grace rubbed Lizzy's back and tried to soothe her. "Lizzy, you didn't bring him into my life. I did." Lizzy looked up at Grace in confusion.

"What do you mean?"

"I didn't want to tell you like this. But my surprise? The reason I wanted you to come over? I got my memory back." She paused and waited while Lizzy absorbed the news, then watched the tightness of her face soften as the realization of what that meant registered.

"Are you serious? When did this happen? How? Why didn't you tell me? Are you okay? Do you remember what happened?" The words tumbled out of her like gumballs out of a candy machine.

"Yes, I'm serious. And yes, I remember everything. Let's go for a walk and I'll tell you the whole story. It's a long one." When Lizzy agreed, she said, "Let me grab a sweater. You can drive us to the park."

The friends strolled around the walking path twice as Grace told her story from the beginning, both shedding tears as she once again re-lived the trauma of the painful nightmare that was her past. They turned onto the wooden bridge to cross the pond, planning to sit on one of the benches in the middle.

"Grace, I'm rarely at a loss for words, but I don't know what to say. You should've told me a long time ago. I have to admit, I'm a little hurt that you didn't feel you could trust me." Lizzy wished she could take the last part back but waited for Grace to respond.

"Danny said the same thing. I do trust you, Lizzy. More than anyone else. But I was so ashamed, and I couldn't bear for you to think I was ca-pable of such a thing. Especially when I found out you couldn't have children. I knew I'd never have the stomach to tell you. Please try not to take it personally, it was something I had to face myself before I could share it with anyone. It just took two decades for me to realize it."

Lizzy took her friend's hand in hers. "I love you, Grace Bradford. You know that. It'll take a lot more than a secret to break this friendship. You're stuck with me."

Squeezing her hand in return, Grace said, "That makes me happy. Now are *you* okay? I mean, with the whole Vince thing. He never hurt you, right?"

"No, he never hurt me. He was always easygoing, polite, and very attentive. We never even had a disagreement. When I think about it, he was a little too close to perfect." Lizzy swallowed and considered her words. "I'll be fine. It's a lot to process right now. I made a lot of changes for him."

Grace hooked an arm through Lizzy's and said, "I'm just glad he's behind bars and can't hurt either of us. I can't believe as long as I was with him, I never knew he was going by a fake name. Hey, how about we go grab the coffee you left at Starbucks?"

As they stood in line at the coffee shop, Grace absently stuck her hands into her sweater pockets, and her fingers brushed something small and cold. She grasped it and pulled out one of Lucy's earrings. "Oh, I forgot Lucy gave these to me to hold for her. Remind me to put them in her jewelry box when we get back to the house, will you? I don't want to accidentally wash them."

"Sure," Lizzy said, checking emails on her phone.

Coffee in hand, the two sat at an outside table. Something was nagging at Grace. A memory in the shadows of her mind. She fingered the earrings in her pocket, but she couldn't figure it out. The past few days had been crazy, so she assumed whatever it was either wasn't important or would come to her later. Sipping at her pistachio latte, she tried to listen as Lizzy told her about her new job. However, her mind kept returning to that feeling that she'd missed something. She told herself to let it go. She shook her head to clear her mind and tried to concentrate on what Lizzy was saying.

"... really going to like this new job. Even though it's a supervisory position, I still plan to be involved on the floor as much as I can. I don't think I could completely give that up. And if I'm out there setting an example, my staff will know exactly what I expect of them."

"Wow, you're pumped about this."

"Yeah, I am. Plus, I'll be home every night, not living out of a hotel." Lizzy fiddled with her napkin. "I suppose this is one good thing that came out of all this."

"It's great to have you home."

"I could say the same about you. And speaking of home, are you ready to go?"

Grace downed the last of her coffee and stood. "Yep, let's go."

* * *

When Grace draped her sweater over the banister, Lizzy said, "Hey, don't forget Lucy's earrings."

"Oh yeah." Grace retrieved them from her pocket. "I'll be right back," she said and climbed the stairs to Lucy's room. As she lifted the ornate lid, the same feeling that she was missing something important tapped at her mind again. She placed the earrings in the box and slowly closed the lid, trying to grasp the memory playing hide and seek with her brain.

Then, like a cloud moving to reveal a full moon, there it was. A twenty-two-year-old memory that might be a clue to everything. But how? She closed Lucy's door behind her and called down the stairs, her excitement building. "Lizzy!"

The women struggled to pull the attic stairs down, then climbed up into the darkness. The space was filled with plastic tubs and a few boxes in one corner, while others were packed with old toys, small pieces of furniture, and a giant Christmas tree. Grace stood for a moment, trying to recall which part of the attic she would've stored the cardboard box.

"Did you really keep this?" Lizzy asked, picking up a dust-covered wooden door hanger in the shape of a rabbit.

Grace turned to see her holding a goofy, googly-eyed Easter bunny wanna be. She laughed and said, "Hey, Lucy loved that bunny and he proudly hung on the front door for a month."

"Lucy was seven, and he needs to be hanging out in a dumpster. Good thing Lucy didn't get her art skills from you. Hey, I know, let's put him in her room," she said, setting the hanger by the steps.

Grace laughed.

"Okay, so what are we looking for, exactly?" Lizzy asked, toeing a small rocking horse.

"A box," Grace said, looking around.

"You're kidding, right?" Lizzy said, waving her arms at the box-filled space. "I don't suppose this box has a big red X on it?"

"Well, my guess would be to start over there," Grace said, pointing to a far corner. "That seems to be where the oldest stuff is. We'll just have to check every box."

"Again, what are we looking for?"

"A wooden jewelry box, about this big." Grace held her hands about twelve inches apart. "Van gave it to me for my eighteenth birthday. It's the only thing I kept. It was gorgeous, and I couldn't bring myself to throw it out. Some of my mom's old costume jewelry is probably still in there. Stuff I wouldn't wear, but wanted to keep, you know?"

For nearly an hour they moved boxes, plastic totes, tricycles, a high chair, a crib, and reams of fabric wrapped in plastic. The dust had them sneezing and sniffling.

"Don't you throw anything away?" Lizzy huffed, moving aside a ream of ugly flower print fabric, then sneezed again as more dust tickled her nostrils.

"I may try to sew again one day," she retorted.

Lizzy returned Grace's glare with a smirk, but wisely pressed her lips together and said nothing.

"This has to be it," Grace said as she tugged at a box that had seen better days. Lifting the flap, she peeked inside and said, "Yes, finally." Sliding the box out into the open, she and Lizzy sat on the floor and began pulling items from the old box. An old leather jacket, some books, and then, near the bottom, the wooden jewelry box she'd loved so much. It didn't hold any fond memories, only ghosts from a troubled past she'd once prayed to forget.

Lizzy reached out to touch the intricate carvings. "Wow, it's beautiful. I see why you didn't want to get rid of it. So, you think Vince-Vincent-Van might've been after this?" she asked doubtfully.

Grace shrugged. "I don't know. I still think it's the money, but why he'd think I'd have it stashed away here is beyond me." She turned the box in her hands, then opened the lid. "When I remembered it, I thought maybe he'd put something in there. But I only remember my mom's things being in there when I put it away. Surely I would've noticed something worth all the trouble he's gone through. She moved pieces of jewelry around with one finger. "None of this is worth anything." Lizzy reached for the box and Grace handed it over, disappointed.

"Huh. Well, it was worth a shot," she said. "What are you going to do with it now?"

"Put it back where it was, I guess. Unless you want it."

Lizzy thrust the box back at her and said, "No, thank you. I don't want anything from that man."

As Grace lowered the box back into its original nest, it slipped from her grip. She tried to catch it but was only able to grab the lid. The old hinge snapped loose, and the bottom fell upside down into the box.

"Ugh. I guess that's my sign to toss it out," she said, picking up the case. She attempted to reattach the lid but noticed the tray of the box had shifted. "Wait. Does this piece come out?"

Lizzy stopped fishing for spilled pieces of jewelry and looked up. "What is it?"

It appeared to Grace that the tray of the box was actually a removable piece. It was tightly fitted, which was why she hadn't noticed it before. Perhaps it was intended to be a hidden compartment. With a final tug, the tray popped loose, revealing an area underneath about a half-inch deep. As if it were a snake that might strike her, Grace used two fingers to lift out the only item in the space, leaving the broken, empty jewelry box in her lap.

Both women jumped when Danny's voice called from the bottom of the attic steps; they hadn't heard him come in. "Up here!" they yelled in unison.

His footsteps were solid and sure as he climbed the narrow steps. "Hey, what're you two up to? Whoa," he said, stunned when he saw what Grace held in her hands.

Grace and Lizzy stared at each other wide-eyed for a moment, then Grace looked up at her husband. "I remembered this old jewelry box, and we were trying to figure out if that was what Van was looking for." She gestured to the broken pieces of wood. "It was in some of my old stuff. I haven't thought about it in years."

She explained to Danny how seeing Lucy's jewelry box had jarred her already overwhelmed brain into recalling her own box that had been stored away. When she reached the end of her story, he shook his head.

"And you think Van hid that away in there?" Danny was skeptical.

"I don't know how else it could've gotten there," Grace said.

Lizzy stood and brushed at her dust-covered jeans, swaying a little after sitting for so long. "Listen, you guys. I'm not sure if it's all the excitement or if I'm coming down with something, but I'm worn out. I'm going to head home." She laid a hand over her stomach and her lip curled.

"You okay, Liz? You look a little pale."

"I'm fine, just a little queasy from all that coffee. I skipped lunch today, so that didn't help."

"Okay, let me know if you need anything. And thanks for helping me dig through all this stuff."

When she had gone, Grace gave Danny a recap of the events of her afternoon with Lizzy. "I think she's more upset about Vince than she's letting on."

"Give her some time. She'll be okay."

* * *

"I've googled everything I can think of and I can't find anything close to it." In her hand, Grace held the key she'd found the day before, willing it to share its secrets.

"Honey, it's probably to some old wardrobe or something."

"But where is this wardrobe? And what's in it?"

Danny raised his hands, palms up. "Clothes?"

"Or a body," Grace offered with a grin.

"A body? Really?" Danny chuckled. "I see your imagination is still intact. It is an interesting piece, though. Maybe you could use it as a fan pull or something."

Grace frowned and held it against her chest. "No way. More like a piece of chunky jewelry." She studied the key in her hand, turning it over and looking at it from all sides.

"I can practically hear the gears in that brain of your turning. What are you thinking?"

Grace shifted her gaze to her husband. "I can't figure out what Van was looking for and why he'd hurt me to get it."

"Who knows what that psycho was thinking?" Danny paused. His nonchalance of the conversation turned to concern as he studied her face. "Grace, what are you thinking? Have you recalled something else?"

"No, nothing like that."

"Then, what?"

"Hear me out, okay?"

"Uh oh." Danny sat up straighter in his chair and pushed the file in front of him aside, giving her his full attention. "I hate it when you say that."

"Can you get me a visit at the prison?" Grace jumped when his palm slapped the desk.

"Absolutely not! Now you've lost your mind for real."

"Danny, listen."

"No. I'm not listening. I don't want you anywhere near that lunatic. Why would you even suggest that?"

"I need to do this. I need closure. Once and for all." Her words were soft, delivered with a finality Danny didn't question.

He pressed his lips into a thin line and nodded.

22

Key to Forgiveness

"Are you sure about this?" Danny asked again. "We can handle this without you having to see him."

Grace understood his apprehension. He was protective, even more so after the events of the past several months. Although the doctors had tried to reassure them, Danny was afraid that any stress or trauma would cause a setback.

"I need to do this, Danny. I've run from this part of my life long enough. It's time to face it so I can finally let it go for good." Lizzy's words echoed in her mind ... "Let me close that chapter so we can continue writing the one we're living." She could see Danny was struggling with a decision he knew wasn't his to make. Finally, he squeezed her hand and nodded.

Pushing the outer door open, he led her into a short hallway with a door on each side. He indicated the door on the left and she stepped over the threshold ahead of him. A guard looked up at them from behind a tall counter, where he was watching several security monitors. "Can I help you?" His voice was gruff with a hint of boredom.

"Bradford to see inmate Vincent Crawley," Danny said authoritatively. He was attorney Daniel Bradford now, all business in his suit and tie. He carried his briefcase which held the letter signed just that morning by a judge. A letter that would get her past the guard should she need it.

Fortunately for the guard, he didn't give Danny any trouble. He slid a worn clipboard toward him and said, "Sign in here, sir." Danny complied and the guard instructed them to place their cell phones, purse, briefcase, and all pocket contents in a plastic bin. After handing over the requested items, they stepped through a metal detector. When they'd passed that test, they collected their belongings and were buzzed through the next door.

They entered another hallway, longer this time. The floors were polished to a shine, but there was a musty smell that was typical of older buildings. Their footsteps echoed in the empty hallway, reminding her of that first visit with Dr. Hyatt. It seemed like ages ago now.

"In here." Danny interrupted her reverie and unlocked a door with a swipe of his badge he'd pulled from his pocket. "The interview rooms are in here," he explained. "Lawyers come in here often, so we get access to this area." He stopped at another counter and spoke with another bored guard who told him the prisoner was on his way. Prisoner, Grace thought. She was going to see a prisoner. Had she lost her mind, again?

Danny ushered her into a small cubicle-like room. It held only a short stool, the kind from her elementary lunchroom, in front of a simple glass window. Danny had described beforehand that it was bulletproof glass. On the other side, she could see a room identical to the one she stood in.

"You'll be able to talk to each other," Danny said. "It's all hands free. No phones or cords." The clenching of his jaw told her he still wasn't keen on the idea of this visit.

"I'll be fine, Danny," she tried to reassure him. "I'm not afraid of him anymore. God's got my back, right?"

He looked down at her with a grim smile. "Right. If you get uncomfortable, just get up and leave. This door doesn't lock. I'll be right across the hall." Danny left, and the door closed as the one on the other side of the glass opened.

Grace approached the window with trepidation at first. But when she looked into the face of the narcissist before her, all nervousness evaporated. He'd put himself there, and he could no longer hurt her.

"Anna," he said. She hadn't expected the tenderness in his voice. She took a breath, momentarily taken aback.

Trust me. There was that familiar nudge, lending her comfort and pushing her forward. Knowing he'd take pride in angering her, she ignored his jab and sat expressionless. Calling her Anna was his way of belittling her; his attempt to control her emotions. She knew that now.

"I knew you'd come. I've missed you." Grace stared blankly back at him, seeing the predator in front of her for what he was.

"So much that you broke into my home and threatened me. Attacked me." The flash of anger that passed over his face was so brief she almost missed it. She waited for the next lie.

"I had to see you, Anna. I couldn't help myself. All those years, Anna. Kate. I had a lot of time to think. I know you were young, innocent, and I hurt you. But I never stopped loving you." There was the lie she'd expected.

"Do you remember the jewelry box I gave you for your birthday, Anna? You loved it so much. Did you keep it?"

Grace twisted her face in mock confusion. "You gave me a jewelry box? All I can remember is you taking from me. You took *everything* from me." The last words left her mouth through gritted teeth.

"So now you're going to pretend you don't remember the box. Just like you pretended you didn't know me at your house. *After* you agreed to meet me at the park that day."

"I didn't know that message was from you. You attacked me and then left me there, bleeding. I had amnesia for months, Van. *Months.* Add that to the endless list of things you took from me." She was trembling inside, but she kept her voice steady, her stare cold.

"That was your fault. You didn't listen." He put his palms to his temples, tried to keep his anger in check. "Anna, stop. You forget how well I know you. I can make this right. Just give me a chance. Get me out of here and let me show you." He was pleading now. He really was crazy.

"What were you after, Van? What were you looking for?"

"You. All I want is you." He placed a palm on the window. "I've missed you. Get me out of here, Anna. You know I don't belong here."

She'd had enough. "No." The single syllable came out firm and final. "You do belong here. I didn't come here to set you free, Van. I came here to free myself."

He looked up, angry and confused. "What are you talking about?"

"I forgive you, Van. Your judgment doesn't belong to me. And after twenty-two long years, I've finally forgiven myself." She pulled out the object she'd tucked into her sweater pocket and held it in her palm. Van's eyes widened and he leaned forward ever so slightly.

She held up a narrow loop of white ribbon, yellowed and worn with age. From it dangled an ornate skeleton key, its age evident by the tarnished surface. An intricate pattern of woven metal made up the bow, then straightened into a twisted rope design that made up the shank. At the end of the piece, the bit and key wards were shaped in a delicate pattern that looked more like a puzzle piece than a key. She let it spin slowly. "Beautiful, isn't it? Is this what you were looking for?"

"I knew you'd find it."

She smiled and continued as though he hadn't spoken. "Everything you've done was for this? A key?"

His eyes were cold. "That key was my mother's. It holds a lot of—sentimental value."

"You were never the sentimental type. There must be more to it than that. After all, you were willing to hurt me to get it."

The muscles in his jaw tightened and a vein in his neck pulsed. "I want it back." Van slammed a fist against the window.

Grace twisted the ribbon and allowed the dangling key to spin.

Then she closed her fingers around it and held it in her hand. "Personal items aren't allowed in prison, Van. I think I'll hang on to it. You know, keep it safe, or maybe I'll turn it over to the police so they know why you attacked me. Goodbye." Grace stood from her chair and turned her back on the man she no longer had to hate.

23

In the Wake of Forgiveness

Lizzy lay in the darkness of her bedroom, staring toward the ceiling. She'd thought she was done crying, but a lone tear escaped and rolled across her temple into her hair.

The devastating words of Dr. Mackey played on an endless loop in her exhausted mind. "I know this is tough for you. It wasn't the news we were expecting. But there are options, Lizzy."

"I'm not ready to discuss options right now." Lizzy was in shock.

"That's understandable. You can take some time to process, but don't wait too long. You're a nurse, Lizzy. You know timing is important, and the sooner we move forward with whatever you decide, the better it will be. I'll see you back in about three weeks, sooner if you need me." Lizzy had nodded absently when the doctor squeezed her shoulder and left the room with a reminder to call him if she needed anything prior to her next appointment.

She needed to call someone. Not her parents. They lived all the way in Michigan, and this wasn't a conversation that should happen over the phone. Lizzy didn't want to talk to anyone. She wanted to hide inside herself and block the outside world and all the sickness, tragedy, and pain that was in it. Unwilling to allow herself any more tears, she lifted her phone and dialed the number for the only person in the world she could call. She picked up her phone and hit the number on her favorites.

"Hey, Lizzy!"

"Grace, can you come over?"

Author's Note

Reading has been a passion of mine for as long as I can remember. As a child I'd read anything I could get my hands on and dreamed of one day writing my own book. A few decades later I had nothing more than a few short stories and barely started manuscripts tossed into a box. I didn't trust myself to create anything worthy of taking up space on a shelf.

Grace from the Grave began as a personal project when I finally vowed to finish something I'd started. When I began writing Grace's story, I wasn't aware she had a secret. In fact, her story turned out to be much different from the one I'd planned. I believe God gives us what we need when we need it. For the past two years Isaiah 60:22 has been my go-to verse when I've had the audacity to question His timing. When the time is right, I the Lord, will make it happen.

Whatever direction this story was destined to take, I wanted it to be pleasing to the Lord. He knew over two decades ago that I would one day pray for Him to place people in my life that would push me to fulfill my dream, so he sent me a very special friend that would help me grow in so many ways over the years that followed. I had no idea what journey I was about to embark on.

That same friend insisted I attend a specific writer's workshop, and thankfully I followed her advice. When I met the amazing Cap Daniels and his precious wife Melissa, I knew immediately God was at work. Do yourself a favor and type Cap Daniels into your search bar. You won't be disappointed. God had placed upon my heart a story, and He expected me to tell it, but I didn't trust myself to do it justice. He knew I'd need guidance, advice, and answers to endless questions, and He delivered a giant vessel. Their encouragement and support are unparalleled. They believed in me when I didn't believe in myself and inspired me to step out of my comfortable little box and into the world. For them, I am eternally grateful.

God didn't stop there. He then led me to a phenomenal editor who taught this amateur more than a few things about writing. I can't say the process was painless, but Nicole worked her magic and managed to guide me through this process without quitting.

Finally, I couldn't have done any of this without the unshakable support of my family. My husband would choose swinging a hammer over reading a book any day of the week, but he sacrificed many evenings in order to attend Cap's workshops with me. Wade and our three girls have been my biggest cheerleaders. Without them, I am nothing.

My job was to trust God and His plan. Trust in itself is a challenge, but forgiveness is on a whole other level. 2 Corinthians 12:9 tells us that God's grace is sufficient. It took a lifetime for me to learn that true forgiveness takes grace. And true grace can only be achieved through the blood of Christ.

In order for Grace to forgive the person who'd hurt her so deeply, she first had to find the courage and strength to forgive herself. But her journey didn't end there. She also had to open her heart to God and accept His forgiveness. Forgiveness that was promised long before she knew she needed it.

I cried and laughed right along with Grace throughout her journey. When she worried, I worried. When she was afraid, so was I. And I was just as surprised by the ending and her forgiveness as she was. Writing this story was just as humbling as it was exciting. In the end, my hope is that you've received as much of a blessing by reading this book as I did by writing it.

Naturally, Pastor Joe always insists on having the last word, so I asked the real Pastor Joe, "What is grace to you?"

His answer: "Grace is God's riches at Christ's expense."

Author Bio

Cindy H. Flowers is a nurse, wife, mother, and proud Gamma. Her fondness for reading sparked the moment she learned to spell her first word. It didn't take long to graduate from Dr. Seuss and Sesame Street to the mystery and suspense novels that quickly became her preferred genre. Her lifelong obsession with reading recently evolved into a passion for writing, initiated by God's demand for obedience.

Cindy describes herself as a lover of the Lord and all things books. Active in church, she writes novels about God's relentless pursuit of humanity amidst their brokenness.

She and her husband reside in Southeast Alabama, and when she isn't working as a nurse in civil service, you'll likely find her soaking up the sun on the beach.